THE GHOST STORIES OF CHARLES DICKENS

BY

CHARLES DICKENS

British Library Cataloguing-in-Publication Data
A catalogue record for this book is available from the
British Library

CONTENTS

CHARLES DICKENS

Charles John Huffam Dickens was born in Landport, Portsmouth in 1812. When he was ten years old, his family settled in Camden Town, a poor neighbourhood of London. A defining moment in the young Dickens' life came only two years later, when his father – the inspiration for the character of Mr Micawber in *David Copperfield* – was imprisoned in the Marshalsea debtor's prison. As a result, Dickens was sent to Warren's blacking factory, where he worked in appalling conditions and gained a first-hand acquaintance with poverty. After three years Dickens resumed his education, but the experience was highly formative for him, and would later be fictionalised in both *David Copperfield* and *Great Expectations*.

Dickens' writing career began in around 1830, when he started to write for the journals *The Mirror of Parliament* and *The True Sun*. Three years later, he became parliamentary journalist for *The Morning Chronicle*, and also began to have some successes with his fiction: His first short story, A 'Dinner at Popular Walk', appeared in the *Monthly Magazine* in December of 1833, and his first book, a collection titled *Sketches by Boz*, was published in 1836. However, his real breakthrough came in 1837, with the serialised publication of *Posthumous Papers of the Pickwick Club* – the work was hugely popular, and transformed Dickens into a well-known literary figure.

Over the next few years, at an almost incredible rate, Dickens wrote *Oliver Twist* (1837-39), *Nicholas Nickleby* (1838-39) and *The Old Curiosity Shop* and *Barnaby Rudge* (1840-41). In 1842, he travelled with his wife to the United States and Canada (where he gave lectures denouncing slavery), and in the years following produced his five 'Christmas Books'. During the fifties, after brief spells living in Italy and Switzerland, he continued to write at a seemingly inexhaustible pace, producing some of his best work: David Copperfield (1849-50), Bleak House (1852-53), Hard Times (1854), Little *Dorrit* (1857), *A Tale of Two Cities* (1859), and *Great Expectations* (1861).

During the latter stages of his life, Dickens turned his focus from writing to giving readings. In 1869, during one such reading, he collapsed, showing symptoms of a mild stroke. He died at home one year later, aged 58. He was buried in the Poets' Corner of Westminster Abbey, where the inscription on his tomb reads: "He was a sympathiser to the poor, the suffering, and the oppressed; and by his death, one of England's greatest writers is lost to the world." Dickens is now regarded as the greatest writer of the Victorian era, and one of the greatest English authors since Shakespeare.

THE HAUNTED MAN AND THE GHOST'S BARGAIN

THE GIFT BESTOWED

Everybody said so. Far be it from me to assert that what everybody says must be true. Everybody is, often, as likely to be wrong as right. In the general experience, everybody has been wrong so often, and it has taken, in most instances, such a weary while to find out how wrong, that authority is proved to be fallible. Everybody may sometimes be right; 'but *that*'s no rule,' as the ghost of Giles Scroggins says in the ballad.

The dread word, GHOST, recalls me.

Everybody said he looked like a haunted man. The extent of my present claim for everybody is, that they were so far right. He did.

Who could have seen his hollow cheek; his sunken, brilliant eye; his black-attired figure, indefinably grim, although well knit and well proportioned; his grizzled hair hanging, like tangled seaweed, about his face – as if he had been, through his whole life, a lonely mark for the chafing and beating of the great deep of humanity – but might have said he looked like a haunted man?

Who could have observed his manner, taciturn, thoughtful, gloomy, shadowed by habitual reserve, retiring always, and jocund never, with a distraught air of reverting to a bygone place and time, or of listening to some old echoes in his mind, but might have said it was the manner of a haunted man?

Who could have heard his voice, slow-speaking, deep, and grave, with a natural fulness and melody in it which he seemed to set himself against and stop, but might have said it was the voice of a haunted man?

Who that had seen him in his inner chamber, part library and part laboratory – for he was, as the world knew, far and wide, a learned man in chemistry, and a teacher on whose lips and hands a crowd of aspiring ears and eyes hung daily – who that had seen him there, upon a winter night, alone, surrounded by his drugs and instruments and books; the shadow of his shaded lamp a monstrous beetle on the wall, motionless among a crowd of spectral shapes raised there by the flickering of the fire upon the quaint objects around him; some of these phantoms (the reflection of glass vessels that held liquids) trembling at heart like things that knew his power to uncombine them, and to give back their component parts to fire and vapour; – who that had seen him then, his work done, and he pondering in his chair before the rusted grate and red flame, moving his thin mouth as if in speech, but silent as the dead, would not have said that the man seemed haunted, and the chamber too?

Who might not, by a very easy flight of fancy, have believed that everything about him took this haunted tone, and that he lived on haunted ground?

His dwelling was so solitary and vault-like – an old, retired part of an ancient endowment for students, once a brave edifice planted in an open place, but now the obsolete whim of forgotten architects; smoke-age-and-weather darkened, squeezed on every side by the overgrowing of the great city, and choked, like an old well, with stones and bricks; its small quadrangles, lying down in very pits formed by the streets and buildings, which, in course of time, had been constructed above its heavy chimney-stacks; its old trees, insulted by the neighbouring smoke, which deigned to droop so low when it was very feeble, and the weather very moody; its grass-plots, struggling with the mildewed earth to be grass, or to win any show of compromise; its silent pavement, unaccustomed to the tread of feet, and even to the observation of eyes, except when a stray face looked down from the upper world, wondering what nook it was; its sun-dial in a little bricked-up corner, where no sun had straggled for a hundred years, but where, in compensation for the sun's neglect, the snow would lie for weeks when it lay nowhere else, and the black east wind would spin like a huge humming-top, when in all other places it was silent and still.

His dwelling at its heart and core – within doors – at his fireside – was so lowering and old, so crazy, yet so strong, with its worm-eaten beams of wood in the ceiling, and its sturdy floor shelving downward to the great oak chimney-piece; so environed and hemmed in by the pressure of the town, yet so remote in fashion, age, and custom; so quiet, yet so thundering with echoes when a distant voice was raised, or a door was shut – echoes not confined to the many low passages and empty rooms, but rumbling and grumbling till they were stifled in the heavy air of the forgotten crypt where the Norman arches were half buried in the earth.

You should have seen him in his dwelling about twilight, in the dead winter-time.

When the wind was blowing shrill and shrewd, with the going down of the blurred sun. When it was just so dark as that the forms of things were indistinct and big – but not wholly lost. When sitters by the fire began to see wild faces and figures, mountains and abysses, ambuscades and armies, in the coals. When people in the streets bent down their heads, and ran before the weather. When those who were obliged to meet it were stopped at angry corners, stung by wandering snow-flakes alighting on the lashes of their eyes – which fell too sparingly, and were blown away too quickly, to leave a trace upon the frozen ground. When windows of private houses closed up tight and warm. When lighted gas began to burst forth in the busy and the quiet streets, fast blackening otherwise. When stray pedestrians, shivering along the latter, looked down at the glowing fires in kitchens, and sharpened their sharp appetites by sniffing up the fragrance of whole miles of dinners.

When travellers by land were bitter cold, and looked wearily on gloomy landscapes, rustling and shuddering in the blast. When mariners at sea, outlying upon icy yards, were tossed and swung above the howling ocean dreadfully. When lighthouses, on rocks and headlands, showed solitary and watchful; and benighted sea birds breasted on against their ponderous lanterns, and fell dead. When little readers of story books, by the firelight, trembled to think of Cassim Baba cut into quarters, hanging in the Robbers' Cave, or had some small misgivings that the fierce little old woman, with the crutch, who used to start out of the box in the merchant Abudah's bedroom, might, one of these nights, be found upon the stairs, in the long, cold, dusky journey up to bed.

When, in rustic places, the last glimmering of daylight died away from the ends of avenues; and the trees, arching overhead, were sullen and black. When, in parks and woods, the high wet fern and sodden moss and beds of fallen leaves, and trunks of trees, were lost to view, in masses of impenetrable shade. When mists arose from dyke, and fen, and river. When lights in old halls and in cottage windows were a cheerful sight. When the mill stopped, the wheelwright and the blacksmith shut their workshops, the turnpike-gate closed, the plough and harrow were left lonely in the fields, the labourer and team went home, and the striking of the church clock had a deeper sound than at noon, and the churchyard wicket would be swung no more that night.

When twilight everywhere released the shadows, prisoned up all day, that now closed in and gathered like mustering swarms of ghosts. When they stood lowering in corners of rooms, and frowned out from behind half-opened doors. When they had full possession of unoccupied apartments. When they danced upon the floors, and walls, and ceilings of inhabited chambers while the fire was low, and withdrew like ebbing waters when it sprung into a blaze. When they fantastically mocked the shapes of household objects, making the nurse an ogress, the rocking-horse a monster, the wondering child, half scared and half amused, a stranger to itself – the very tongs upon the hearth a straddling giant with his arms a-kimbo, evidently smelling the blood of Englishmen, and wanting to grind people's bones to make his bread.

When these shadows brought into the minds of older people other thoughts, and showed them different images. When they stole from their retreats, in the likenesses of forms and faces from the past, from the grave, from the deep, deep gulf, where the things that might have been, and never were, are always wandering.

When he sat, as already mentioned, gazing at the fire. When, as it rose and fell, the shadows went and came. When he took no heed of them with his bodily eyes; but, let them come or let them go, looked fixedly at the fire. You should have seen him then.

When the sounds that had arisen with the shadows, and come out of their lurking-places at the twilight summons, seemed to make a deeper stillness all about him. When the wind was rumbling in the chimney, and sometimes crooning, sometimes howling, in the house. When the old trees outward were so shaken and beaten, that one querulous old rook, unable to sleep, protested now and then in a feeble, dozy, high-up 'Caw!' When, at intervals, the window trembled, the rusty vane upon the turret-top complained, the clock beneath it recorded that another quarter of an hour was gone, or the fire collapsed and fell in with a rattle.

—When a knock came at his door, in short, as he was sitting so, and roused him.

'Who's that?' said he. 'Come in!'

Surely there had been no figure leaning on the back of his chair; no face looking over it. It is certain that no gliding footstep touched the floor as he lifted up his head with a start, and spoke. And yet there was no mirror in the room on whose surface his own form could have cast its shadow for a moment: and Something had passed darkly and gone!

'I'm humbly fearful, sir,' said a fresh-coloured busy man, holding the door open with his foot for the admission of himself and a wooden tray he carried, and letting it go again by very gentle and careful degrees, when he and the tray had got in, lest it should close noisily, 'that it's a good bit past the time tonight. But Mrs William had been taken off her legs so often——'

'By the wind? Ay! I have heard it rising.'

'—By the wind, sir – that it's a mercy she got home at all. Oh dear, yes! Yes. It was by the wind, Mr Redlaw. By the wind.'

He had, by this time, put down the tray for dinner, and was employed in lighting the lamp, and spreading a cloth on the table. From this employment he desisted in a hurry, to stir and feed the fire, and then resumed it; the lamp he had lighted, and the blaze that rose under his hand, so quickly changing the appearance of the room, that it seemed as if the mere coming in of his fresh red face and active manner had made the pleasant alteration.

'Mrs William is of course subject at any time, sir, to be taken off her balance by the elements. She is not formed superior to *that*.'

'No,' returned Mr Redlaw good-naturedly, though abruptly.

'No, sir. Mrs William may be taken off her balance by Earth; as, for example, last Sunday week, when sloppy and greasy, and she going out to tea with her newest sister-in-law, and having a pride in herself, and wishing to appear perfectly spotless, though pedestrian. Mrs William may be taken off her balance by Air; as being once over-persuaded by a friend to try a swing at Peckham Fair, which acted on her constitution instantly like a steamboat. Mrs William may be taken off her balance by Fire; as on a false alarm of engines at her mother and when she went two mile in her nightcap. Mrs William may be taken off her balance by Water; as at Battersea, when rowed into the piers by her young nephew, Charley Swidger, junior, aged twelve, which had no idea of boats whatever. But these are elements. Mrs William must be taken out of elements for the strength of *her* character to come into play.'

As he stopped for a reply, the reply was 'Yes,' in the same tone as before.

'Yes, sir. Oh dear, yes!' said Mr Swidger, still proceeding with his preparations, and checking them off as he made them. 'That's where it is, sir. That's what I always say myself, sir. Such a many of us Swidgers! Pepper. Why, there's my father, sir, superannuated keeper and custodian of this Institution, eighty-seven year old. He's a Swidger! Spoon.'

'True, William,' was the patient and abstracted answer when he stopped again.

'Yes, sir,' said Mr Swidger. 'That's what I always say, sir. You may call him the trunk of the tree! Bread. Then you come to his successor, my unworthy self – salt – and Mrs William, Swidgers both. Knife and fork. Then you come to all my brothers and their families, Swidgers, man and woman, boy and girl. Why, what with cousins, uncles, aunts, and relationships of this, that, and t'other degree, and what-not degree, and marriages, and lyings-in, the Swidgers – tumbler – might take hold of hands, and make a ring round England!'

Receiving no reply at all here from the thoughtful man whom he addressed, Mr William approached him nearer, and made a feint of accidentally knocking the table with a decanter to rouse him. The moment he succeeded, he went on, as if in great alacrity of aquiescence.

'Yes, sir! That's just what I say myself, sir. Mrs William and me have often said so. "There's Swidgers enough," we say, "without *our* voluntary contributions. Butter. In fact, sir, my father is a family in himself – casters – to take care of; and it happens all for the best that we have no child of our own, though it's made Mrs William rather quiet-like, too. Quite ready for the fowl and mashed potatoes, sir? Mrs William said she'd dish in ten minutes when I left the Lodge.'

'I am quite ready,' said the other, waking as from a dream, and walking slowly to and fro.

'Mrs William has been at it again, sir!' said the keeper, as he stood warming a plate at the fire, and pleasantly shading his face with it. Mr Redlaw stopped in his walking, and an expression of interest appeared in him.

'What I always say myself, sir. She *will* do it! There's a motherly feeling in Mrs William's breast that must and will have went.'

'What has she done?'

'Why, sir, not satisfied with being a sort of mother to all the young gentlemen that come up from a variety of parts, to attend your courses of lectures at this ancient foundation——It's surprising how stone-chaney catches the heat, this frosty weather, to be sure!' Here he turned the plates, and cooled his fingers.

'Well?' said Mr Redlaw.

'That's just what I say myself, sir,' returned Mr William, speaking over his shoulder, as if in ready and delighted assent. 'That's exactly where it is, sir! There ain't one of our students but appears to regard Mrs William in that light. Every day, right through the course, they put their heads into the Lodge, one after another, and have all got something to tell her, or something to ask her. "Swidge" is the appellation by which they speak of Mrs William in general, among themselves, I'm told; but that's what I say, sir. Better be called ever so far out of your name, if it's done in real liking, than have it made ever so much of, and not cared about! What's a name for? To know a person by. If Mrs William is known by something better than her name – I allude to Mrs William's qualities and disposition – never mind her name, though it *is* Swidger, by rights. Let 'em call her Swidge, Widge, Bridge – Lord! London Bridge, Black-friars, Chelsea, Putney, Waterloo, or Hammersmith Suspension – if they like!"

The close of this triumphant oration brought him and the plate to the table, upon which he half laid and half dropped it, with a lively sense of its being thoroughly heated, just as the subject of his praises entered the room, bearing another tray and a lantern, and followed by a venerable old man with long grey hair.

Mrs William, like Mr William, was a simple innocent-looking person, in whose smooth cheeks the cheerful red of her husband's official waistcoat was very pleasantly repeated. But whereas Mr William's light hair stood on end all over his head, and seemed to draw his eyes up with it in an excess of bustling readiness for anything, the dark brown hair of

Mrs William was carefully smoothed down, and waved away under a trim, tidy cap, in the most exact and quiet manner imaginable. Whereas Mr William's very trousers hitched themselves up at the ankles, as if it were not in their iron-grey nature to rest without looking about them. Mrs William's neatly-flowered skirts – red and white, like her own pretty face – were as composed and orderly as if the very wind that blew so hard out of doors could not disturb one of their folds. Whereas his coat had something of a fly-away and half-off appearance about the collar and breast, her little bodice was so placid and neat, that there should have been protection for her in it, had she needed any, with the roughest people. Who could have had the heart to make so calm a bosom swell with grief, or throb with fear, or flutter with a thought of shame? To whom would its repose and peace have not appealed against disturbance, like the innocent slumber of a child?

'Punctual, of coure, Milly,' said her husband, relieving her of the tray, 'or it wouldn't be you. Here's Mrs William, sir! He looks lonelier than ever tonight,' whispering to his wife as he was taking the tray, 'and ghostlier altogether.'

Without any show of hurry or noise, or any show of herself even, she was so calm and quiet, Milly set the dishes she had brought upon the table, Mr William, after much clattering and running about, having only gained possession of a butter-boat of gravy, which he stood ready to serve.

'What is that the old man has in his arms?' asked Mr Redlaw as he sat down to his solitary meal.

'Holly, sir,' replied the quiet voice of Milly.

'That's what I say myself, sir,' interposed Mr William, striking in with the butter-boat. 'Berries is so seasonable to the time of year! Brown gravy!'

'Another Christmas come, another year gone!' murmured the Chemist with a gloomy sigh. 'More figures in the lengthening sum of recollection that we work and work at to our torment, till Death idly jumbles all together, and rubs all out. So, Philip!' breaking off, and raising his voice as he addressed the old man standing apart, with his glistening burden in his arms, from which the quiet Mrs William took small branches, which she noiselessly trimmed with his scissors, and decorated the room with, while her aged father-in-law looked on, much interested in the ceremony.

'My duty to you, sir,' returned the old man. 'Should have spoke before, sir, but know your ways, Mr Redlaw – proud to say – and wait till spoke to! Merry Christmas, sir, and happy New Year, and many of 'em. Have had a pretty many of 'em myself – ha, ha! – and may take the liberty of wishing 'em. I'm eighty-seven!'

'Haven't you had so many that were merry and happy?' asked the other.

'Ay, sir, ever so many,' returned the old man.

'Is his memory impaired with age? It is to be expected now,' said Mr Redlaw, turning to the son, and speaking lower.

'Not a morsel of it, sir,' replied Mr William. 'That's exactly what I say myself, sir. There never was such a memory as my father's. He's the most wonderful man in the world. He don't know what forgetting means. It's the very observation I'm always making to Mrs William, sir, if you'll believe me!'

Mr Swidger, in his polite desire to seem to acquiesce at all events, delivered this as if there were no iota of contradiction in it, and it were all said in unbounded and unqualified assent.

The Chemist pushed his plate away, and, rising from the table, walked across the room to where the old man stood looking at a little sprig of holly in his hand.

'It recalls the time when many of those years were old and new, then?' he said, observing him attentively, and touching him on the shoulder. 'Does it?'

'Oh, many, many!' said Philip, half awaking from his reverie. 'I'm eighty-seven!'

'Merry and happy, was it?' asked the Chemist in a low voice. 'Merry and happy, old man?'

'Maybe as high as that, no higher,' said the old man, holding out his hand a little way above the level of his knee, and looking retrospectively at his questioner, 'when I first remember 'em! Cold, sunshiny day it was, out a walking, when someone – it was my mother as sure as you stand there, though I don't know what her blessed face was like, for she took ill and died that Christmas-time – told me they were food for birds. The pretty little fellow thought – that's me, you understand – that birds' eyes were so bright, perhaps, because the berries that they lived on in the winter were so bright. I recollect that. And I'm eighty-seven!'

'Merry and happy!' mused the other, bending his dark eyes upon the stooping figure, with a smile of compassion. 'Merry and happy – and remember well?'

'Ay, ay, ay!' resumed the old man, catching the last words. 'I remember 'em well in my school-time, year after year, and all the merry-making that used to come along with them. I was a strong chap then, Mr Redlaw; and, if you'll believe me, hadn't my match at football within ten mile. Where's my son William? Hadn't my match at football, William, within ten mile!'

'That's what I always say, father!' returned the son promptly, and with great respect. 'You *are* a Swidger, if ever there was one of the family!'

'Dear!' said the old man, shaking his head as he again looked at the holly. 'His mother – my son William's my youngest son – and I, have sat among 'em all, boys and girls, little children and babies, many a year, when the berries like these were not shining half so bright all round us, as their bright faces. Many of 'em are gone; she's gone; and my son George (our eldest, who was her pride more than all the rest) is fallen very low: but I can see them, when I look here, alive and healthy, as they used to be in those days; and I can see him, thank God, in his innocence. It's a blessed thing to me, at eighty-seven.'

The keen look that had been fixed upon him with so much earnestness had gradually sought the ground.

'When my circumstances got to be not so good as formerly, through not being honestly dealt by, and I first come here to be custodian,' said the old man, ' – which was upwards of fifty years ago – where's my son William? More than half a century ago, William!'

'That's what I say, father,' replied the son as promptly and dutifully as before, 'that's exactly where it is. Two times ought's an ought, and twice five ten, and there's a hundred of 'em.'

' – It was quite a pleasure to know that one of our founders – or, more correctly speaking,' said the old man, with a great glory in his subject and his knowledge of it, 'one of the learned gentlemen that helped endow us in Queen Elizabeth's time, for we were founded afore her day – left in his will, among the other bequests he made us, so much to buy holly, for garnishing the walls and windows come Christmas. There was something homely and friendly in it. Being but strange here then, and coming at Christmas-time, we took a liking for his very picter that hangs in what used to be, anciently, afore our ten poor gentlemen commuted for an annual stipend in money, our great Dinner Hall. A sedate gentleman in a peaked beard, with a ruff round his neck, and a scroll below him, in old English letters, "Lord, keep my memory green!" You know all about him, Mr Redlaw?'

'I know the portrait hangs there, Philip.'

'Yes, sure, it's the second on the right, above the panelling. I was going to say – he has helped to keep *my* memory green, I thank him; for going round the building every year, as I'm a doing now, and freshening up the bare rooms with these branches and berries, freshens up my bare old brain. One year brings back another, and that year another, and those others numbers! At last, it seems to me as if the birth-time of our Lord was the birth-time of all I have ever had affection for, or mourned for, or delighted in, and they're a pretty many, for I'm eighty-seven!'

'Merry and happy,' murmured Redlaw to himself.

The room began to darken strangely.

'So you see, sir,' pursued old Philip, whose hale, wintry cheek had warmed into a ruddier glow and whose blue eyes had brightened, while he spoke, 'I have plenty to keep, when

I keep this present season. Now, where's my quiet Mouse? Chattering's the sin of my time of life, and there's half the building to do yet, if the cold don't freeze us first, or the wind don't blow us away, or the darkness don't swallow us up.'

The quiet Mouse had brought her calm face to his side, and silently taken his arm, before he finished speaking.

'Come away, my dear,' said the old man. 'Mr Redlaw won't settle to his dinner, otherwise, till it's cold as the winter. I hope you'll excuse me rambling on, sir, and I wish you good night, and, once again, a merry——'

'Stay!' said Mr Redlaw, resuming his place at the table, more, it would have seemed from his manner, to reassure the old keeper, than in any remembrance of his own appetite. 'Spare me another moment, Philip. William, you were going to tell me something to your excellent wife's honour. It will not be disagreeable to her to hear you praise her. What was it?'

'Why, that's where it is, you see, sir,' returned Mr William Swidger, looking towards his wife in considerable embarrassment. 'Mrs William's got her eye upon me.'

'But you're not afraid of Mrs William's eye?'

'Why, no, sir,' returned Mr Swidger, 'that's what I say myself. It wasn't made to be afraid of. It wouldn't have been made so mild, if that was the intention. But I wouldn't like to – Milly! – him, you know. Down in the Buildings.'

Mr William, standing behind the table, and rummaging disconcertedly among the objects upon it, directed persuasive glances at Mrs William, and secret jerks of his head and thumb at Mr Redlaw, as alluring her towards him.

'Him, you know, my love,' said Mr William. 'Down in the Buildings. Tell, my dear! You're the works of Shakespeare in comparison with myself. Down in the Buildings, you know, my love. Student.'

'Student!' repeated Mr Redlaw, raising his head.

'That's what I say, sir!' cried Mr William in the utmost animation of assent. 'If it wasn't the poor student down in the Buildings, why should you wish to hear it from Mrs William's lips? Mrs William, my dear – Buildings.'

'I didn't know,' said Milly with a quiet frankness, free from any haste or confusion, 'that William had said anything about it, or I wouldn't have come. I asked him not to. It's a sick young gentleman, sir – and very poor, I am afraid – who is too ill to go home this holiday-time, and lives, unknown to any one, in but a common kind of lodging for a gentleman, down in Jerusalem Buildings. That's all, sir.'

'Why have I never heard of him?' said the Chemist, rising hurriedly. 'Why has he not made his situation known to me? Sick! Give me my hat and cloak. Poor! What house? – what number?'

'Oh, you mustn't go there, sir!' said Milly, leaving her father-in-law, and calmly confronting him with her collected little face and folded hands.

'Not go there?'

'Oh dear, no!' said Milly, shaking her head as at a most manifest and self-evident impossibility. 'It couldn't be thought of!'

'What do you mean? Why not?'

'Why, you see, sir,' said Mr William Swidger persuasively and confidentially, 'that's what I say. Depend upon it, the young gentleman would never have made his situation known to one of his own sex. Mrs William has got into his confidence, but that's quite different. They all confide in Mrs William; they all trust *her*. A man, sir, couldn't have got a whisper out of him; but woman, sir, and Mrs William combined——!'

'There is good sense and delicacy in what you say, William,' returned Mr Redlaw, observant of the gentle and composed face at his shoulder. And laying his finger on his lip, he secretly put his purse into her hand.

'Oh dear, no, sir!' cried Milly, giving it back again. 'Worse and worse! Couldn't be dreamed of!'

Such a staid, matter-of-fact housewife she was, and so unruffled by the momentary haste of this rejection, that, an instant afterwards, she was tidily picking up a few leaves which had strayed from between her scissors and her apron when she had arranged the holly.

Finding, when she rose from her stooping posture, that Mr Redlaw was still regarding her with doubt and astonishment, she quietly repeated – looking about, the while, for any other fragments that might have escaped her observation:

'Oh dear, no, sir! He said that of all the world he would not be known to you, or receive help from you – though he is a student in your class. I have made no terms of secrecy with you, but I trust to your honour completely.'

'Why did he say so?'

'Indeed I can't tell, sir,' said Milly, after thinking a little, 'because I am not at all clever, you know; and I wanted to be useful to him in making things neat and comfortable about him, and employed myself that way. But I know he is poor and lonely, and I think he is somehow neglected too. How dark it is!'

The room had darkened more and more. There was a very heavy gloom and shadow gathering behind the Chemist's chair.

'What more about him?' he asked.

'He is engaged to be married when he can afford it,' said Milly, 'and is studying, I think, to qualify himself to earn a living. I have seen, a long time, that he has studied hard, and denied himself much. How very dark it is!'

'It's turned colder, too,' said the old man, rubbing his hands. 'There's a chill and dismal feeling in the room. Where's my son William? William, my boy, turn the lamp, and rouse the fire!'

Milly's voice resumed, like quiet music very softly played: 'He muttered in his broken sleep yesterday afternoon, after talking to me' (this was to herself), 'about someone dead, and some great wrong done that could never be forgotten; but whether to him or to another person, I don't know. Not *by* him, I am sure.'

'And, in short, Mrs William, you see – which she wouldn't say herself, Mr Redlaw, if she was to stop here till the new year after this next one,' said Mr William, coming up to him to speak in his ear – 'has done him worlds of good! Bless you, worlds of good! All at home just the same as ever – my father made as snug and comfortable – not a crumb of litter to be found in the house, if you were to offer fifty pound ready money for it – Mrs William apparently never out of the way – yet Mrs William backwards and forwards, backwards and forwards, up and down, up and down, a mother to him!'

The room turned darker and colder, and the gloom and shadow gathering behind the chair was heavier.

'Not content with this, sir, Mrs William goes and finds, this very night, when she was coming home (why, it's not above a couple of hours ago), a creature more like a young wild beast than a young child, shivering upon a doorstep. What does Mrs William do, but brings it home to dry it, and feed it, and keep it till our old Bounty of food and flannel is given away on Christmas morning! If it ever felt a fire before, it's as much as it ever did; for it's sitting in the old Lodge chimney, staring at ours as if its ravenous eyes would never shut again. It's sitting there, at least,' said Mr William, correcting himself, on reflection, 'unless it's bolted!'

'Heaven keep her happy!' said the Chemist aloud, 'and you too, Philip! and you, William! I must consider what to do in this. I may desire to see this student. I'll not detain you longer now. Good night!'

'I thankee, sir, I thankee!' said the old man, 'for Mouse, and for my son William, and for myself. Where's my son William? William, you take the lantern, and go on first, through them long dark passages, as you did last year and the year afore. Ha, ha! *I* remember – though I'm eighty-seven! "Lord, keep my memory green!" It's a very good prayer, Mr Redlaw, that of the learned gentleman in the peaked beard, with a ruff round his neck-hangs up, second on the right above the panelling, in what used to be, afore our ten poor gentlemen commuted, our great Dinner Hall. "Lord, keep my memory green!" It's very good and pious, sir. Amen! Amen!'

As they passed out and shut the heavy door, which,

however carefully withheld, fired a long train of thundering reverberations when it shut at last, the room turned darker.

As he fell a musing in his chair alone, the healthy holly withered on the wall, and dropped – dead branches.

As the gloom and shadow thickened behind him, in that place where it had been gathering so darkly, it took, by slow degrees, or out of it there came, by some unreal, unsubstantial process, not to be traced by any human sense, an awful likeness of himself.

Ghastly and cold, colourless in its leaden face and hands, but with his features, and his bright eyes, and his grizzled hair, and dressed in the gloomy shadow of his dress, it came into its terrible appearance of existence, motionless, without a sound. As *he* leaned his arm upon the elbow of his chair, ruminating before the fire, *it* leaned upon the chair-back, close above him, with its appalling copy of his face looking where his face looked, and bearing the expression his face bore.

This, then, was the Something that had passed and gone already. This was the dread companion of the haunted man!

It took, for some moments, no more apparent heed of him than he of it. The Christmas Waits were playing somewhere in the distance, and, through his thoughtfulness, he seemed to listen to the music. It seemed to listen too.

At length he spoke; without moving or lifting up

his face.

'Here again!' he said.

'Here again!' replied the Phantom.

'I see you in the fire,' said the haunted man. 'I hear you in music, in the wind, in the dead stillness of the night.'

The Phantom moved his head, assenting.

'Why do you come to haunt me thus?'

'I come as I am called,' replied the Ghost.

'No. Unbidden!' exclaimed the Chemist.

'Unbidden be it,' said the Spectre. 'It is enough. I am here.'

Hitherto the light of the fire had shone on the two faces – if the dread lineaments behind the chair might be called a face – both addressed towards it, as at first, and neither looking at the other. But, now, the haunted man turned suddenly, and stared upon the Ghost. The Ghost, as sudden in its motion, passed to before the chair, and stared on him.

The living man, and the animated image of himself dead, might so have looked, the one upon the other. An awful survey, in a lonely and remote part of an empty old pile of building, on a winter night, with the loud wind going by upon its journey of mystery – whence, or whither, no man knowing since the world began – and the stars, in unimaginable millions, glittering through it, from eternal space, where the world's bulk is as a grain, and its hoary age is infancy.

'Look upon me!' said the Spectre. 'I am he, neglected in my youth, and miserably poor, who strove and suffered, and still strove and suffered, until I hewed out knowledge from the mine where it was buried, and made rugged steps thereof, for my worn feet to rest and rise on.'

'I *am* that man,' returned the Chemist.

'No mother's self-denying love,' pursued the Phantom, 'no father's counsel, aided *me*. A stranger came into my father's place when I was but a child, and I was easily an alien from my mother's heart. My parents, at the best, were of that sort whose care soon ends, and whose duty is soon done; who cast their offspring loose early, as birds do theirs; and, if they do well, claim the merit; and, if ill, the pity.'

It paused, and seemed to tempt and goad him with its look, and with the manner of its speech, and with its smile.

'I am he,' pursued the Phantom, 'who, in this struggle upward, found a friend. I made him – won him – bound him to me! We worked together, side by side. All the love and confidence that in my earlier youth had had no outlet, and found no expression, I bestowed on him.'

'Not all,' said Redlaw hoarsely.

'No, not all,' returned the Phantom. 'I had a sister.'

The haunted man, with his head resting on his hands,

replied, 'I had!' The Phantom, with an evil smile, drew closer to the chair, and resting its chin upon its folded hands, its folded hands upon the back, and looking down into his face with searching eyes, that seemed instinct with fire, went on:

'Such glimpses of the light of home as I had ever known, had streamed from her. How young she was, how fair, how loving! I took her to the first poor roof that I was master of, and made it rich. She came into the darkness of my life, and made it bright. She is before me!'

'I saw her, in the fire, but now. I hear her in music, in the wind, in the dead stillness of the night,' returned the haunted man.

'*Did* he love her?' said the Phantom, echoing his contemplative tone. 'I think he did once. I am sure he did. Better had she loved him less – less secretly, less dearly, from the shallower depths of a more divided heart!'

'Let me forget it,' said the Chemist with an angry motion of his hand. 'Let me blot it from my memory!'

The Spectre, without stirring, and with its unwinking, cruel eyes still fixed upon his face, went on: 'A dream, like hers, stole upon my own life.'

'It did,' said Redlaw.

'A love, as like hers,' pursued the Phantom, 'as my inferior nature might cherish, arose in my own heart. I was too poor to bind its object to my fortune, then, by any thread of promise or entreaty. I loved her far too well to seek to do it. But, more than ever I had striven in my life, I strove to climb! Only an inch gained, brought me something nearer to the height. I toiled up! In the late pauses of my labour at that time – my sister (sweet companion!) still sharing with me the expiring embers and the cooling hearth – when day was breaking, what pictures of the future did I see!'

'I saw them in the fire but now,' he murmured. 'They come back to me in music, in the wind, in the dead stillness of the night, in the revolving years.'

'—Pictures of my own domestic life, in after-time, with her who was the inspiration of my toil. Pictures of my sister, made the wife of my dear friend, on equal terms – for he had some inheritance, we none – pictures of our sobered age and mellowed happiness, and of the golden links, extending back so far, that should bind us, and our children, in a radiant garland,' said the Phantom.

'Pictures,' said the haunted man, 'that were delusions. Why is it my doom to remember them too well?'

'Delusions,' echoed the Phantom in its changeless voice, and glaring on him with its changeless eyes. 'For my friend (in whose breast my confidence was locked as in my own), passing between me and the centre of the system of my hopes and struggles, won her to himself, and shattered my frail universe. My sister, doubly dear, doubly devoted, doubly cheerful in my home, lived on to see me famous, and my old ambition so rewarded when its spring was broken, and then——'

'Then died,' he interposed. 'Died, gentle as ever, happy, and with no concern but for her brother. Peace!'

The Phantom watched him silently.

'Remembered!' said the haunted man after a pause. 'Yes. So well remembered, that even now, when years have passed, and nothing is more idle or more visionary to me than the boyish love so long outlived, I think of it with sympathy, as if it were a younger brother's or a son's. Sometimes I ever wonder when her heart first inclined to him, and how it had been affected towards me. Not lightly, once, I think.—But that is nothing. Early unhappiness, a wound from a hand I loved and trusted, and a loss that nothing can replace, outlive such fancies.'

'Thus,' said the Phantom, 'I bear within me a Sorrow and a Wrong. Thus I prey upon myself. Thus, memory is my curse; and, if I could forget my sorrow and my wrong, I would!'

'Mocker!' said the Chemist, leaping up, and making, with a wrathful hand, at the throat of his other self. 'Why have I always that taunt in my ears?'

'Forbear!' exclaimed the Spectre in an awful voice. 'Lay a hand on me, and die!'

He stopped midway, as if its words had paralysed him, and stood looking on it. It had glided from him; it had its arm raised high in warning; and a smile passed over its unearthly features as it reared its dark figure in triumph.

'If I could forget my sorrow and wrong, I would,' the Ghost repeated. 'If I could forget my sorrow and wrong, I would!'

'Evil spirit of myself,' returned the haunted man in a low, trembling tone, 'my life is darkened by that incessant whisper.'

'It is an echo,' said the Phantom.

'If it be an echo of my thoughts – as now, indeed, I know it is,' rejoined the haunted man, 'why should I, therefore, be tormented? It is not a selfish thought. I suffer it to range beyond myself. All men and women have their sorrows, most of them their wrongs; ingratitude, and sordid jealousy, and interest besetting all degrees of life. Who would not forget their sorrows and their wrongs?'

'Who would not, truly, and be the happier and better for it?' said the Phantom.

'These revolutions of years, which we commemorate,' proceeded Redlaw, 'what do *they* recall? Are there any minds in which they do not re-awaken some sorrow, or some trouble? What is the remembrance of the old man who was here tonight? A tissue of sorrow and trouble.'

'But common natures,' said the Phantom, with its evil smile upon its glassy face, 'unenlightened minds and ordinary spirits, do not feel or reason on these things like men of higher cultivation and profounder thought.'

'Tempter,' answered Redlaw, 'whose hollow look and voice I dread more than words can express, and from whom some dim foreshadowing of greater fear is stealing over me while I speak, I hear again an echo of my own mind.'

'Receive it as a proof that I am powerful,' returned the Ghost. 'Hear what I offer! Forget the sorrow, wrong, and trouble you have known!'

'Forget them!' he repeated.

'I have the power to cancel their remembrance – to leave but very faint, confused traces of them, that will die out soon,' returned the Spectre. 'Say! Is it done?'

'Stay!' cried the haunted man, arresting by a terrified gesture the uplifted hand. 'I tremble with distrust and doubt of you; and the dim fear you cast upon me deepens into a nameless horror I can hardly bear. I would not deprive myself of any kindly recollection, or any sympathy that is good for me, or others. What shall I lose if I assent to this? What else will pass from my remembrance?'

'No knowledge; no result of study; nothing but the intertwisted chain of feelings and associations, each in its turn dependent on, and nourished by, the banished recollections.

Those will go.'

'Are they so many?' said the haunted man, reflecting in alarm.

'They have been wont to show themselves in the fire, in music, in the wind, in the dead stillness of the night, in the revolving years,' returned the Phantom scornfully.

'In nothing else?'

The Phantom held its peace.

But, having stood before him, silent, for a little while, it moved towards the fire; then stopped.

'Decide!' it said, 'before the opportunity is lost!'

'A moment! I call Heaven to witness,' said the agitated man, 'that I have never been a hater of my kind – never morose, indifferent, or hard to anything around me. If, living here alone, I have made too much of all that was and might have been, and too little of what is, the evil, I believe, has fallen on me, and not on others. But, if there were poison in my body, should I not, possessed of antidotes and knowledge how to use them, use them? If there be poison in my mind, and through this fearful shadow I can cast it out, shall I not cast it out?'

'Say,' said the Spectre, 'is it done?'

'A moment longer!' he answered hurriedly. '*I would forget it if I could*! Have *I* thought that alone, or has it been the thought of thousands upon thousands, generation after generation? All human memory is fraught with sorrow and trouble. My memory is as the memory of other men, but other men have not this choice. Yes, I close the bargain. Yes! I *will* forget my sorrow, wrong and trouble!'

'Say,' said the Spectre, 'is it done?'

'It is!'

'*It is*. And take this with you, man whom I here renounce! The gift that I have given, you shall give again, go where you will. Without recovering yourself the power that you have yielded up, you shall henceforth destroy its like in all whom you approach. Your wisdom has discovered that the memory of sorrow, wrong, and trouble is the lot of all mankind, and that mankind would be the happier, in its other memories, without it. Go! Be its benefactor! Freed from such remembrance, from this hour, carry involuntarily the blessing of such freedom with you. Its diffusion is inseparable and inalienable from you. Go! Be happy in the good you have won, and in the good you do!'

The Phantom, which had held its bloodless hand above him while it spoke, as if in some unholy invocation, or some ban; and which had gradually advanced its eyes so close to his, that he could see how they did not participate in the terrible smile upon its face, but were a fixed, unalterable, steady horror; melted from before him, and was gone.

As he stood rooted to the spot, possessed by fear and

wonder, and imagining he heard repeated in melancholy echoes, dying away fainter and fainter, the words, 'Destroy its like in all whom you approach!' a shrill cry reached his ears. It came, not from the passages beyond the door, but from another part of the old building, and sounded like the cry of some one in the dark who had lost the way.

He looked confusedly upon his hands and limbs, as if to be assured of his identity, and then shouted in reply, loudly and wildly; for there was a strangeness and terror upon him, as if he, too, were lost.

The cry responding, and being nearer, he caught up the lamp, and raised a heavy curtain in the wall, by which he was accustomed to pass into and out of the theatre where he lectured, which adjoined his room. Associated with youth and animation, and a high amphitheatre of faces which his entrance charmed to interest in a moment, it was a ghostly place when all this life was faded out of it, and stared upon him like an emblem of Death.

'Holloa!' he cried. 'Holloa! This way! Come to the light!' When, as he held the curtain with one hand, and with the other raised the lamp and tried to pierce the gloom that filled the place, something rushed past him into the room like a wild cat, and crouched down in a corner.

'What is it?' he said hastily.

He might have asked, 'What is it?' even had he seen it well, as presently he did when he stood looking at it gathered up in its corner.

A bundle of tatters, held together by a hand, in size and form almost an infant's, but in its greedy, desperate little clutch, a bad old man's. A face round and smoothed by some half-dozen years, but pinched and twisted by the experiences of a life. Bright eyes, but not youthful. Naked feet, beautiful in their childish delicacy, ugly in the blood and dirt that cracked upon them. A baby savage, a young monster, a child who had never been a child, a creature who might live to take the outward form of man, but who, within, would live and perish a mere beast.

Used, already, to be worried and hunted like a beast, the boy crouched down as he was looked at, and looked back again, and interposed his arm to ward off the expected blow.

'I'll bite,' he said, 'if you hit me!'

The time had been, and not many minutes since, when such a sight as this would have wrung the Chemist's heart. He looked upon it now coldly; but with a heavy effort to remember something – he did not know what – he asked the boy what he did there, and whence he came.

'Where's the woman?' he replied. 'I want to find the woman.'

'Who?'

'The woman. Her that brought me here, and set me by the large fire. She was so long gone, that I went to look for her, and lost myself. I don't want you. I want the woman.'

He made a spring, so suddenly, to get away, that the dull sound of his naked feet upon the floor was near the curtain, when Redlaw caught him by his rags.

'Come! you let me go!' muttered the boy, struggling, and clenching his teeth. 'I've done nothing to you. Let me go, will you, to the woman?'

'That is not the way. There is a nearer one,' said Redlaw, detaining him, in the same blank effort to remember some association that ought of right to bear upon this monstrous object. 'What is your name?'

'Got none.'

'Where do you live?'

'Live! What's that?'

The boy shook his hair from his eyes to look at him for a moment, and then, twisting round his legs and wrestling with him, broke again into his repetition of, 'You let me go, will you? I want to find the woman.'

The Chemist led him to the door. 'This way,' he said, looking at him still confusedly, but with repugnance and avoidance, growing out of his coldness. 'I'll take you to her.'

The sharp eyes in the child's head, wandering round the room, lighted on the table where the remnants of the dinner were.

'Give me some of that!' he said covetously.

'Has she not fed you?'

'I shall be hungry again tomorrow, shan't I? Ain't I hungry every day?'

Finding himself released, he bounded at the table like some small animal of prey, and hugging to his breast bread and meat, and his own rags, all together, said:

'There! Now take me to the woman!'

As the Chemist, with a new-born dislike to touch him, sternly motioned him to follow, and was going out of the door, he trembled and stopped.

'The gift that I have given, you shall give again, go where you will.'

The Phantom's words were blowing in the wind, and the wind blew chill upon him.

'I'll not go there tonight,' he murmured faintly. 'I'll go nowhere tonight. Boy! straight down this long arched passage, and past the great dark door into the yard, you will see the fire shining on a window there.'

'The woman's fire?' inquired the boy.

He nodded, and the naked feet had sprung away. He came back with his lamp, locked his door hastily, and sat down in his chair, covering his face like me who was frightened at himself.

For now he was indeed alone. Alone, alone.

THE GIFT DIFFUSED

A small man sat in a small parlour, partitioned off from a small shop by a small screen, pasted all over with small scraps of newspapers. In company with the small man was almost any amount of small children you may please to name – at least, it seemed so; they made, in that very limited sphere of action, such an imposing effect, in point of numbers.

Of these small fry, two had, by some strong machinery, been got into bed in a corner, where they might have reposed snugly enough in the sleep of innocence, but for a constitutional propensity to keep awake, and also to scuffle in and out of bed. The immediate occasion of these predatory dashes at the waking world was the construction of an oyster-shell wall in a corner, by two other youths of tender age; on which fortification the two in bed made harassing descents (like those accursed Picts and Scots who beleaguer the early historical studies of most young Britons), and then withdrew to their own territory.

In addition to the stir attendant on these inroads, and the retorts of the invaded, who pursued hotly, and made lunges at the bedclothes, under which the marauders took refuge, another little boy, in another little bed, contributed his mite of confusion to the family stock, by casting his boots upon the waters; in other words, by launching these and several small objects, inoffensive in themselves, though of a hard substance considered as missiles, at the disturbers of his repose, who were not slow to return these compliments.

Besides which, another little boy – the biggest there, but still little – was tottering to and fro, bent on one side, and considerably affected in his knees by the weight of a large baby, which he was supposed, by a fiction that obtains sometimes in sanguine families, to be hushing to sleep. But oh! the inexhaustible regions of contemplation and watchfulness into which this baby's eyes were then only beginning to compose themselves to stare over his unconscious shoulder!

It was a very Moloch of a baby, on whose insatiate altar the whole existence of this particular young brother was offered up a daily sacrifice. Its personality may be said to have consisted in its never being quiet, in any one place, for five consecutive minutes, and never going to sleep when required. 'Tetterby's baby' was as well known in the neighbourhood as the postman or the potboy. It roved from door-step to door-step, in the arms of little Johnny Tetterby, and lagged heavily at the rear of troops of juveniles who followed the Tumblers or the Monkey, and came up, all on one side, a little too late for everything that was attractive, from Monday morning until Saturday night. Wherever childhood congregated to play, there was little Moloch making Johnny fag and toil. Wherever Johnny desired to stay, little Moloch became fractious, and would not remain. Whenever Johnny wanted to go out, Moloch was asleep, and must be watched. Whenever Johnny wanted to stay at home, Moloch was awake, and must be taken out. Yet Johnny was verily persuaded that it was a faultless baby, without its peer in the realm of England; and was quite content to catch meek glimpses of things in general from behind its skirts, or over its limp flapping bonnet, and to go staggering about with it like a very little porter with a very large parcel, which was not directed to anybody, and could never be delivered anywhere.

The small man who sat in the small parlour, making fruitless attempts to read his newspaper peaceably in the midst of this disturbance, was the father of the family, and the chief of the firm described in the inscription over the little shop-front, by the name and title of A. TETTERBY AND CO., NEWSMEN. Indeed, strictly speaking, he was the only personage answering to that designation; as Co. was a merely poetical abstraction, altogether baseless and impersonal.

Tetterby's was the corner shop in Jerusalem Buildings. There was a good show of literature in the window, chiefly consisting of picture-newspapers out of date, and serial pirates and footpads. Walking-sticks, likewise, and marbles, were included in the stock-in-trade. It had once extended into the light confectionery line; but it would seem that those elegancies of life were not in demand about Jerusalem Buildings, for nothing connected with that branch of commerce remained in the window, except a sort of small glass lantern containing a languishing mass of bull's-eyes, which had melted in the summer and congealed in the winter, until all hope of ever getting them out, or of eating them without eating the lantern too, was gone for ever. Tetterby's had tried its hand at several things. It had once made a feeble little dart at the toy business; for, in another lantern, there was a heap of minute wax dolls, all sticking together upside down, in the direst confusion, with their feet on one another's heads, and a precipitate of broken arms and legs at the bottom. It had made a move in the millinery direction, which a few dry, wiry bonnet-shapes remained in a corner of the window to attest. It had fancied that a living might lie hidden in the tobacco trade, and had stuck up a representation of a native of each of the three integral portions of the British empire in the act of consuming that fragrant weed; with a poetic legend attached, importing that united in one cause they sat and joked, one chewed tobacco, one took snuff, one smoked: but nothing seemed to have come of it – except flies. Time had been when it had put a forlorn trust in imitative jewellery, for in one pane of glass there was a card of cheap seals, and another of pencil-cases, and a mysterious black amulet of inscrutable intention labelled ninepence. But, to that hour, Jerusalem Buildings had bought none of them. In short, Tetterby's had tried so hard to get a livelihood out of Jerusalem Buildings in one way or other, and appeared to have done so indifferently in all, that the best position in the firm was too evidently Co.'s; Co., as a bodiless creation, being untroubled with the vulgar inconveniences of hunger and thirst, being chargeable neither to the poor's-rates nor the assessed taxes, and having no family to provide for.

Tetterby himself, however, in his little parlour, as already mentioned, having the presence of a young family impressed upon his mind in a manner too clamorous to be disregarded, or to comport with the quiet perusal of a newspaper, laid down his paper, wheeled, in his distraction, a few times round the parlour like an undecided carrier pigeon, made an ineffectual rush at one or two flying little figures in bedgowns that skimmed past him, and then, bearing suddenly down upon the only unoffending member of the family, boxed the ears of little Moloch's nurse.

'You bad boy!' said Mr Tetterby; 'haven't you any feeling for your poor father after the fatigues and anxieties of a hard winter's day, since five o'clock in the morning, but must you wither his rest, and corrode his latest intelligence, with *your* vicious tricks? Isn't it enough, sir, that your brother 'Dolphus is toiling and moiling in the fog and cold, and you rolling in the lap of luxury with a – with a baby, and everythink you can wish for,' said Mr Tetterby, heaping this up as a great climax of blessings, 'but must you make a wilderness of home, and maniacs of your parents? Must you, Johnny? Hey?' At each interrogation, Mr Tetterby made a feint of boxing his ears again, but thought better of it, and held his hand.

'Oh, father!' whimpered Johnny, 'when I wasn't doing anything, I'm sure, but taking such care of Sally, and getting her to sleep. Oh, father!'

'I wish my little woman would come home!' said Mr Tetterby, relenting and repenting; 'I only wish my little woman would come home! I ain't fit to deal with 'em. They make my head go round, and get the better of me. Oh, Johnny! Isn't it enough that your dear mother has provided you with that sweet sister?' indicating Moloch; 'isn't it enough that you were seven boys before, without a ray of gal, and that your dear mother went through what she *did* go through, on purpose that you might all of you have a little sister, but must you so behave yourself as to make my head swim?'

Softening more and more as his own tender feelings, and those of his injured son, were worked on, Mr Tetterby concluded by embracing him, and immediately breaking away to catch one of the real delinquents. A reasonably good start occurring, he succeeded, after a short but smart run, and some rather severe cross-country work under and over the bedsteads, and in and out among the intricacies of the chairs, in capturing this infant, whom he condignly punished, and bore to bed. This example had a powerful, and apparently mesmeric, influence on him of the boots, who instantly fell into a deep sleep, though he had been, but a moment before, broad awake, and in the highest possible feather. Nor was it lost upon the two young architects, who retired to bed, in an adjoining closet, with great privacy and speed. The comrade of the Intercepted One also shrinking into his nest with similar discretion, Mr Tetterby, when he paused for breath, found himself unexpectedly in a scene of peace.

'My little woman herself,' said Mr Tetterby, wiping his flushed face, 'could hardly have done it better! I only wish my little woman had had it to do, I do indeed!'

Mr Tetterby sought upon his screen for a passage appropriate to be impressed upon his children's minds on the occasion, and read the following: ' "It is an undoubted fact that all remarkable men have had remarkable mothers, and have respected them in after life as their best friends." Think of your own remarkable mother, my boys,' said Mr Tetterby, 'and know her value while she is still among you!'

He sat down again in his chair by the fire, and composed himself, cross-legged, over his newspaper.

'Let anybody, I don't care who it is, get out of bed again,' said Tetterby as a general proclamation, delivered in a very soft-hearted manner, 'and astonishment will be the portion of that respected contemporary!' – which expression Mr Tetterby selected from his screen. 'Johnny, my child, take care of your only sister, Sally; for she's the brightest gem that ever sparkled on your early brow.'

Johnny sat down on a little stool, and devotedly crushed himself beneath the weight of Moloch.

'Ah, what a gift that baby is to you, Johnny!' said his father; 'and how thankful you ought to be! "It is not generally known," Johnny,' – he was now referring to the screen again – ' "but it is a fact ascertained, by accurate calculations, that the following immense percentage of babies never attain to two years old; that is to say——" '

'Oh, don't, father, please!' cried Johnny. 'I can't bear it when I think of Sally.'

Mr Tetterby desisting, Johnny, with a profounder sense of his trust, wiped his eyes, and hushed his sister.

'Your brother 'Dolphus,' said his father, poking the fire, 'is late tonight, Johnny, and will come home like a lump of ice. What's got your precious mother?'

'Here's mother, and 'Dolphus too, father,' exclaimed

Johnny, 'I think!'

'You're right!' returned his father, listening. 'Yes, that's the footstep of my little woman.'

The process of induction, by which Mr Tetterby had come to the conclusion that his wife was a little woman, was his own secret. She would have made two editions of himself very easily. Considered as an individual, she was rather remarkable for being robust and portly; but, considered with reference to her husband, her dimensions became magnificent. Nor did they assume a less imposing proportion when studied with reference to the size of her seven sons, who were but diminutive. In the case of Sally, however, Mrs Tetterby had asserted herself at last; as nobody knew better than the victim Johnny, who weighed and measured that exacting idol every hour in the day.

Mrs Tetterby, who had been marketing, and carried a basket, threw back her bonnet and shawl, and sitting down, fatigued, commanded Johnny to bring his sweet charge to her straightway for a kiss. Johnny having complied, and gone back to his stool, and again crushed himself, Master Adolphus Tetterby, who had by this time unwound his torso out of a prismatic comforter, apparently interminable, requested the same favour. Johnny having again complied, and again gone back to his stool, and again crushed himself, Mr Tetterby, struck by a sudden thought, preferred the same claim on his own parental part. The satisfaction of this third desire, completely exhausted the sacrifice, who had hardly breath enough left to get back to his stool, crush himself again, and pant at his relations.

'Whatever you do, Johnny,' said Mrs Tetterby, shaking her head, 'take care of her, or never look your mother in the face again.'

'Nor your brother,' said Adolphus.

'Nor your father, Johnny,' added Mr Tetterby.

Johnny, much affected by this conditional renunciation of him, looked down at Moloch's eyes to see that they were all right, so far, and skilfully patted her back (which was uppermost), and rocked her with his foot.

'Are you wet, 'Dolphus, my boy?' said his father. 'Come and take my chair, and dry yourself.'

'No, father, thankee,' said Adolphus, smoothing himself down with his hands. 'I an't very wet, I don't think. Does my face shine much, father?'

'Well, it *does* look waxy, my boy,' returned Mr Tetterby.

'It's the weather, father,' said Adolphus, polishing his cheeks on the worn sleeve of his jacket. 'What with rain, and sleet, and wind, and snow, and fog, my face gets quite brought out into a rash sometimes. And shines, it does–oh, don't it, though!'

Master Adolphus was also in the newspaper line of life,

being employed, by a more thriving firm than his father and Co., to vend newspapers at a railway station, where his chubby little person, like a shabbily-disguised Cupid, and his shrill little voice (he was not much more than ten years old), were as well known as the hoarse panting of the locomotives running in and out. His juvenility might have been at some loss for a harmless outlet, in this early application to traffic, but for a fortunate discovery he made of a means of entertaining himself, and of dividing the long day into stages of interest, without neglecting business. This ingenious invention, remarkable, like many great discoveries, for its simplicity, consisted in varying the first vowel in the word 'paper,' and substituting in its stead, at different periods of the day, all the other vowels in grammatical succession. Thus, before daylight in the wintertime, he went to and fro, in his little oil-skin cap and cape, and his big comforter, piercing the heavy air with his cry of 'Morn-ing Pa-per!' which, about an hour before noon, changed to 'Morn-ing Pepper!' which, at about two, changed to 'Morn-ing Pip-per!' which, in a couple of hours, changed to 'Morn-ing Pop-per!' and so declined with the sun into 'Eve-ning Pup-per!' to the great relief and comfort of this young gentleman's spirits.

Mrs Tetterby, his lady mother, who had been sitting with her bonnet and shawl thrown back, as aforesaid, thoughtfully turning her wedding-ring round and round upon her finger, now rose, and, divesting herself of her out-of-door attire, began to lay the cloth for supper.

'Ah, dear me, dear me, dear me!' said Mrs Tetterby. 'That's the way the world goes!'

'Which is the way the world goes, my dear?' asked Mr Tetterby, looking around.

'Oh, nothing!' said Mrs Tetterby.

Mr Tetterby elevated his eyebrows, folded his newspaper afresh, and carried his eyes up it, and down it, and across it, but was wandering in his attention, and not reading it.

Mrs Tetterby, at the same time, laid the cloth, but rather as if she were punishing the table than preparing the family supper; hitting it unnecessarily hard with the knives and forks, slapping it with the plates, dinting it with the saltcellar, and coming heavily down upon it with the loaf.

'Ah, dear me, dear me, dear me!' said Mrs Tetterby. 'That's the way the world goes!'

'My duck,' returned her husband, looking round again, 'you said that before. Which is the way the world goes?'

'Oh, nothing!' said Mrs Tetterby.

'Sophia!' remonstrated her husband, 'you said *that* before, too.'

'Well, I'll say it again if you like,' returned Mrs Tetterby. 'Oh, nothing – there! And again if you like. Oh, nothing – there! And again if you like. Oh, nothing – now then!'

Mr Tetterby brought his eye to bear upon the partner of his bosom, and said, in mild astonishment: 'My little woman, what has put you out?'

'I'm sure *I* don't know,' she retorted. 'Don't ask me. Who said I was put out at all? *I* never did.'

Mr Tetterby gave up the perusal of his newspaper as a bad job, and, taking a slow walk across the room, with his hands behind him, and his shoulders raised – his gait according perfectly with the resignation of his manner – addressed himself to his two eldest offspring.

'Your supper will be ready in a minute, 'Dolphus,' said Mr Tetterby. 'Your mother has been out in the wet, to the cook's shop, to buy it. It was very good of your mother so to do. *You* shall get some supper too, very soon, Johnny. Your mother's pleased with you, my man, for being so attentive to your precious sister.'

Mrs Tetterby, without any remark, but with a decided subsidence of her animosity towards the table, finished her preparations, and took from her ample basket a substantial slab of hot pease-pudding wrapped in paper, and a basin covered with a saucer, which, on being uncovered, sent forth an odour so agreeable, that the three pair of eyes in the two beds opened wide, and fixed themselves upon the banquet. Mr Tetterby, without regarding this tacit invitation to be seated, stood repeating slowly, 'Yes, yes, your supper will be ready in a minute, 'Dolphus – your mother went out in the wet, to the cook's shop, to buy it. It was very good of your mother so to do' – until Mrs Tetterby, who had been exhibiting sundry tokens of contrition behind him, caught him round the neck, and wept.

'Oh, 'Dolphus!' said Mrs Tetterby, 'how could I go and behave so?'

This reconciliation affected Adolphus the younger and Johnny to that degree, that they both, as with one accord, raised a dismal cry, which had the effect of immediately shutting up the round eyes in the beds, and utterly routing the two remaining little Tetterbys, just then stealing in from the adjoining closet to see what was going on in the eating way.

'I am sure, 'Dolphus,' sobbed Mrs Tetterby, 'coming home, I had no more idea than a child unborn——'

Mr Tetterby seemed to dislike this figure of speech, and observed, 'Say than the baby, my dear.'

'—Had no more idea than the baby,' said Mrs Tetterby. 'Johnny, don't look at me, but look at her, or she'll fall out of your lap and be killed, and then you'll die in agonies of a broken heart, and serve you right. No more idea, I hadn't, than that darling, of being cross when I came home; but somehow, 'Dolphus——' Mrs Tetterby paused, and again turned her wedding-ring round and round upon her finger.

'I see!' said Mr Tetterby. 'I understand! My little woman was put out. Hard times, and hard weather, and hard work, make it trying now and then. I see, bless your soul! No wonder! 'Dolf, my man,' continued Mr Tetterby, exploring the basin with a fork, 'here's your mother been and bought, at the cook's shop, besides pease-pudding, a whole knuckle of a lovely roast leg of pork, with lots of crackling left upon it, and with seasoning, gravy, and mustard quite unlimited. Hand in your plate, my boy, and begin while it's simmering.'

Master Adolphus, needing no second summons, received his portion with eyes rendered moist by appetite, and, withdrawing to his particular stool, fell upon his supper tooth and nail. Johnny was not forgotten, but received his rations on bread, lest he should, in a flush of gravy, trickle any on the baby. He was required, for similar reasons, to keep his pudding, when not on active service, in his pocket.

There might have been more pork on the knuckle-bone – which knuckle-bone the carver at the cook's shop had assuredly not forgotten in carving for previous customers – but there was no stint of seasoning, and that is an accessory dreamily suggesting pork, and pleasantly cheating the sense of taste. The pease-pudding, too, the gravy and mustard, like the Eastern rose in respect of the nightingale, if they were not absolutely pork, had lived near it; so, upon the whole, there was the flavour of a middle-sized pig. It was irresistible to the Tetterbys in bed, who, though professing to slumber peacefully, crawled out when unseen by their parents, and silently appealed to their brothers for any gastronomic token of fraternal affection. They, not hard of heart, presenting scraps in return, it resulted that a party of light skirmishers in nightgowns were careering about the parlour all through supper, which harassed Mr Tetterby exceedingly, and once or twice imposed upon him the necessity of a charge, before which these guerrilla troops retired in all directions, and in great confusion.

Mrs Tetterby did not enjoy her supper. There seemed to be something on Mrs Tetterby's mind. At one time she laughed without reason, and at another time she cried without reason, and at last she laughed and cried together in a manner so very unreasonable that her husband was confounded.

'My little woman,' said Mr Tetterby, 'if the world goes that way, it appears to go the wrong way, and to choke you.'

'Give me a drop of water,' said Mrs Tetterby, struggling with herself, 'and don't speak to me for the present, or take any notice of it. Don't do it!'

Mr Tetterby, having administered the water, turned suddenly on the unlucky Johnny (who was full of sympathy), and demanded why he was wallowing there in gluttony and idleness, instead of coming forward with the baby, that the sight of her might revive his mother. Johnny immediately approached, borne down by its weight; but Mrs Tetterby holding out her hand to signify that she was not in a condition to bear that trying appeal to her feelings, he was interdicted from advancing another inch, on pain of perpetual hatred from all his dearest connections; and accordingly retired to his stool again, and crushed himself as before.

After a pause Mrs Tetterby said she was better now, and began to laugh.

'My little woman,' said her husband dubiously, 'are you quite sure you're better? Or are you, Sophia, about to break out in a fresh direction?'

'No, 'Dolphus, no,' replied his wife. 'I'm quite myself.' With that, settling her hair, and pressing the palms of her hands upon her eyes, she laughed again.

'What a wicked fool I was to think so for a moment!' said Mrs Tetterby. 'Come nearer, 'Dolphus, and let me ease my mind, and tell you what I mean. Let me tell you all about it.'

Mr Tetterby bringing his chair closer, Mrs Tetterby laughed again, gave him a hug, and wiped her eyes.

'You know, 'Dolphus, my dear,' said Mrs Tetterby, 'that when I was single, I might have given myself away in several directions. At one time, four after me at once; two of them were sons of Mars.'

'We're all sons of Ma's, my dear,' said Mr Tetterby, 'jointly with Pa's.'

'I don't mean that,' replied his wife; 'I mean soldiers – sergeants.'

'Oh!' said Mr Tetterby.

'Well, 'Dolphus, I'm sure I never think of such things now, to regret them; and I'm sure I've got as good a husband, and would do as much to prove that I was fond of him, as——'

'As any little woman in the world,' said Mr Tetterby. 'Very good. *Very* good.'

If Mr Tetterby had been ten feet high, he could not have expressed a gentler consideration for Mrs Tetterby's fairylike stature; and, if Mrs Tetterby had been two feet high she could not have felt it more appropriately her due.

'But you see, 'Dolphus,' said Mrs Tetterby, 'this being Christmas-time, when all people who can, make holiday, and when all people who have got money like to spend some, I did, somehow, get a little out of sorts when I was in the streets just now. There were so many things to be sold – such delicious things to eat, such fine things to look at, such delightful things to have – and there was so much calculating and calculating necessary, before I durst lay out a sixpence for the commonest thing; and the basket was so large, and wanted so much in it; and my stock of money was so small, and would go such a little way——You hate me, don't you, 'Dolphus?'

'Not quite,' said Mr Tetterby, 'as yet.'

'Well! I'll tell you the whole truth,' pursued his wife penitently, 'and then perhaps you will. I felt all this so much, when I was trudging about in the cold, and when I saw a lot of other calculating faces and large baskets trudging about too, that I began to think whether I mightn't have done better, and been happier, if I hadn't——' The wedding-ring went round again, and Mrs Tetterby shook her downcast head as she turned it.

'I see,' said her husband quietly; 'if you hadn't married at all, or if you had married somebody else?'

'Yes,' sobbed Mrs Tetterby. 'That's really what I thought. Do you hate me now, 'Dolphus?'

'Why, no,' said Mr Tetterby, 'I don't find that I do as yet.'

Mrs Tetterby gave him a thankful kiss, and went on.

'I begin to hope you won't, now, 'Dolphus, though I am afraid I haven't told you the worst. I can't think what came over me. I don't know whether I was ill, or mad, or what I was, but I couldn't call up anything that seemed to bind us to each other, or to reconcile me to my fortune. All the pleasures and enjoyments we had ever had – *they* seemed so poor and insignificant, I hated them. I could have trodden on them. And I could think of nothing else except our being poor, and the number of mouths there were at home.'

'Well, well, my dear,' said Mr Tetterby, shaking her hand encouragingly, 'that's truth, after all. We *are* poor, and there *are* a number of mouths at home here.'

'Ah! but, Dolf, Dolf!' cried his wife, laying her hands upon his neck, 'my good, kind, patient fellow, when I had been at home a very little while – how different! Oh, Dolf dear, how different it was! I felt as if there was a rush of recollection on me, all at once, that softened my hard heart, and filled it up till it was bursting. All our struggles for a livelihood, all our cares and wants since we have been married, all the times of sickness, all the hours of watching, we have ever had, by one another, or by the children, seemed to speak to me, and say that they had made us one, and that I never might have been, or could have been, or would have been, any other than the wife and mother I am. Then the cheap enjoyments that I could have trodden on so cruelly, got to be so precious to me – oh, so priceless and dear! – that I couldn't bear to think how much I had wronged them; and I said, and say again a hundred times, how could I ever behave so, 'Dolphus? how could I ever have the heart to do it?'

The good woman, quite carried away by her honest tenderness and remorse, was weeping with all her heart, when she started up with a scream, and ran behind her husband. Her cry was so terrified, that the children started from their sleep and from their beds, and clung about her. Nor did her gaze belie her voice as she pointed to a pale man in a black cloak who had come into the room.

'Look at that man! Look there! What does he want?'

'My dear,' returned her husband, 'I'll ask him if you'll let me go. What's the matter? How you shake!'

'I saw him in the street when I was out just now. He looked at me, and stood near me. I am afraid of him.'

'Afraid of him! Why?'

'I don't know why – I – stop! husband!' for he was going towards the stranger.

She had one hand pressed upon her forehead, and one upon her breast; and there was a peculiar fluttering all over her, and a hurried unsteady motion of her eyes, as if she had lost something.

'Are you ill, my dear?'

'What is it that is going from me again?' she muttered in a low voice. 'What *is* this that is going away?'

Then she abruptly answered: 'Ill? No, I am quite well,' and stood looking vacantly at the floor.

Her husband, who had not been altogether free from the infection of her fear at first, and whom the present strangeness of her manner did not tend to reassure, addressed himself to the pale visitor in the black cloak, who stood still, and whose eyes were bent upon the ground.

'What may be your pleasure, sir,' he asked, 'with us?'

'I fear that my coming in unperceived,' returned the visitor, 'has alarmed you; but you were talking, and did not hear me.'

'My little woman says – perhaps you heard her say it,' returned Mr Tetterby, 'that it's not the first time you have alarmed her tonight.'

'I am sorry for it. I remember to have observed her, for a few moments only, in the street. I had no intention of frightening her.'

As he raised his eyes in speaking, she raised hers. It was extraordinary to see what dread she had of him, and with what dread he observed it – and yet how narrowly and closely.

'My name,' he said, 'is Redlaw. I come from the old College hard by. A young gentleman, who is a student there, lodges in your house, does he not?'

'Mr Denham?' said Tetterby.

'Yes.'

It was a natural action, and so slight as to be hardly noticeable; but the little man, before speaking again, passed his hand across his forehead, and looked quickly round the room, as though he were sensible of some change in its atmosphere. The Chemist, instantly transferring to him the look of dread he had directed towards the wife, stepped back, and his face turned paler.

'The gentleman's room,' said Tetterby, 'is upstairs, sir. There's a more convenient private entrance; but, as you have come in here, it will save your going out into the cold, if you'll take this little staircase,' showing one communicating directly with the parlour, 'and go up to him that way, if you wish to see him.'

'Yes, I wish to see him,' said the Chemist. 'Can you spare alight?'

The watchfulness of his haggard look, and the inexplicable distrust that darkened it, seemed to trouble Mr Tetterby. He paused; and, looking fixedly at him in return, stood for a minute or so, like a man stupefied or fascinated.

At length he said, 'I'll light you, sir, if you'll follow me.'

'No,' replied the Chemist, 'I don't wish to be attended, or announced to him. He does not expect me. I would rather go alone. Please to give me the light, if you can spare it, and I'll find the way.'

In the quickness of his expression of this desire, and in taking the candle from the newsman, he touched him on the breast. Withdrawing his hand hastily, almost as though he had wounded him by accident (for he did not know in what part of himself his new power resided, or how it was communicated, or how the manner of its reception varied in different persons), he turned and ascended the stair.

But, when he reached the top, he stopped and looked

down. The wife was standing in the same place, twisting her ring round and round upon her finger. The husband, with his head bent forward on his breast, was musing heavily and sullenly. The children, still clustering about the mother, gazed timidly after the visitor, and nestled together when they saw him looking down.

'Come!' said the father roughly. 'There's enough of this. Get to bed here!'

'The place is inconvenient and small enough,' the mother added, 'without you. Get to bed!'

The whole brood, scared and sad, crept away: little Johnny and the baby lagging last. The mother glancing contemptuously round the sordid room, and tossing from her the fragments of their meal, stopped on the threshold of her task of clearing the table, and sat down, pondering idly and dejectedly. The father betook himself to the chimney-corner, and, impatiently raking the small fire together, bent over it as if he would monopolise it all. They did not interchange a word.

The Chemist, paler than before, stole upward like a thief; looking back upon the change below, and dreading equally to go on or return.

'What have I done?' he said confusedly. 'What am I going to do?'

'To be the benefactor of mankind,' he thought he heard a

voice reply.

He looked round, but there was nothing there; and a passage now shutting out the little parlour from his view, he went on, directing his eyes before him at the way he went.

'It is only since last night,' he muttered gloomily, 'that I have remained shut up, and yet all things are strange to me. I am strange to myself. I am here as in a dream. What interest have I in this place, or in any place that I can bring to my remembrance? My mind is going blind!'

There was a door before him, and he knocked at it. Being invited, by a voice within, to enter, he complied.

'Is that my kind nurse?' said the voice. 'But I need not ask her. There was no one else to come here.'

It spoke cheerfully, though in a languid tone, and attracted his attention to a young man lying on a couch, drawn before the chimney-piece, with the back towards the door. A meagre, scanty stove, pinched and hollowed like a sick man's cheeks, and bricked into the centre of a hearth that it could scarcely warm, contained the fire, to which his face was turned. Being sp near the windy housetop, it wasted quickly, and with a busy sound, and the burning ashes dropped down fast.

'They chink when they shoot out here,' said the student, smiling; 'so, according to the gossips, they are not coffins, but purses. I shall be well and rich yet, some day, if it please God, and shall live, perhaps, to love a daughter Milly, in remembrance of the kindest nature and the gentlest heart in the world.'

He put up his hands as if expecting her to take it, but, being weakened, he lay still, with his face resting on his other hand, and did not turn round.

The Chemist glanced about the room; at the student's books and papers, piled upon a table in a corner, where they, and his extinguished reading-lamp, now prohibited and put away, told of the attentive hours that had gone before this illness, and perhaps caused it; at such signs of his old health and freedom as the out-of-door attire that hung idle on the wall; at those remembrances of other and less solitary scenes, the little miniatures upon the chimney-piece, and the drawing of home; at that token of his emulation, perhaps, in some sort, of his personal attachment, too, the framed engraving of himself, the looker-on. The time had been, only yesterday, when not one of these objects, in its remotest association of interest with the living figure before him, would have been lost on Redlaw. Now, they were but objects; or, if any gleam of such connection shot upon him, it perplexed, and not enlightened him, as he stood looking round with a dull wonder.

The student, recalling the thin hand which had remained so long untouched, raised himself on the couch, and turned his head.

'Mr Redlaw!' he exclaimed, and started up.

Redlaw put out his arm.

'Don't come near to me. I will sit here. Remain you where you are!'

He sat down on a chair near the door, and, having glanced at the young man standing leaning with his hand upon the couch, spoke with his eyes averted towards the ground.

'I heard, by an accident, by what accident is no matter, that one of my class was ill and solitary. I received no other description of him than that he lived in this street. Beginning my inquiries at the first house in it, I have found him.'

'I have been ill, sir,' returned the student, not merely with a modest hesitation, but with a kind of awe of him, 'but am greatly better. An attack of fever – of the brain, I believe – has weakened me, but I am much better. I cannot say I have been solitary in my illness, or I should forget the ministering that has been near me.'

'You are speaking of the keeper's wife?' said Redlaw.

'Yes.' The student bent his head, as if he rendered her some silent homage.

The Chemist, in whom there was a cold, monotonous apathy, which rendered him more like a marble image on the tomb of the man who had started from his dinner yesterday at the first mention of this student's case, than the breathing man himself, glanced again at the student leaning with his hand upon the couch, and looked upon the ground, and in the air, as if for light for his blinded mind.

'I remembered your name,' he said, 'when it was mentioned to me downstairs just now; and I recollect your face. We have held but very little personal communication together?'

'Very little.'

'You have retired and withdrawn from me, more than any of the rest, I think?'

The student signified assent.

'And why?' said the Chemist; not with the least expression of interest, but with a moody, wayward kind of curiosity. 'Why? How comes it that you have sought to keep especially from me the knowledge of your remaining here, at this season, when all the rest have dispersed, and of your being ill? I want to know why this is?'

The young man, who had heard him with increasing agitation, raised his downcast eyes to his face, and, clasping his hands together, cried with sudden earnestness, and with trembling lips:

'Mr Redlaw! You have discovered me. You know my secret!'

'Secret?' said the Chemist harshly. '*I* know?'

'Yes! Your manner, so different from the interest and sympathy which endear you to so many hearts, your altered voice, the constraint there is in everything you say, and in your looks,' replied the student, 'warn me that you know me. That you would conceal it, even now, is but a proof to me (God knows I need none!) of your natural kindness, and of the bar there is between us.'

A vacant and contemptuous laugh was all his answer.

'But Mr Redlaw,' said the student, 'as a just man, and a good man, think how innocent I am, except in name and descent, of participation in any wrong inflicted on you, or in any sorrow you have borne.'

'Sorrow!' said Redlaw, laughing. 'Wrong! What are those to me?'

'For Heaven's sake,' entreated the shrinking student, 'do not let the mere interchange of a few words with me change you like this, sir! Let me pass again from your knowledge and notice. Let me occupy my old reserved and distant place among those whom you instruct. Know me only by the name I have assumed, and not by that of Longford——'

'Longford!' exclaimed the other.

He clasped his head with both his hands, and for a moment turned upon the young man his own intelligent and thoughtful face. But the light passed from it like the sunbeam of an instant, and it clouded as before.

'The name my mother bears, sir,' faltered the young man, 'the name she took, when she might, perhaps, have taken one more honoured. Mr Redlaw,' hesitating, 'I believe I know that history. Where my information halts, my guesses at what is wanting may supply something not remote from the truth. I am the child of a marriage that has not proved itself a well-assorted or a happy one. From infancy I have heard you spoken of with honour and respect – with something that was almost reverence. I have heard of such devotion, of such fortitude and tenderness, of such rising up against the obstacles which press men down, that my fancy, since I learnt my little lesson from my mother, has shed a lustre on your name. At last, a poor student myself, from whom could I learn but you?'

Redlaw, unmoved, unchanged, and looking at him with a staring frown, answered by no word or sign.

'I cannot say,' pursued the other, 'I should try in vain to say, how much it has impressed me, and affected me, to find the gracious traces of the past, in that certain power of winning gratitude and confidence which is associated among us students (among the humblest of us most) with Mr Redlaw's generous name. Our ages and positions are so different, sir, and I am so accustomed to regard you from a distance, that I wonder at my own presumption when I touch, however lightly, on that theme. But to one who – I may say, who felt no common interest in my mother once – it may be something to hear, now that is all past, with what indescribable feelings of affection I have, in my obscurity, regarded him; with what pain and reluctance I have kept aloof from his encouragement, when a word of it would have made me rich; yet how I have felt it fit that I should hold my course, content to know him, and to be unknown. Mr Redlaw,' said the student faintly, 'what I would have said, I have said ill, for my strength is strange to me as yet; but, for anything unworthy in this fraud of mine, forgive me, and for all the rest forget me!'

The staring frown remained on Redlaw's face, and yielded to no other expression until the student, with these words, advanced towards him, as if to touch his hand, when he drew back and cried to him:

'Don't come nearer to me!'

The young man stopped, shocked by the eagerness of his recoil, and by the sternness of his repulsion; and he passed his hand thoughtfully across his forehead.

'The past is past,' said the Chemist. 'It dies like the brutes. Who talks to me of its traces in my life? He raves or lies! What have I to do with your distempered dreams? If you want money, here it is. I came to offer it; and that is all I came for. There can be nothing else that brings me here,' he muttered, holding his head again with both his hands. 'There *can* be nothing else, and yet——'

He had tossed his purse upon the table. As he fell into this dim cogitation with himself, the student took it up, and held it out to him.

'Take it back, sir,' he said proudly, though not angrily. 'I wish you could take from me, with it, the remembrance of your words and offer.'

'You do?' he retorted, with a wild light in his eyes. 'You do?'

'I do!'

The Chemist went close to him for the first time, and took the purse, and turned him by the arm, and looked him in the face.

'There is sorrow and trouble in sickness, is there not?' he demanded with a laugh.

The wondering student answered, 'Yes.'

'In its unrest, in its anxiety, in its suspense, in all its train of physical and mental miseries?' said the Chemist with a wild, unearthly exultation. 'All best forgotten, are they not?'

The student did not answer, but again passed his hand confusedly across his forehead. Redlaw still held him by the sleeve, when Milly's voice was heard outside.

'I can see very well now,' she said, 'thank you, Dolf. Don't cry, dear. Father and mother will be comfortable again tomorrow, and home will be comfortable too. A gentleman with him, is there?'

Redlaw released his hold as he listened.

'I have feared, from the first moment,' he murmured to

himself, 'to meet her. There is a steady quality of goodness in her that I dread to influence. I may be the murderer of what is tenderest and best within her bosom.'

She was knocking at the door.

'Shall I dismiss it as an idle foreboding, or still avoid her?' he muttered, looking uneasily around.

She was knocking at the door again.

'Of all the visitors who could come here,' he said in a hoarse, alarmed voice, turning to his companion, 'this is the one I should desire most to avoid. Hide me!'

The student opened a frail door in the wall, communicating, where the garret roof began to slope towards the floor, with a small inner room. Redlaw passed in haste, and shut it after him.

The student then resumed his place upon the couch, and called to her to enter.

'Dear Mr Edmund,' said Milly, looking round, 'they told me there was a gentleman here.'

'There is no one here but I.'

'There has been someone?'

'Yes, yes, there has been someone.'

She put her little basket on the table, and went up to the back of the couch, as if to take the extended hand – but it was not there. A little surprised, in her quiet way, she leaned over to look at his face, and gently touched him on the brow.

'Are you quite as well tonight? Your head is not so cool as in the afternoon.'

'Tut!' said the student petulantly, 'very little ails me.'

A little more surprise, but no reproach, was expressed in her face, as she withdrew to the other side of the table, and took a small packet of needlework from her basket. But she laid it down again, on second thoughts, and going noiselessly about the room, set everything exactly in its place, and in the neatest order; even to the cushions on the couch, which she touched with so light a hand, that he hardly seemed to know it, as he lay looking at the fire. When all this was done, and she had swept the hearth, she sat down, in her modest little bonnet, to her work, and was quietly busy on it directly.

'It's the new muslin curtain for the window, Mr Edmund,' said Milly, stitching away as she talked. 'It will look very clean and nice, though it costs very little, and will save your eyes, too, from the light. Mr William says the room should not be too light just now, when you are recovering so well, or the glare might make you giddy.'

He said nothing; but there was something so fretful and impatient in his change of position, that her quick fingers stopped, and she looked at him anxiously.

'The pillows are not comfortable,' she said, laying down her work and rising. 'I will soon put them right.'

'They were very well,' he answered. 'Leave them alone,

pray. You make so much of everything.'

He raised his head to say this, and looked at her so thanklessly, that, after he had thrown himself down again, she stood timidly pausing. However, she resumed her seat, and her needle, without having directed even a murmuring look towards him, and was soon as busy as before.

'I have been thinking, Mr Edmund, that *you* have been often thinking of late, when I have been sitting by, how true the saying is, that adversity is a good teacher. Health will be more precious to you, after this illness, than it has ever been. And years hence, when this time of year comes round, and you remember the days when you lay here sick, alone, that the knowledge of your illness might not afflict those who are dearest to you, your home will be doubly dear and doubly blessed. Now, isn't that a good, true thing?'

She was too intent upon her work, and too earnest in what she said, and too composed and quiet altogether, to be on the watch for any look he might direct towards her in reply; so the shaft of his ungrateful glance fell harmless, and did not wound her.

'Ah!' said Milly, with her pretty head inclining thoughtfully on one side, as she looked down, following her busy fingers with her eyes. 'Even on me – and I am very different from you, Mr Edmund, for I have no learning, and don't know how to think properly – this view of such things has made a great impression since you have been lying ill. When I have seen you so touched by the kindness and attention of the poor people down-stairs, I have felt that you thought even that experience some repayment for the loss of health, and I have read in your face, as plain as if it was a book, that but for some trouble and sorrow we should never know half the good there is about us.'

His getting up from the couch interrupted her, or she was going on to say more.

'We needn't magnify the merit, Mrs William,' he rejoined slightingly. 'The people downstairs will be paid in good time, I dare say, for any little extra service they may have rendered me; and perhaps they anticipate no less. I am much obliged to you, too.'

Her fingers stopped, and she looked at him.

'I can't be made to feel the more obliged by your exaggerating the case,' he said. 'I am sensible that you have been interested in me, and I say I am much obliged to you. What more would you have?'

Her work fell on her lap, as she still looked at him walking to and fro with an intolerant air, and stopping now and then.

'I say again, I am much obliged to you. Why weaken my sense of what is your due in obligation, by preferring enormous claims upon me? Trouble, sorrow, affliction, adversity! One might suppose I had been dying a score of deaths here.'

'Do you believe, Mr Edmund,' she asked, rising and going nearer to him, 'that I spoke of the poor people of the house with any reference to myself? To me?' laying her hand upon her bosom with a simple and innocent smile of astonishment.

'Oh! I think nothing about it, my good creature,' he returned. 'I have had an indisposition, which your solicitude – observe! I say solicitude – makes a great deal more of than it merits; and it's over, and we can't perpetuate it.'

He coldly took a book, and sat down at the table.

She watched him for a little while, until her smile was quite gone, and then, returning to where her basket was, said gently:

'Mr Edmund, would you rather be alone?'

'There is no reason why I should detain you here,' he replied.

'Except——' said Milly, hesitating, and showing her work.

'Oh! the curtain,' he answered with a supercilious laugh. 'That's not worth staying for.'

She made up the little packet again, and put it in her basket. Then, standing before him with such an air of patient entreaty that he could not choose but look at her, she said:

'If you should want me, I will come back willingly. When you did want me I was quite happy to come; there was no merit in it. I think you must be afraid that, now you are getting well, I may be troublesome to you; but I should not have been, indeed. I should have come no longer than your weakness and confinement lasted. You owe me nothing; but it is right that you should deal as justly by me as if I was a lady – even the very lady that you love; and, if you suspect me of meanly making much of the little I have tried to do to comfort your sick-room, you do yourself more wrong than ever you can do me. That is why I am sorry. That is why I am very sorry.'

If she had been as passionate as she was quiet, as indignant as she was calm, as angry in her look as she was gentle, as loud of tone as she was low and clear, she might have left no sense of her departure in the room, compared with that which fell upon the lonely student when she went away.

He was gazing drearily upon the place where she had been, when Redlaw came out of his concealment, and came to the door.

'When sickness lays its hand on you again,' he said looking fiercely back at him – 'may it be soon! – die here! Rot here!'

'What have you done?' returned the other catching at his cloak. 'What change have you wrought in me? What curse have you brought upon me? Give me back myself!'

'Give me back *myself*!' exclaimed Redlaw like a madman. 'I am infected. I am infectious! I am charged with poison for my own mind, and the minds of all mankind. Where I felt interest, compassion, sympathy, I am turning into stone. Selfishness and ingratitude spring up in my blighting footsteps. I am only so much less base than the wretches whom I make so, that in the moment of their transformation I can hate them.'

As he spoke – the young man still holding to his cloak – he cast him off, and struck him; then wildly hurried out into the night air where the wind was blowing, the snow falling, the cloud-drift sweeping on, the moon dimly shining; and where, blowing in the wind, falling with the snow, drifting with the clouds, shining in the moonlight, and heavily looming in the darkness, were the Phantom's words, 'The gift that I have given, you shall give again, go where you will!'

Wither he went he neither knew nor cared, so that he avoided company. The change he felt within him made the busy streets a desert, and himself a desert, and the multitude around him, in their manifold endurances and ways of life, a mighty waste of sand, which the winds tossed into unintelligible heaps, and made a ruinous confusion of. Those traces in his breast which the Phantom had told him would 'die out soon' were not, as yet, so far upon their way to death, but that he understood enough of what he was, and what he made of others, to desire to be alone.

This put it in his mind – he suddenly bethought himself, as he was going along, of the boy who had rushed into his room. And then he recollected that, of those with whom he had communicated since the Phantom's disappearance, that boy alone had shown no sign of being changed.

Monstrous and odious as the wild thing was to him, he determined to seek it out, and prove if this were really so; and also to seek it with another intention, which came into his thoughts at the same time.

So, resolving with some difficulty where he was, he directed his steps back to the old College, and to that part of it where the general porch was, and where, alone, the pavement was worn by the tread of students' feet.

The keeper's house stood just within the iron gates, forming a part of the chief quadrangle. There was a little cloister outside, and from that sheltered place he knew he could look in at the window of their ordinary room, and see who was within. The iron gates were shut, but his hand was familiar with the fastening, and, drawing it back by thrusting in his wrist between the bars, he passed through softly, shut it again, and crept up to the window, crumbling the thin crust of snow with his feet.

The fire, to which he had directed the boy last night, shining brightly through the glass, made an illuminated place upon the ground. Instinctively avoiding this, and going round it, he looked in at the window. At first he thought that there was no one there, and that the blaze was reddening only the old beams in the ceiling and the dark walls; but, peering in more narrowly, he saw the object of his search coiled asleep before it on the floor. He passed quickly to the door, opened it, and went in.

The creature lay in such a fiery heat, that, as the Chemist stooped to rouse him, it scorched his head. So soon as he was touched, the boy, not half awake, clutched his rags together with the instinct of flight upon him, half rolled and half ran into a distant corner of the room, where, heaped upon the ground, he struck his foot out to defend himself.

'Get up!' said the Chemist. 'You have not forgotten me?'

'You let me alone!' returned the boy. 'This is the woman's house – not yours.'

The Chemist's steady eye controlled him somewhat, or inspired him with enough submission to be raised upon his feet, and looked at.

'Who washed them, and put those bandages where they were bruised and cracked?' asked the Chemist, pointing to their altered state.

'The woman did.'

'And is it she who has made you cleaner in the face, too?'

'Yes, the woman.'

Redlaw asked these questions to attract his eyes towards himself, and, with the same intent, now held him by the chin, and threw his wild hair back, though he loathed to touch him. The boy watched his eyes keenly, as if he thought it needful to his own defence, not knowing what he might do next; and Redlaw could see well that no change came over him.

'Where are they?' he inquired.

'The woman's out.'

'I know she is. Where is the old man with the white hair, and his son?'

'The woman's husband, d'ye mean?' inquired the boy.

'Ay. Where are those two?'

'Out. Something's the matter somewhere. They were fetched out in a hurry, and told me to stop here.'

'Come with me,' said the Chemist, 'and I'll give you money.'

'Come where? and how much will you give?'

'I'll give you more shillings than you ever saw, and bring you back soon. Do you know your way to where you came from?'

'You let me go,' returned the boy, suddenly twisting out of his grasp. 'I'm not a-going to take you there. Let me be, or I'll heave some fire at you!'

He was down before it, and ready, with his savage little hand, to pluck the burning coals out.

What the Chemist had felt, in observing the effect of his charmed influence stealing over those with whom he came in contact, was not nearly equal to the cold vague terror with which he saw this baby-monster put it at defiance. It chilled his blood to look on the immovable, impenetrable thing, in the likeness of a child, with its sharp malignant face turned up to his, and its almost infant hand ready at the bars.

'Listen, boy!' he said. 'You shall take me where you please, so that you take me where the people are very miserable or very wicked. I want to do them good, and not to harm them. You shall have money, as I have told you, and I will bring you back. Get up! Come quickly!' He made a hasty step towards the door, afraid of her returning.

'Will you let me walk by myself, and never hold me, nor yet touch me?' said the boy, slowly withdrawing the hand with which he threatened, and beginning to get up.

'And let me go before, behind, or anyways I like?'

'I will!'

'Give me some money first, then, and I'll go.'

The Chemist laid a few shillings, one by one, in his extended hand. To count them was beyond the boy's knowledge, but he said, 'one,' every time, and avariciously looked at each as it was given, and at the donor. He had nowhere to put them, out of his hand, but in his mouth; and he put them there.

Redlaw then wrote with his pencil, on a leaf of his pocket-book, that the boy was with him; and, laying it on the table, signed to him to follow. Keeping his rags together, as usual, the boy complied, and went out with his bare head and his naked feet into the winter night.

Preferring not to depart by the iron gate by which he had entered, where they were in danger of meeting her whom he so anxiously avoided, the Chemist led the way, through some of those passages among which the boy had lost himself, and by that portion of the building where he lived, to a small door of which he had the key. When they got into the street, he stopped to ask his guide – who instantly retreated from him – if he knew where they were.

The savage thing looked here and there, and at length, nodding his head, pointed in the direction he designed to take. Redlaw going on at once, he followed, somewhat less suspiciously; shifting his money from his mouth into his hand, and back again into his mouth, and stealthily rubbing it bright upon his shreds of dress, as he went along.

Three times, in their progress, they were side by side. Three times they stopped, being side by side. Three times the Chemist glanced down at his face, and shuddered as it forced upon him one reflection.

The first occasion was when they were crossing an old

churchyard, and Redlaw stopped among the graves, utterly at a loss how to connect them with any tender, softening, or consolatory thought.

The second was when the breaking forth of the moon induced him to look up at the heavens, where he saw her in her glory, surrounded by a host of stars he still knew by the names and histories which human science has appended to them; but where he saw nothing else he had been wont to see, felt nothing he had been wont to feel, in looking up there on a bright night.

The third was when he stopped to listen to a plaintive strain of music, but could only hear a tune, made manifest to him by the dry mechanism of the instruments and his own ears, with no address to any mystery within him, without a whisper in it of the past, or of the future, powerless upon him as the sound of last year's running water, or the rushing o.f last year's wind.

At each of these three times he saw, with horror, that in spite of the vast intellectual distance between them, and their being unlike each other in all physical respects, the expression on the boy's face was the expression on his own.

They journeyed on for some time – now through such crowded places, that he often looked over his shoulder, thinking he had lost his guide, but generally finding him within his shadow on his other side; now by ways so quiet, that he could have counted his short, quick, naked footsteps coming on behind – until they arrived at a ruinous collection of houses, and the boy touched him and stopped.

'In there!' he said, pointing out one house where there were scattered lights in the windows, and a dim lantern in the doorway, with 'Lodgings for Travellers' painted on it.

Redlaw looked about him; from the houses, to the waste piece of ground on which the houses stood, or rather, did not altogether tumble down, unfenced, undrained, unlighted, and bordered by a sluggish ditch; from that, to the sloping line of arches, part of some neighbouring viaduct or bridge with which it was surrounded, and which lessened gradually towards them, until the last but one was a mere kennel for a dog, the last a plundered little heap of bricks; from that, to the child, close to him, cowering and trembling with the cold, and limping on one little foot, while he coiled the other round his leg to warm it, yet staring at all these things with that frightful likeness of expression so apparent in his face, that Redlaw started from him.

'In there!' said the boy, pointing out the house again. 'I'll wait.'

'Will they let me in?' asked Redlaw.

'Say you're a doctor,' he answered with a nod. 'There's plenty ill here.'

Looking back on his way to the house-door, Redlaw saw

him trail himself upon the dust, and crawl within the shelter of the smallest arch, as if he were a rat. He had no pity for the thing, but he was afraid of it; and when it looked out of its den at him, he hurried to the house as a retreat.

'Sorrow, wrong, and trouble,' said the Chemist, with a painful effort at some more distinct remembrance, 'at least haunt this place darkly. He can do no harm who brings forgetfulness of such things here!'

With these words he pushed the yielding door, and went in.

There was a woman sitting on the stairs, either asleep or forlorn, whose head was bent down on her hands and knees. As it was not easy to pass without treading on her, and as she was perfectly regardless of his near approach, he stopped, and touched her on the shoulder. Looking up, she showed him quite a young face, but one whose bloom and promise were all swept away, as if the haggard winter should unnaturally kill the spring.

With little or no show of concern on his account, she moved nearer to the wall to leave him a wider passage.

'What are you?' said Redlaw, pausing, with his hand upon the broken stair-rail.

'What do you think I am?' she answered, showing him her face again.

He looked upon the ruined temple of God, so lately

made, so soon disfigured; and something, which was not compassion – for the springs in which a true compassion for such miseries has its rise were dried up in his breast – but which was nearer to it, for the moment, than any feeling that had lately struggled into the darkening, but not yet wholly darkened, night of his mind – mingled a touch of softness with his next words.

'I am come here to give relief, if I can,' he said. 'Are you thinking of any wrong?'

She frowned at him, and then laughed; and then her laugh prolonged itself into a shivering sigh, as she dropped her head again, and hid her fingers in her hair.

'Are you thinking of a wrong?' he asked once more.

'I am thinking of my life,' she said with a momentary look at him.

He had a perception that she was one of many, and that he saw the type of thousands when he saw her drooping at his feet.

'What are your parents?' he demanded.

'I had a good home once. My father was a gardener, far away into the country.'

'Is he dead?'

'He's dead to me. All such things are dead to me. You a gentleman, and not know that!' She raised her eyes again, and laughed at him.

'Girl!' said Redlaw sternly, 'before this death of all such things was brought about, was there no wrong done to you? In spite of all that you can do, does no remembrance of wrong cleave to you? Are there not times upon times when it is misery to you?'

So little of what was womanly was left in her appearance, that now, when she burst into tears, he stood amazed. But he was more amazed, and much disquieted, to note that, in her awakened recollection of this wrong, the first trace of her old humanity and frozen tenderness appeared to show itself.

He drew a little off, and, in doing so, observed that her arms were black, her face cut, and her bosom bruised.

'What brutal hand has hurt you so?' he asked.

'My own. I did it myself!' she answered quickly.

'It is impossible.'

'I'll swear I did! He didn't touch me. I did it to myself in a passion, and threw myself down here. He wasn't near me. He never laid a hand upon me!'

In the white determination of her face, confronting him with this untruth, he saw enough of the last perversion and distortion of good surviving in that miserable breast, to be stricken with remorse that he had ever come near here.

'Sorrow, wrong, and trouble!' he muttered, turning his fearful gaze away. 'All that connects her with the state from which she has fallen has those roots! In the name of God, let me go by!'

Afraid to look at her again, afraid to touch her, afraid to think of having sundered the last thread by which she held upon the mercy of Heaven, he gathered his cloak about him, and glided swiftly up the stairs.

Opposite to him, on the landing, was a door, which stood partly open, and which, as he ascended, a man with a candle in his hand came forward from within to shut. But this man, on seeing him, drew back, with much emotion in his manner, and, as if by a sudden impulse, mentioned his name aloud.

In the surprise of such a recognition there, he stopped, endeavouring to recollect the wan and startled face. He had no time to consider it, for, to his yet greater amazement, old Philip came out of the room, and took him by the hand.

'Mr Redlaw,' said the old man, 'this is like you, this is like you, sir! You have heard of it, and have come after us to render any help you can. Ah, too late, too late!'

Redlaw, with a bewildered look, submitted to be led into the room. A man lay there on a truckle-bed, and William Swidger stood at the bedside.

'Too late!' murmured the old man, looking wistfully into the Chemist's face; and the tears stole down his cheeks.

'That's what I say, father,' interposed his son in a low voice. 'That's where it is exactly. To keep as quiet as ever we can while he's a dozing is the only thing to do. You're right, father!'

Redlaw paused at the bedside, and looked down on the figure that was stretched upon the mattress. It was that of a man who should have been in the vigour of his life, but on whom it was not likely that the sun would ever shine again. The vices of his forty or fifty years' career had so branded him, that, in comparison with their effects upon his face, the heavy hand of time upon the old man's face who watched him had been merciful and beautifying.

'Who is this?' asked the Chemist, looking round.

'My son George, Mr Redlaw,' said the old man, wringing his hands. 'My eldest son, George, who was more his mother's pride than all the rest!'

Redlaw's eyes wandered from the old man's grey head, as he laid it down upon the bed, to the person who had recognised him, and who had kept aloof in the remotest corner of the room. He seemed to be about his own age; and, although he knew no such hopeless decay and broken man as he appeared to be, there was something in the turn of his figure, as he stood with his back towards him, and now went out at the door, that made him pass his hand uneasily across his brow.

'William,' he said in a gloomy whisper, 'who is that man?'

'Why, you see, sir,' returned Mr William, 'that's what I say myself. Why should a man ever go and gamble, and the like of that, and let himself down inch by inch till he can't let himself down any lower?'

'Has *he* done so?' asked Redlaw, glancing after him with the same uneasy action as before.

'Just exactly that, sir,' returned William Swidger, 'as I'm told. He knows a little about medicine, sir, it seems; and having been wayfaring towards London with my unhappy brother that you see here,' – Mr William passed his coat-sleeve across his eyes – 'and being lodging upstairs for the night – what I say, you see, is, that strange companions come together here sometimes – he looked in to attend upon him, and came for us at his request. What a mournful spectacle, sir! But that's where it is. It's enough to kill my father!'

Redlaw looked up at these words, and, recalling where he was and with whom, and the spell he carried with him – which his surprise had obscured – retired a little, hurriedly, debating with himself whether to shun the house that moment, or remain.

Yielding to a certain sullen doggedness, which it seemed to be part of his condition to struggle with, he argued for remaining.

'Was it only yesterday,' he said, 'when I observed the memory of this old man to be a tissue of sorrow and trouble, and shall I be afraid, tonight, to shake it? Are such remembrances as I can drive away so precious to this dying man, that I need fear for *him*? No, I'll stay here.'

But he stayed in fear and trembling none the less for these words; and, shrouded in his black cloak with his face turned from them, stood away from the bedside, listening to what they said, as if he felt himself a demon in the place.

'Father!' murmured the sick man, rallying a little from his stupor.

'My boy! My son George!' said old Philip.

'You spoke, just now, of my being mother's favourite long ago. It's a dreadful thing to think, now, of long ago!'

'No, no, no!' returned the old man. 'Think of it. Don't say it's dreadful. It's not dreadful to me, my son.'

'It cuts you to the heart, father.' For the old man's tears were falling on him.

'Yes, yes,' said Philip, 'so it does; but it does me good. It's a heavy sorrow to think of that time, but it does me good, George. Oh, think of it too, think of it too, and your heart will be softened more and more! Where's my son William? William, my boy, your mother loved him dearly to the last, and with her latest breath said, "Tell him I forgave him, blessed him, and prayed for him." Those were her words to me. I have never forgotten them, and I'm eighty-seven!'

'Father!' said the man upon the bed, 'I am dying, I know.

I am so far gone, that I can hardly speak, even of what my mind most runs on. Is there any hope for me beyond this bed?'

'There is hope,' returned the old man, 'for all who are softened and penitent. There is hope for all such. Oh!' he exclaimed, clasping his hands and looking up, 'I was thankful, only yesterday, that I could remember this unhappy son when he was an innocent child. But what a comfort is it, now, to think that even God himself has that remembrance of him!'

Redlaw spread his hands upon his face, and shrunk like a murderer.

'Ah!' feebly moaned the man upon the bed. 'The waste since then, the waste of life since then!'

'But he was a child once,' said the old man. 'He played with children. Before he lay down on his bed at night, and fell into his guiltless rest, he said his prayers at his poor mother's knee. I have seen him do it many a time; and seen her lay his head upon her breast and kiss him. Sorrowful as it was to her, and to me, to think of this, when he went so wrong, and when our hopes and plans for him were all broken, this gave him still ahold upon us, that nothing else could have given. Oh, Father, so much better than the fathers upon earth! Oh, Father, so much more afflicted by the errors of thy children! take this wanderer back! Not as he is, but as he was then, let him cry to thee, as he has so often seemed to cry to us!'

As the old man lifted up his trembling hands, the son, for whom he made the supplication, laid his sinking head against him for support and comfort, as if he were indeed the child of whom he spoke.

When did man ever tremble as Redlaw trembled in the silence that ensued? He knew it must come upon them, knew that it was coming fast.

'My time is very short, my breath is shorter,' said the sick man, supporting himself on one arm, and with the other groping in the air, 'and I remember there is something on my mind concerning the man who was here just now. Father and William – wait! – is there really anything in black out there?'

'Yes, yes, it is real,' said his aged father.

'Is it a man?'

'What I say myself George,' interposed his brother, bending kindly over him. 'It's Mr Redlaw.'

'I thought I had dreamed of him. Ask him to come here.'

The Chemist, whiter than the dying man, appeared before him. Obedient to the motion of his hand, he sat upon the bed.

'It has been so ripped up tonight, sir,' said the sick man, laying his hand upon his heart, with a look in which the mute, imploring agony of his condition was concentrated, 'by the sight of my poor old father, and the thought of all the trouble I have been the cause of, and all the wrong and sorrow lying at my door that—'

Was it the extremity to which he had come, or was it the dawning of another change, that made him stop?

'—That what I *can* do right, with my mind running on so much, so fast, I'll try to do. There was another man here. Did you see him?'

Redlaw could not reply by any word; for when he saw that fatal sign he knew so well now, of the wandering hand upon the forehead, his voice died at his lips. But he made some indication of assent.

'He is penniless, hungry, and destitute. He is completely beaten down, and has no resource at all. Look after him! Lose no time! I know he has it in his mind to kill himself.'

It was working. It was on his face. His face was changing, hardening, deepening in all its shades, and losing all its sorrow.

'Don't you remember? Don't you know him?' he pursued.

He shut his face out for a moment with the hand that again wandered over his forehead, and then it lowered on Redlaw, reckless, ruffianly, and callous.

'Why, d—n you!' he said, scowling round, 'what have you been doing to me here? I have lived bold, and I mean to die bold. To the Devil with you!'

And so lay down upon his bed, and put his arms up over his head and ears, as resolute from that time to keep out all access, and to die in his indifference.

If Redlaw had been struck by lightning, it could not have struck him from the bedside with a more tremendous shock. But the old man, who had left the bed while his son was speaking to him, now returning, avoided it quickly likewise, and with abhorrence.

'Where's my boy William?' said the, old man hurriedly. 'William, come away from here. We'll go home.'

'Home, father!' returned William. 'Are you going to leave your own son?'

'Where's my own son?' replied the old man.

'Where? Why, there!'

'That's no son of mine,' said Philip, trembling with resentment. 'No such wretch as that has any claim on me. My children are pleasant to look at, and they wait upon me, and get my meat and drink ready, and are useful to me. I've a right to it! I'm eighty-seven!'

'You're old enough to be no older,' muttered William, looking at him grudgingly, with his hands in his pockets. 'I don't know what good you are myself. We could have a deal more pleasure without you.'

'*My* son, Mr Redlaw!' said the old man. '*My* son, too! The boy talking to me of *my* son! Why, what has he ever done to give me any pleasure, I should like to know?'

'I don't know what you have ever done to give *me* any pleasure,' said William sulkily.

'Let me think,' said the old man. 'For how many Christmas-times running have I sat in my warm place, and never had to come out in the cold night air; and have made good cheer, without being disturbed by any such uncomfortable, wretched sight as him there? Is it twenty, William?'

'Nigh forty, it seems,' he muttered. 'Why, when I look at my father, sir, and come to think of it,' addressing Redlaw with an impatience and an irritation that where quite new, 'I'm whipped if I can see anything in him but a calendar of ever so many years of eating, and drinking, and making himself comfortable over and over again.'

'I – I'm eighty-seven,' said the old man, rambling on, childishly and weakly, 'and I don't know as I ever was much put out by anything. I'm not a-going to begin now, because of what he calls my son. He's not my son. I've had a power of pleasant times. I recollect once – no, I don't – no, it's broken off. It was something about a game of cricket and a friend of mine, but it's somehow broken off. I wonder who he was – I suppose I liked him? And I wonder what became of him – I suppose he died? But I don't know. And I don't care, neither; I don't care a bit.'

In his drowsy chuckling, and the shaking of his head, he put his hands into his waistcoat pockets. In one of them he found a bit of holly (left there, probably, last night), which he now took out, and looked at.

'Berries, eh?' said the old man. 'Ah! It's a pity they're not good to eat. I recollect when I was a little chap about as high as that, and out a walking with – let me see – who was I out a walking with? – no, I don't remember how that was. I don't remember as I ever walked with any one particular, or cared for any one, or any one for me. Berries, eh? There's good cheer when there's berries. Well, I ought to have my share of it, and to be waited on, and kept warm and comfortable; for I'm eighty-seven, and a poor old man. I'm eighty-seven. Eighty-seven!'

The drivelling, pitiable manner in which, as he repeated this, he nibbled at the leaves, and spat the morsels out; the cold, uninterested eye with which his youngest son (so changed) regarded him; the determined apathy with which his eldest son lay hardened in his sin; impressed themselves no more on Redlaw's observation; for he broke his way from the spot to which his feet seemed to have been fixed, and ran out of the house.

His guide came crawling forth from his place of refuge, and was ready for him before he reached the arches.

'Back to the woman's?' he inquired.

'Back quickly!' answered Redlaw. 'Stop nowhere on the way!'

For a short distance the boy went on before; but their return was more like a flight than a walk, and it was as much as his bare feet could do to keep pace with the Chemist's rapid strides. Shrinking from all who passed, shrouded in his cloak, and keeping it drawn closely about him, as though there were mortal contagion in any fluttering touch of his garments, he made no pause until they reached the door by which they had come out. He unlocked it with his key, went in, accompanied by the boy, and hastened through the dark passages to his own chamber.

The boy watched him as he made the door fast, and withdrew behind the table when he looked round.

'Come!' he said. 'Don't you touch me! You've not brought me here to take my money away.'

Redlaw threw some more upon the ground. He flung his body on it immediately, as if to hide it from him, lest the sight of it should tempt him to reclaim it; and not until he saw him seated by his lamp, with his face hidden in his hands, began furtively to pick it up. When he had done so, he crept near the fire, and, sitting down in a great chair before it, took from his breast some broken scraps of food, and fell to munching, and to staring at the blaze, and now and then to glancing at his shillings, which he kept clenched up in a bunch in one hand.

'And this,' said Redlaw, gazing on him with increasing repugnance and fear, 'is the only one companion I have left on earth!'

How long it was before he was aroused from his contemplation of this creature whom he dreaded so – whether half an hour, or half the night – he knew not. But the stillness of the room was broken by the boy (whom he had seen listening) starting up, and running towards the door.

'Here's the woman coming!' he exclaimed.

The Chemist stopped him on his way, at the moment when she knocked.

'Let me go to her, will you?' said the boy.

'Not now,' returned the Chemist. 'Stay here. Nobody must pass in or out of the room now. Who's that?'

'It's I, sir,' cried Milly. 'Pray, sir, let me in.'

'No! not for the world!' he said.

'Mr Redlaw, Mr Redlaw, pray, sir, let me in!'

'What is the matter?' he said, holding the boy.

'The miserable man you saw is worse, and nothing I can say will wake him from his terrible infatuation. William's father has turned childish in a moment. William himself is changed. The shock has been too sudden for him; I cannot understand him: he is not like himself. Oh, Mr Redlaw, pray advise me, help me!'

'No! No! No!' he answered.

'Mr Redlaw! Dear sir! George has been muttering in his doze about the man you saw there, who, he fears, will kill himself.'

'Better he should do it than come near me!'

'He says, in his wandering, that you know him; that he was your friend once, long ago; that he is the ruined father of a student here – my mind misgives me, of the young gentleman who has been ill. What is to be done? How is he to be followed? How is he to be saved? Mr Redlaw, pray, oh, pray advise me! Help me!'

All this time he held the boy, who was half mad to pass him, and let her in.

'Phantoms! Punishers of impious thoughts!' cried Redlaw, gazing round in anguish. 'Look upon me! From the darkness of my mind, let the glimmering of contrition that I know is there, shine up and show my misery! In the material world, as I have long taught, nothing can be spared; no step or atom in the wondrous structure could be lost, without a blank being made in the great universe. I know, now, that it is the same with good and evil, happiness and sorrow, in the memories of men. Pity me! Relieve me!'

There was no response but her 'Help me, help me, let me in!' and the boy's struggling to get to her.

'Shadow of myself! Spirit of my darker hours!' cried Redlaw in distraction. 'Come back, and haunt me day and night, but take this gift away! Or, if it must still rest with me, deprive me of the dreadful power of giving it to others. Undo what I have done. Leave me benighted, but restore the day to those whom I have cursed. As I have spared this woman from the first, and as I never will go forth again, but will die here, with no hand to tend me, save this creature's who is proof against me – hear me!'

The only reply still was, the boy struggling to get to her, while he held him back; and the cry increasing in its energy, 'Help! let me in! He was your friend once: how shall he be followed, how shall he be saved? They are all changed, there is no one else to help me: pray, pray let me in!'

THE GIFT REVERSED

Night was still heavy in the sky. On open plains, from hill-tops, and from the decks of solitary ships at sea, a distant low-lying line, that promised by-and-by to change to light, was visible in the dim horizon; but its promise was remote and doubtful, and the moon was striving with the night clouds busily.

The shadows upon Redlaw's mind succeeded thick and fast to one another, and obscured its light as the night clouds hovered between the moon and earth, and kept the latter veiled in darkness. Fitful and uncertain as the shadows which the night clouds cast were their concealments from him, and imperfect revelations to him; and, like the night clouds still, if the clear light broke forth for a moment, it was only that they might sweep over it, and make the darkness deeper than before.

Without, there was a profound and solemn hush upon the ancient pile of building, and its buttresses and angles made dark shapes of mystery upon the ground, which now seemed to retire into the smooth white snow, and now seemed to come out of it, as the moon's path was more or less beset. Within, the Chemist's room was indistinct and murky, by the light of the expiring lamp; a ghostly silence had succeeded to the knocking and the voice outside; nothing was audible but, now and then, a low sound among the whitened ashes of the fire, as of its yielding up its last breath. Before it, on the ground, the boy lay fast asleep. In his chair the Chemist sat, as he had sat there since the calling at his door had ceased – like a man turned to stone.

At such a time the Christmas music he had heard before began to play. He listened to it, at first, as he had listened in the churchyard; but presently – it playing still, and being borne towards him on the night air, in a low, sweet melancholy strain – he rose, and stood stretching his hands about him, as if there were some friend approaching within his reach, on whom his desolate touch might rest, yet do no harm. As he did this, his face became less fixed and wondering; a gentle trembling came upon him; and at last his eyes filled with tears, and he put his hands before them, and bowed down his head.

His memory of sorrow, wrong, and trouble had not come back to him; he knew that it was not restored; he had no passing belief or hope that it was. But some dumb stir within him made him capable, again, of being moved by what was hidden, afar off, in the music. If it were only that it told him sorrowfully the value of what he had lost, he thanked Heaven for it with a fervent gratitude.

As the last chord died upon his ear, he raised his head to listen to its lingering vibration. Beyond the boy, so that his sleeping figure lay at its feet, the Phantom stood, immovable and silent, with its eyes upon him.

Ghastly it was, as it had ever been, but not so cruel and relentless in its aspect – or he thought or hoped so, as he looked upon it, trembling. It was not alone, but in its shadowy hand it held another hand.

And whose was that? Was the form that stood beside it indeed Milly's, or but her shade and picture? The quiet head was bent a little, as her manner was, and her eyes were looking down, as if in pity, on the sleeping child. A radiant light fell on her face, but did not touch the Phantom; for, though close beside her, it was dark and colourless as ever.

'Spectre!' said the Chemist, newly troubled as he looked, 'I have not been stubborn or presumptuous in respect of her. Oh, do not bring her here! Spare me that!'

'This is but a shadow,' said the Phantom; 'when the morning shines, seek out the reality whose image I present before you.'

'Is it my inexorable doom to do so?' cried the Chemist.

'It is,' replied the Phantom.

'To destroy her peace, her goodness; to make her what I am myself, and what I have made of others?'

'I have said, "Seek her out," ' returned the Phantom. 'I have said no more.'

'Oh, tell me!' exclaimed Redlaw, catching at the hope

which he fancied might lie hidden in the words. 'Can I undo what I have done?'

'No,' returned the Phantom.

'I do not ask for restoration to myself,' said Redlaw. 'What I abandoned, I abandoned of my own will, and have justly lost. But for those to whom I have transferred the fatal gift; who never sought it; who unknowingly received a curse of which they had no warning, and which they had no power to shun; can I do nothing?'

'Nothing,' said the Phantom.

'If I cannot, can anyone?'

The Phantom, standing like a statue, kept its gaze upon him for awhile; then turned its head suddenly, and looked upon the shadow at its side.

'Ah! Can she?' cried Redlaw, still looking upon the shade.

The Phantom released the hand it had retained till now, and softly raised its own with a gesture of dismissal. Upon that, her shadow, still preserving the same attitude, began to move or melt away.

'Stay!' cried Redlaw with an earnestness to which he could not give enough expression. 'For a moment! As an act of mercy! I know that some change fell upon me when those sounds were in the air just now. Tell me, have I lost the power of harming her? May I go near her without dread? Oh, let her give me any sign of hope!'

The Phantom looked upon the shade as he did – not at him – and gave no answer.

'At least, say this – has she, henceforth, the consciousness of any power to set right what I have done?'

'She has not,' the Phantom answered.

'Has she the power bestowed on her without the consciousness?'

The Phantom answered: 'Seek her out.' And her shadow slowly vanished.

They were face to face again, and looking on each other as intently and awfully as at the time of the bestowal of the gift, across the boy who still lay on the ground between them, at the Phantom's feet.

'Terrible instructor,' said the Chemist, sinking on his knee before it in an attitude of supplication, 'by whom I was renounced, but by whom I am revisited (in which, and in whose milder aspect, I would fain believe I have a gleam of hope), I will obey without inquiry, praying that the cry I have sent up in the anguish of my soul has been, or will be, heard in behalf of those whom I have injured beyond human reparation. But there is one thing——'

'You speak to me of what is lying here,' the Phantom interposed, and pointed with its finger to the boy.

'I do,' returned the Chemist. 'You know what I would ask. Why has this child alone been proof against my influence, and why, why have I detected in its thoughts a terrible companionship with mine?'

'This,' said the Phantom, pointing to the boy, 'is the last, completest illustration of a human creature utterly bereft of such remembrances as you have yielded up. No softening memory of sorrow, wrong, or trouble enters here, because this wretched mortal from his birth has been abandoned to a worse condition than the beasts, and has, within his knowledge, no one contrast, no humanising touch to make a grain of such a memory spring up in his hardened breast. All within this desolate creature is barren wilderness. All within the man bereft of what you have resigned is the same barren wilderness. Woe to such a man! Woe, tenfold, to the nation that shall count its monsters such as this, lying here by hundreds and by thousands!'

Redlaw shrunk, appalled, from what he heard.

'There is not,' said the Phantom, 'one of these – not one – but sows a harvest that mankind *must* reap. From every seed of evil in this boy a field of ruin is grown that shall be gathered in, and garnered up, and sown again in many places in the world, until regions are overspread with wickedness enough to raise the waters of another Deluge. Open and unpunished murder in a city's streets would be less guilty in its daily toleration than one such spectacle as this.'

It seemed to look down upon the boy in his sleep. Redlaw,

too, looked down upon him with a new emotion.

'There is not a father,' said the Phantom, 'by whose side, in his daily or his nightly walk, these creatures pass; there is not a mother among all the ranks of loving mothers in this land; there is no one risen from the state of childhood, but shall be responsible in his or her degree for this enormity. There is not a country throughout the earth on which it would not bring a curse. There is no religion upon earth that it would not deny; there is no people upon earth it would not put to shame.'

The Chemist clasped his hands, and looked, with trembling fear and pity, from the sleeping boy to the Phantom, standing above him with its finger pointing down.

'Behold, I say,' pursued the Spectre, 'the perfect type of what it was your choice to be. Your influence is powerless here, because from this child's bosom you can banish nothing. His thoughts have been in "terrible companionship" with yours, because you have gone down to his unnatural level. He is the growth of man's indifference; you are the growth of man's presumption. The beneficent design of Heaven is, in each case, overthrown, and from the two poles of the immaterial world you come together.'

The Chemist stooped upon the ground beside the boy, and, with the same kind of compassion for him that he now felt for himself, covered him as he slept, and no longer shrunk from him with abhorrence or indifference.

Soon, now, the distant line on the horizon brightened, the darkness faded, the sun rose red and glorious, and the chimney-stacks and gables of the ancient building gleamed in the clear air, which turned the smoke and vapour of the city into a cloud of gold. The very sun-dial in his shady corner, where the wind was used to spin with such unwindy constancy, shook off the finer particles of snow that had accumulated on his dull old face in the night, and looked out at the little white wreaths eddying round and round him. Doubtless some blind groping of the morning made its way down into the forgotten crypt, so cold and earthy, where the Norman arches were half buried in the ground, and stirred the dull sap in the lazy vegetation hanging to the walls, and quickened the slow principle of life within the little world of wonderful and delicate creation which existed there, with some faint knowledge that the sun was up.

The Tetterbys were up, and doing. Mr Tetterby took down the shutters of the shop, and, strip by strip, revealed the treasures of the window to the eyes, so proof against their seductions, of Jerusalem Buildings. Adolphus had been out so long already, that he was half-way on to Morning Pepper. Five small Tetterbys, whose ten round eyes were much inflamed by soap and friction, were in the tortures of a cool wash in the back-kitchen; Mrs Tetterby presiding.

Johnny, who was pushed and hustled through his toilet with great rapidity when Moloch chanced to be in an exacting frame of mind (which was always the case), staggered up and down with his charge before the shop-door, under greater difficulties than usual; the weight of Moloch being much increased by a complication of defences against the cold, composed of knitted worsted-work, and forming a complete suit of chain-armour, with a head-piece and blue gaiters.

It was a peculiarity of this baby to be always cutting teeth. Whether they never came, or whether they came and went away again, is not in evidence; but it had certainly cut enough, on the showing of Mrs Tetterby, to make a handsome dental provision for the sign of the Bull and Mouth. All sorts of objects were impressed for the rubbing of its gums, notwithstanding that it always carried, dangling at its waist (which was immediately under its chin), a bone ring, large enough to have represented the rosary of a young nun. Knife handles, umbrella tops, the heads of walking-sticks selected from the stock, the fingers of the family in general, but especially of Johnny, nutmeg-graters, crusts, the handles of doors, and the cool knobs on the tops of pokers, were among the commonest instruments indiscriminately applied for this baby's relief. The amount of electricity that must have been rubbed out of it in a week is not to be calculated. Still Mrs Tetterby always said 'it was coming through, and then the child would be herself;' and still it never did come through, and the child continued to be somebody else.

The tempers of the little Tetterbys had sadly changed with a few hours. Mr and Mrs Tetterby themselves were not more altered than their offspring. Usually they were an unselfish, good-natured, yielding little race, sharing short commons when it happened (which was pretty often) contentedly, and even generously, and taking a great deal of enjoyment out of a very little meat. But they were fighting now, not only for the soap-and-water, but even for the breakfast which was yet in perspective. The hand of every little Tetterby was against the other little Tetterby's; and even Johnny's hand – the patient, much-enduring, and devoted Johnny – rose against the baby! Yes. Mrs Tetterby, going to the door by a mere accident, saw him viciously pick out a weak place in the suit of armour, where a slap would tell, and slap that blessed child.

Mrs Tetterby had him into the parlour, by the collar, in that same flash of time, and repaid him the assault with usury thereto.

'You brute, you murdering little boy!' said Mrs Tetterby. 'Had you the heart to do it?'

'Why don't her teeth come through, then,' retorted Johnny in a loud rebellious voice, 'instead of bothering me? How would you like it yourself?'

'Like it, sir!' said Mrs Tetterby, relieving him of his dishonoured load.

'Yes, like it,' said Johnny. 'How would you? Not at all. If you was me, you'd go for a soldier. I will, too. There an't no babies in the army.'

Mr Tetterby, who had arrived upon the scene of action, rubbed his chin thoughtfully, instead of correcting the rebel, and seemed rather struck by this view of a military life.

'I wish I was in the army myself, if the child's in the right,' said Mrs Tetterby, looking at her husband, 'for I have no peace of my life here. I'm a slave – a Virginia slave,' some indistinct association with their weak descent on the tobacco trade, perhaps, suggested this aggravated expression to Mrs Tetterby. 'I never have a holiday, or any pleasure at all, from year's end to year's end! Why, Lord bless and save the child,' said Mrs Tetterby, shaking the baby with an irritability hardly suited to so pious an aspiration, 'what's the matter with her now?'

Not being able to discover, and not rendering the subject much clearer by shaking it, Mrs Tetterby put the baby away in a cradle, and, folding her arms, sat rocking it angrily with her foot.

'How you stand there, 'Dolphus!' said Mrs Tetterby to her husband. 'Why don't you do something?'

'Because I don't care about doing anything,' Mr Tetterby

replied.

'I'm sure *I* don't,' said Mrs Tetterby.

'I'll take my oath *I* don't,' said Mr Tetterby.

A diversion arose here among Johnny and his five younger brothers, who, in preparing the family breakfast-table, had fallen to skirmishing for the temporary possession of the loaf, and were buffeting one another with great heartiness; the smallest boy of all, with precocious discretion, hovering outside the knot of combatants, and harassing their legs. Into the midst of this fray Mr and Mrs Tetterby both precipitated themselves with great ardour, as if such ground were the only ground on which they could now agree; and having, with no visible remains of their late soft-heartedness, laid about them without any lenity, and done much execution, resumed their former relative positions.

'You had better read your paper than do nothing at all,' said Mrs Tetterby.

'What's there to read in a paper?' returned Mr Tetterby with excessive discontent.

'What?' said Mrs Tetterby. 'Police.'

'It's nothing to me,' said Tetterby. 'What do I care what people do, or are done to?"

'Suicides,' suggested Mrs Tetterby.

'No business of mine,' replied her husband.

'Births, deaths, and marriages, are those nothing to you?'

said Mrs Tetterby.

'If the births were all over for good and all today; and the deaths were all to begin to come off tomorrow; I don't see why it should interest me, till I thought it was a-coming to my turn,' grumbled Tetterby. 'As to marriages, I've done it myself. I know quite enough about *them.*'

To judge from the dissatisfied expression of her face and manner, Mrs Tetterby appeared to entertain the same opinions as her husband; but she opposed him, nevertheless, for the gratification of quarrelling with him.

'Oh! you're a consistent man,' said Mrs Tetterby, 'an't you? You, with the screen of your own making there, made of nothing else but bits of newspapers, which you sit and read to the children by the half-hour together!'

'Say used to, if you please,' returned her husband. 'You won't find me doing so any more. I'm wiser now.'

'Bah! Wiser, indeed!' said Mrs Tetterby. 'Are you better?'

The question sounded some discordant note in Mr Tetterby's breast. He ruminated dejectedly, and passed his hand across and across his forehead.

'Better!' murmured Mr Tetterby. 'I don't know as any of us are better, or happier either. Better is it?'

He turned to the screen, and traced about it with his finger, until he found a certain paragraph of which he was in quest.

'This used to be one of the family favourites, I recollect,' said Tetterby in a forlorn and stupid way, 'and used to draw tears from the children, and make 'em good, if there was any little bickering or discontent among 'em, next to the story of the robin redbreasts in the wood. "Melancholy case of destitution. Yesterday a small man, with a baby in his arms, and surrounded by half-a-dozen ragged little ones, of various ages between ten and two, the whole of whom were evidently in a famishing condition, appeared before the worthy magistrate, and made the following recital." Ha! I don't understand it, I'm sure,' said Tetterby; 'I don't see what it has got to do with us.'

'How old and shabby he looks!' said Mrs Tetterby, watching him. 'I never saw such a change in a man. Ah! dear me, dear me, dear me, it was a sacrifice!'

'What was a sacrifice?' her husband sourly inquired.

Mrs Tetterby shook her head; and, without replying in words, raised a complete sea-storm about the baby by her violent agitation of the cradle.

'If you mean your marriage was a sacrifice, my good woman——' said her husband.

'I *do* mean it,' said his wife.

'Why, then, I mean to say,' pursued Mr Tetterby as sulkily and surlily as she, 'that there are two sides to that affair; and that *I* was the sacrifice; and that I wish the sacrifice hadn't been accepted.'

'I wish it hadn't,' Tetterby, with all my heart and soul, I do assure you,' said his wife. 'You can't wish it more than I do, Tetterby.'

'I don't know what I saw in her,' muttered the newsman, 'I'm sure; certainly, if I saw anything, it's not there now. I was thinking so last night, after supper, by the fire. She's fat, she's ageing, she won't bear comparison with most other women.'

'He's common-looking, he has no air with him, he's small, he's beginning to stoop, and he's getting bald,' muttered Mrs Tetterby.

'I must have been half out of my mind when I did it,' muttered Mr Tetterby.

'My senses must have forsook me. That's the only way in which I can explain it to myself,' said Mrs Tetterby with elaboration.

In this mood they sat down to breakfast. The little Tetterbys were not habituated to regard that meal in the light of a sedentary occupation, but discussed it as a dance or trot; rather resembling a savage ceremony, in the occasional shrill whoops and brandishings of bread-and-butter with which it was accompanied, as well as in the intricate filings off into the street and back again, and the hoppings up and down the door-steps, which were incidental to the performance.

In the present instance, the contentions between these Tetterby children for the milk-and-water jug, common to all, which stood upon the table, presented so lamentable an instance of angry passions risen very high indeed, that it was an outrage on the memory of Doctor Watts, It was not until Mr Tetterby had driven the whole herd out of the front-door that a moment's peace was secured; and even that was broken by the discovery that Johnny had surreptitiously come back, and was at that instant choking in the jug like a ventriloquist, in his indecent and rapacious haste.

'These children will be the death of me at last!' said Mrs Tetterby after banishing the culprit. 'And the sooner the better, I think.'

'Poor people,' said Mr Tetterby, 'ought not to have children at all. They give *us* no pleasure.'

He was at that moment taking up the cup which Mrs Tetterby had rudely pushed towards him, and Mrs Tetterby was lifting her own cup to her lips, when they both stopped, as if they were transfixed.

'Here! Mother! Father!' cried Johnny, running into the room. 'Here's Mrs William coming down the street!'

And if ever, since the world began, a young boy took a baby from a cradle with the care of an old nurse, and hushed and soothed it tenderly, and tottered away with it cheerfully, Johnny was that boy, and Moloch was that baby, as they went out together.

Mr Tetterby put down his cup; Mrs Tetterby put down her cup. Mr Tetterby rubbed his forehead; Mrs Tetterby rubbed hers. Mr Tetterby's face began to smooth and brighten; Mrs Tetterby's began to smooth and brighten.

'Why, Lord forgive me,' said Mr Tetterby to himself, 'what evil tempers have I been giving way to? What has been the matter here?'

'How could I ever treat him ill again, after all I said and felt last night?' sobbed Mrs Tetterby, with her apron to her eyes.

'Am I a brute,' said Mr Tetterby, 'or is there any good in me at all? Sophia! My little woman!'

''Dolphus dear!' returned his wife.

'I – I've been in a state of mind,' said Mr Tetterby, 'that I can't abear to think of, Sophy.'

'Oh! It's nothing to what I've been in, Dolf,' cried his wife in a great burst of grief.

'My Sophia,' said Mr Tetterby, 'don't take on! I never shall forgive myself. I must have nearly broke your heart, I know.'

'No, Dolf, no. It was me! Me!' cried Mrs Tetterby.

'My little woman,' said her husband, 'don't. You make me reproach myself dreadful when you show such a noble spirit. Sophia, my dear, you don't know what I thought. I showed it bad enough, no doubt; but what I thought, my little woman——'

'Oh dear Dolf, don't! Don't!' cried his wife.

'Sophia,' said Mr Tetterby, 'I must reveal it. I couldn't rest in my conscience unless I mentioned it. My little woman——'

'Mrs William's very nearly here!' screamed Johnny at the door.

'My little woman, I wondered how,' gasped Mr Tetterby, supporting himself by his chair, 'I wondered how I had ever admired you – I forgot the precious children you have brought about me, and thought you didn't look as slim as I could wish. I – I never gave a recollection,' said Mr Tetterby with severe self-accusation, 'to the cares you've had as my wife, and along of me and mine, when you might have had hardly any with another man, who got on better and was luckier than me (anybody might have found such a man easily, I am sure); and I quarrelled with you for having aged a little in the rough years you've lightened for me. Can you believe it, my little woman? I hardly can myself.'

Mrs Tetterby, in a whirlwind of laughing and crying, caught his face within her hands, and held it there.

'Oh, Dolf!' she cried. 'I am so happy that you thought so; I am so grateful that you thought so! For I thought that you were common-looking, Dolf; and so you are, my dear, and may you be the commonest of all sights in my eyes, till you close them with your own good hands! I thought that you were small; and so you are, and I'll make much of you because you are, and more of you because I love my husband. I thought that you began to stoop; and so you do, and you shall lean on me, and I'll do all I can to keep you up. I thought there was no air about you; but there is, and it's the air of home, and that's the purest and the best there is, and *God* bless home once more, and all belonging to it, Dolf!'

'Hurrah! Here's Mrs William!' cried Johnny.

So she was, and all the children with her; and, as she came in, they kissed her, and kissed one another, and kissed the baby, and kissed their father and mother, and then ran back and flocked and danced about her, trooping on with her in triumph.

Mr and Mrs Tetterby were not a bit behind-hand in the warmth of their reception. They were as much attracted to her as the children were; they ran towards her, kissed her hands, pressed round her, could not receive her ardently or enthusiastically enough. She came among them like the spirit of all goodness, affection, gentle consideration, love, and domesticity.

'What! are *you* all so glad to see me, too, this bright Christmas morning?' said Milly, clapping her hands in a pleasant wonder. 'Oh dear, how delightful this is!'

More shouting from the children, more kissing, more trooping round her, more happiness, more love, more joy, more honour, on all sides, than she could bear.

'Oh dear!' said Milly, 'what delicious tears you make me shed! How can I ever have deserved this? What have I done to be so loved?'

'Who can help it?' cried Mr Tetterby.

'Who can help it?' cried Mrs Tetterby.

'Who can help it?' echoed the children in a joyful chorus. And they danced and trooped about her again, and clung to her, and laid their rosy faces against her dress, and kissed and fondled it, and could not fondle it, or her, enough.

'I never was so moved,' said Milly, drying her eyes, 'as I have been this morning. I must tell you as soon as I can speak – Mr Redlaw came to me at sunrise, and with a tenderness in his manner, more as if I had been his darling daughter than myself, implored me to go with him to where William's brother George is lying ill. We went together, and all the way along he was so kind, and so subdued, and seemed to put such trust and hope in me, that I could not help crying with pleasure. When we got to the house, we met a woman at the door (somebody had bruised and hurt her, I am afraid), who caught me by the hand, and blessed me as I passed.'

'She was right,' said Mr Tetterby. Mrs Tetterby said she

was right. All the children cried out she was right.

'Ah! but there's more than that,' said Milly. 'When we got upstairs into the room, the sick man, who had lain for hours in a state from which no effort could rouse him, rose up in his bed, and, bursting into tears, stretched out his arms to me, and said that he had led a misspent life, but that he was truly repentant now in his sorrow for the past, which was all as plain to him as a great prospect from which a dense black cloud had cleared away, and that he entreated me to ask his poor old father for his pardon and his blessing, and to say a prayer beside his bed. And, when I did so, Mr Redlaw joined in it so fervently, and then so thanked and thanked me, and thanked Heaven, that my heart quite overflowed, and I could have done nothing but sob and cry, if the sick man had not begged me to sit down by him – which made me quiet, of course. As I sat there, he held my hand in his until he sunk in a doze; and even then, when I withdrew my hand to leave him to come here (which Mr Redlaw was very earnest indeed in wishing me to do), his hand felt for mine, so that some one else was obliged to take my place, and make believe to give him my hand back. Oh dear, oh dear!' said Milly, sobbing. 'How thankful and how happy I should feel, and do feel, for all this!'

While she was speaking Redlaw had come in, and, after pausing for a moment to observe the group of which she was the centre, had silently ascended the stairs. Upon those stairs he now appeared again; remaining there while the young student passed him, and came running down.

'Kind nurse, gentlest, best of creatures,' he said, falling on his knee to her, and catching at her hand, 'forgive my cruel ingratitude!'

'Oh dear, oh dear!' cried Milly innocently, 'here's another of them! Oh dear, here's somebody else who likes me! What shall I ever do?'

The guileless, simple way in which she said it, and in which she put her hands before her eyes and wept for very happiness, was as touching as it was delightful.

'I was not myself,' he said. 'I don't know what it was – it was some consequence of my disorder, perhaps – I was mad. But I am so no longer. Almost as I speak I am restored. I heard the children crying out your name, and the shade passed from me at the very sound of it. Oh, don't weep! Dear Milly, if you could read my heart, and only know with what affection and what grateful homage it is glowing, you would not let me see you weep. It is such deep reproach.'

'No, no,' said Milly, 'it's not that. It's not, indeed. It's joy. It's wonder that you should think it necessary to ask me to forgive so little, and yet it's pleasure that you do.'

'And will you come again? and will you finish the little curtain?'

'No,' said Milly, drying her eyes, and shaking her head. 'You won't care for *my* needlework now.'

'Is it forgiving me to say that?'

She beckoned him aside, and whispered in his ear.

'There is news from your home, Mr Edmund.'

'News? How?'

'Either your not writing when you were very ill, or the change in your handwriting when you began to be better, created some suspicion of the truth. However, that is—— But you're sure you'll not be the worse for any news, if it's not bad news?'

'Sure.'

'Then there's some one come!' said Milly.

'My mother?' asked the student, glancing round involuntarily towards Redlaw, who had come down from the stairs.

'Hush! No,' said Milly.

'It can be no one else.'

'Indeed!' said Milly. 'Are you sure?'

'It is not——' Before he could say more, she put her hand upon his mouth.

'Yes, it is!' said Milly. 'The young lady (she is very like the miniature, Mr Edmund, but she is prettier) was too unhappy to rest without satisfying her doubts, and came up last night, with a little servant-maid. As you always dated your letters from the College, she came there; and, before I saw Mr Redlaw this morning, I saw her. *She* likes me too!' said Milly. 'Oh dear, that's another!'

'This morning! Where is she now?'

'Why, she is now,' said Milly advancing her lips to his ear, 'in my little parlour in the Lodge, and waiting to see you.'

He pressed her hand, and was darting off, but she detained him.

'Mr Redlaw is much altered, and has told me this morning that his memory is impaired. Be very considerate to him, Mr Edmund; he needs that from us all.'

The young man assured her, by a look, that her caution was not ill bestowed; and, as he passed the Chemist on his way out, bent respectfully and with an obvious interest before him.

Redlaw returned the salutation courteously, and even humbly, and looked after him as he passed on. He dropped his head upon his hand too, as trying to re-awaken something he had lost. But it was gone.

The abiding change that had come upon him since the influence of the music, and the Phantom's reappearance, was, that now he truly felt how much he had lost, and could compassionate his own condition, and contrast it, clearly, with the natural state of those who were around him. In this, an interest in those who were around him was revived, and a meek, submissive sense of his calamity was bred, resembling that which sometimes obtains in age, when its mental powers are weakened, without insensibility or sullenness being added to the list of its infirmities.

He was conscious that, as he redeemed, through Milly, more and more of the evil he had done, and as he was more and more with her, this change ripened itself within him. Therefore, and because of the attachment she inspired him with (but without other hope), he felt that he was quite dependent on her, and that she was his staff in his affliction.

So, when she asked him whether they should go home now to where the old man and her husband were, and he readily replied, 'Yes' – being anxious in that regard – he put his arm through hers, and walked beside her; not as if he were the wise and learned man to whom the wonders of nature were an open book, and hers were the uninstructed mind, but as if their two positions were reversed, and he knew nothing, and she all.

He saw the children throng about her, and caress her, as he and she went away together thus out of the house; he heard the ringing of their laughter, and their merry voices; he saw their bright faces clustering round him like flowers, he witnessed the renewed contentment and affection of their parents; he breathed the simple air of their poor home, restored to its tranquillity; he thought of the unwholesome blight he had shed upon it, and might, but for her, have been diffusing then; and perhaps it is no wonder that he walked submissively beside her, and drew her gentle bosom nearer to his own.

When they arrived at the Lodge, the old man was sitting in his chair in the chimney-corner, with his eyes fixed on the ground, and his son was leaning against the opposite side of the fire-place, looking at him. As she came in at the door, both started and turned round towards her, and a radiant change came upon their faces.

'Oh dear, dear, dear, they are pleased to see me, like the rest!' cried Milly, clapping her hands in an ecstasy, and stopping short. 'Here are two more!'

Pleased to see her! Pleasure was no word for it. She ran into her husband's arms, thrown wide open to receive her, and he would have been glad to have her there, with her head lying on his shoulder, through the short winter's day. But the old man couldn't spare her. He had arms for her too, and he locked her in them.

'Why, where has my quiet Mouse been all this time?' said the old man. 'She has been a long while away. I find that it's impossible for me to get on without Mouse. I – where's my son William? – I fancy I have been dreaming, William.'

'That's what I say myself, father,' returned his son. '*I* have been in an ugly sort of dream, I think. How are you, father? Are you pretty well?'

'Strong and brave, my boy,' returned the old man.

It was quite a sight to see Mr William shaking hands with his father, and patting him on the back, and rubbing him gently down with his hand, as if he could not possibly do enough to show an interest in him.

'What a wonderful man you are, father! How are you, father? Are you really pretty hearty, though?' said William, shaking hands with him again, and patting him again, and rubbing him gently down again.

'I never was fresher or stouter in my life, my boy.'

'What a wonderful man you are, father! But that's exactly where it is,' said Mr William with enthusiasm. 'When I think of all that my father's gone through, and all the chances and changes, and sorrows and troubles, that have happened to him in the course of his long life, and under which his head has grown grey, and years upon years have gathered on it, I feel as if we couldn't do enough to honour the old gentleman, and make his old age easy. How are you, father? Are you really pretty well, though?'

Mr William might never have left off repeating this inquiry and shaking hands with him again, and patting him again, and rubbing him down again, if the old man had not espied the Chemist, whom until now he had not seen.

'I ask your pardon, Mr Redlaw,' said Philip, 'but didn't know you were here, sir, or should have made less free. It reminds me, Mr Redlaw, seeing you here on a Christmas morning, of the time when you was a student yourself, and worked so hard that you was backwards and forwards in our library even at Christmas-time. Ha, ha! I'm old enough to remember that; and I remember it right well, I do, though I am eighty-seven. It was after you left here that my poor wife died. You remember my poor wife, Mr Redlaw?'

The Chemist answered, 'Yes.'

'Yes,' said the old man. 'She was a dear creetur.—I recollect you come here one Christmas morning with a young lady – I ask your pardon, Mr Redlaw, but I think it was a sister you was very much attached to?'

The Chemist looked at him, and shook his head. 'I had a sister,' he said vacantly. He knew no more.

'One Christmas morning,' pursued the old man, 'that you come here with her – and it began to snow, and my wife invited the young lady to walk in, and sit by the fire that is always a burning on Christmas Day in what used to be, before our ten poor gentlemen commuted, our great Dinner Hall. I was there; and I recollect, as I was stirring up the blaze for the young lady to warm her pretty feet by, she read the scroll out loud, that is underneath that picter. "Lord, keep my memory green!" She and my poor wife fell a talking about it; and it's a strange thing to think of, now, that they both said (both being so unlike to die) that it was a good prayer, and that it was one they would put up very earnestly, if they were called away young, with reference to those who were dearest to them. "My brother," says the young lady – "My husband," says my poor wife – "Lord, keep his memory of me green, and do not let me be forgotten!" '

Tears more painful and more bitter than he had ever shed in all his life coursed down Redlaw's face. Philip, fully occupied in recalling his story, had not observed him until now, nor Milly's anxiety that he should not proceed.

'Philip!' said Redlaw, laying his hand upon his arm, 'I am a stricken man, on whom the hand of Providence has fallen heavily, although deservedly. You speak to me, my friend, of what I cannot follow; my memory is gone.'

'Merciful power!' cried the old man.

'I have lost my memory of sorrow, wrong, and trouble,' said the Chemist; 'and with that I have lost all man would remember!'

To see old Philip's pity for him, to see him wheel his own great chair for him to rest in, and look down upon him with a solemn sense of his bereavement, was to know, in some degree, how precious to old age such recollections are.

The boy came running in, and ran to Milly.

'Here's the man,' he said, 'in the other room. I don't

want *him.*'

'What man does he mean?' asked Mr William.

'Hush!' said Milly.

Obedient to a sign from her, he and his old father softly withdrew. As they went out unnoticed, Redlaw beckoned to the boy to come to him.

'I like the woman best,' he answered holding to her skirts.

'You are right,' said Redlaw with a faint smile. 'But you needn't fear to come to me. I am gentler than I was. Of all the world, to you, poor child!'

The boy still held back at first; but yielding little by little to her urging, he consented to approach, and even to sit down at his feet. As Redlaw laid his hand upon the shoulder of the child, looking on him with compassion and a fellow-feeling, he put out his other hand to Milly. She stooped down on that side of him, so that she could look into his face; and, after silence, said: 'Mr Redlaw, may I speak to you?'

'Yes,' he answered, fixing his eyes upon her. 'Your voice and music are the same to me.'

'May I ask you something?'

'What you will.'

'Do you remember what I said when I knocked at your door last night? About one who was your friend once, and who stood on the verge of destruction?'

'Yes. I remember,' he said with some hesitation.

'Do you understand it?'

He smoothed the boy's hair – looking at her fixedly the while, and shook his head.

'This person,' said Milly in her clear, soft voice, which her mild eyes, looking at him, made clearer and softer, 'I found soon afterwards. I went back to the house, and, with Heaven's help, traced him. I was not too soon. A very little, and I should have been too late.'

He took his hand from the boy, and, laying it on the back of that hand of hers, whose timid and yet earnest touch addressed him no less appealingly than her voice and eyes, looked more intently on her.

'He *is* the father of Mr Edmund, the young gentleman we saw just now. His real name is Longford. You recollect the name?'

'I recollect the name.'

'And the man?'

'No, not the man. Did he ever wrong me?'

'Yes!'

'Ah! Then it's hopeless – hopeless.'

He shook his head, and softly beat upon the hand he held, as though mutely asking her commiseration.

'I did not go to Mr Edmund last night,' said Milly. 'You will listen to me just the same as if you did remember all?'

'To every syllable you say.'

'Both because I did not know, then, that this really was his father, and because I was fearful of the effect of such intelligence upon him, after his illness, if it should be. Since I have known who this person is, I have not gone either; but that is for another reason. He has long been separated from his wife and son – has been a stranger to his home almost from his son's infancy, I learn from him – and has abandoned and deserted what he should have held most dear. In all that time he has been falling from the state of a gentleman, more and more, until——' She rose up hastily, and, going out for a moment, returned, accompanied by the wreck that Redlaw had beheld last night.

'Do you know me?' asked the Chemist.

'I should be glad,' returned the other, 'and that is an unwonted word for me to use, if I could answer no.'

The Chemist looked at the man standing, in self-abasement and degradation before him, and would have looked longer, in an ineffectual struggle for enlightenment, but that Milly resumed her late position by his side, and attracted his attentive gaze to her own face.

'See how low he is sunk, how lost he is!' she whispered, stretching out her arm towards him, without looking from the Chemist's face. 'If you could remember all that is connected with him, do you not think it would move your pity to reflect that one you ever loved (do not let us mind how long ago, or in what belief that he has forfeited), should come to this?'

'I hope it would,' he answered. 'I believe it would.'

His eyes wandered to the figure standing near the door, but came back speedily to her, on whom he gazed intently, as if he strove to learn some lesson from every tone of her voice, and every beam of her eyes.

'I have no learning, and you have much,' said Milly; 'I am not used to think, and you are always thinking. May I tell you why it seems to me a good thing for us to remember wrong that has been done us?'

'Yes.'

'That we may forgive it.'

'Pardon me, great Heaven!' said Redlaw, lifting up his eyes, 'for having thrown away thine own high attribute!'

'And if,' said Milly, 'if your memory should one day be restored, as we will hope and pray it may be, would it not be a blessing to you to recall at once a wrong and its forgiveness?'

He looked at the figure by the door, and fastened his attentive eyes on her again. A ray of clearer light appeared to him to shine into his mind from her bright face.

'He cannot go to his abandoned home. He does not seek to go there. He knows that he could only carry shame and trouble to those he has so cruelly neglected; and that the best reparation he can make them now is to avoid them. A very little money, carefully bestowed, would remove him to some distant place, where he might live and do no wrong, and make such atonement as is left within his power for the wrong he has done. To the unfortunate lady who is his wife, and to his son, this would be the best and kindest boon that their best friend could give them – one, too, that they need never know of; and to him, shattered in reputation, mind, and body, it might be salvation.

He took her head between his hands, and kissed it, and said: 'It shall be done. I trust to you to do it for me, now and secretly; and to tell him that I would forgive him, if I were so happy as to know for what.'

As she rose, and turned her beaming face towards the fallen man, implying that her mediation had been successful, he advanced a step, and, without raising his eyes, addressed himself to Redlaw.

'You are so generous,' he said, 'you ever were – that you will try to banish your rising sense of retribution in the spectacle that is before you. I do not try to banish it from myself, Redlaw. If you can, believe me.'

The Chemist entreated Milly, by a gesture, to come nearer to him; and, as he listened, looked in her face, as if to find in it the clue to what he heard.

'I am too decayed a wretch to make professions; I recollect my own career too well to array any such before you. But from the day on which I made my first step downward, in dealing falsely by you, I have gone down with a certain, steady, doomed progression. That I say.'

Redlaw, keeping her close at his side, turned his face towards the speaker, and there was sorrow in it. Something like mournful recognition too.

'I might have been another man, my life might have been another life, if I had avoided that first fatal step. I don't know that it would have been. I claim nothing for the possibility. Your sister is at rest, and better than she could have been with me, if I had continued even what you thought me: even what I once supposed myself to be.'

Redlaw made a hasty motion with his hand, as if he would have put that subject on one side.

'I speak,' the other went on, 'like a man taken from the grave. I should have made my own grave last night, had it not been for this blessed hand.'

'Oh dear, he likes me too!' sobbed Milly under her breath. 'That's another!'

'I could not have put myself in your way last night, even for bread. But, today, my recollection of what has been between us is so strongly stirred, and is presented to me, I don't know how, so vividly, that I have dared to come at her suggestion, and to take your bounty, and to thank you for it, and to beg you, Redlaw, in your dying hour, to be as merciful to me in your thoughts as you are in your deeds.'

He turned towards the door, and stopped a moment on his way forth.

'I hope my son may interest you, for his mother's sake. I hope he may deserve to do so. Unless my life should be preserved a long time, and I should know that I have not misused your aid, I shall never look upon him more.'

Going out, he raised his eyes to Redlaw for the first time. Redlaw, whose steadfast gaze was fixed upon him, dreamily held out his hand. He returned and touched it – little more – with both his own – and, bending down his head, went slowly out.

In the few moments that elapsed while Milly silently took him to the gate, the Chemist dropped into his chair, and covered his face with his hands. Seeing him thus when she came back, accompanied by her husband and his father (who were both greatly concerned for him), she avoided disturbing him, or permitting him to be disturbed; and kneeled down near the chair to put some warm clothing on the boy.

'That's exactly where it is. That's what I always say, father!' exclaimed her admiring husband. 'There's a motherly feeling in Mrs William's breast that must and will have went!'

'Ay, ay,' said the old man; 'you're right. My son William's

right!'

'It happens all for the best, Milly dear, no doubt,' said Mr William tenderly, 'that we have no children of our own; and yet I sometimes wish you had one to love and cherish. Our little dead child that you built such hopes upon, and that never breathed the breath of life – it has made you quietlike, Milly.'

'I am very happy in the recollection of it, William dear,' she answered. 'I think of it every day.'

'I was afraid you thought of it a good deal.'

'Don't say afraid; it is a comfort to me; it speaks to me in so many ways. The innocent thing that never lived on earth is like an angel to me, William.'

'You are like an angel to father and me,' said Mr William softly. 'I know that.'

'When I think of all those hopes I built upon it, and the many times I sat and pictured to myself the little smiling face upon my bosom, that never lay there, and the sweet eyes turned up to mine that never opened to the light,' said Milly, 'I can feel a greater tenderness, I think, for all the disappointed hopes in which there is no harm. When I see a beautiful child in its fond mother's arms, I love it all the better, thinking that my child might have been like that, and might have made my heart as proud and happy.'

Redlaw raised his head, and looked towards her.

'All through life, it seems by me,' she continued, 'to tell me something. For poor neglected children my little child pleads as if it were alive, and had a voice I knew, with which to speak to me. When I hear of youth in suffering or shame, I think that my child might have come to that, perhaps, and that God took it from me in his mercy. Even in age and grey hair, such as father's, it is present: saying that it too might have lived to be old, long and long after you and I were gone, and to have needed the respect and love of younger people.'

Her quiet voice was quieter than ever as she took her husband's arm, and laid her head against it.

'Children love me so, that sometimes I half fancy – it's a silly fancy, William – they have some way I don't know of, of feeling for my little child, and me, and understanding why their love is precious to me. If I have been quiet since, I have been more happy, William, in a hundred ways. Not least happy, dear, in this – that even when my little child was born and dead but a few days, and I was weak and sorrowful, and could not help grieving a little, the thought arose that, if I tried to lead a good life, I should meet in Heaven a bright creature who would call me Mother!'

Redlaw fell upon his knees with a loud cry.

'O Thou,' he said, 'who, through the teaching of pure love, hast graciously restored me to the memory which was the memory of Christ upon the cross, and of all the good who perished in His cause, receive my thanks, and bless her!'

Then he folded her to his heart; and Milly, sobbing more than ever, cried, as she laughed, 'He is come back to himself! He likes me very much indeed, too! Oh dear, dear, dear me, here's another!'

Then, the student entered, leading by the hand a lovely girl, who was afraid to come. And Redlaw, so changed towards him, seeing in him, and in his youthful choice, the softened shadow of that chastening passage in his own life, to which, as to a shady tree, the dove so long imprisoned in his solitary ark might fly for rest and company, fell upon his neck, entreating them to be his children.

Then, as Christmas is a time in which, of all times in the year, the memory of every remediable sorrow, wrong, and trouble in the world around us, should be active with us, not less than our own experiences, for all good, he laid his hand upon the boy, and, silently calling Him to witness who laid His hand on children in old time, rebuking, in the majesty of His prophetic knowledge, those who kept them from him, vowed to protect him, teach him, and reclaim him.

Then, he gave his right hand cheerily to Philip, and said that they would that day hold a Christmas dinner in what used to be, before the ten poor gentlemen commuted, their great Dinner Hall; and that they would bid to it as many of that Swidger family, who, his son had told him, were so numerous that they might join hands and make a ring round England, as could be brought together on so short a notice.

And it was that day done. There were so many Swidgers there, grown up and children, that an attempt to state them in round numbers might engender doubts, in the distrustful, of the veracity of this history. Therefore the attempt shall not be made. But there they were, by dozens and scores – and there was good news and good hope there, ready for them, of George, who had been visited again by his father and brother, and by Milly, and again left in a quiet sleep. There, present at the dinner too, were the Tetterbys, including young Adolphus, who arrived in his prismatic comforter, in good time for the beef. Johnny and the baby were too late, of course, and came in all on one side, the one exhausted, the other in a supposed state of double-tooth; but that was customary, and not alarming.

It was sad to see the child who had no name or lineage watching the other children as they played, not knowing how to talk with them, or sport with them, and more strange to the ways of childhood than a rough dog. It was sad, though in a different way, to see what an instinctive knowledge the youngest children there had of his being different from all the rest, and how they made timid approaches to him with soft words and touches, and with little presents, that he might not be unhappy. But he kept by Milly, and began to love her – that was another, as she said! – and, as they all liked her dearly, they were glad of that, and when they saw him peeping at them from behind her chair, they were pleased that he was so close to it.

All this the Chemist, sitting with the student and his bride that was to be, and Philip, and the rest, saw.

Some people have said since that he only thought what has been herein set down; others, that he read it in the fire, one winter night about the twilight-time; others, that the Ghost was but the representation of his gloomy thoughts, and Milly the embodiment of his better wisdom. *I* say nothing.

——Except this. That as they were assembled in the old Hall, by no other light than that of a great fire (having dined early), the shadows once more stole out of their hiding-places, and danced about the room, showing the children marvellous shapes and faces on the walls, and gradually changing what was real and familiar there to what was wild and magical. But that there was one thing in the Hall to which the eyes of Redlaw, and of Milly and her husband, and of the old man, and of the student, and his bride that was to be, were often turned, which the shadows did not obscure or change. Deepened in its gravity by the fire-light, and gazing from the darkness of the panelled wall like life, the sedate face in the portrait, with the beard and ruff, looked down at them from under its verdant wreath of holly, as they looked up at it, and, clear and plain below, as if a voice had uttered them, were the words:

'Lord, keep my Memory Green!'

A CHILD'S DREAM OF A STAR

There was once a child, and he strolled about a good deal, and thought of a number of things. He had a sister, who was a child too, and his constant companion. These two used to wonder all day long. They wondered at the beauty of the flowers; they wondered at the height and blueness of the sky; they wondered at the depth of the bright water; they wondered at the goodness and the power of God who made the lovely world.

They used to say to one another, sometimes, Supposing all the children upon earth were to die, would the flowers, and the water, and the sky, be sorry? They believed they would be sorry. For, said they, the buds are the children of the flowers, and the little playful streams that gambol down the hill-sides are the children of the water; and the smallest bright specks playing at hide-and-seek in the sky all night must surely be the children of the stars; and they would all be grieved to see their playmates, the children of men, no more.

There was one clear shining star that used to come out in the sky before the rest, near the church spire, above the graves. It was larger and more beautiful, they thought, than all the others, and every night they watched for it, standing hand in hand at a window. Whoever saw it first, cried out, 'I see the star!' And often they cried out both together, knowing so well when it would rise, and where. So they grew to be such friends with it, that, before lying down in their beds, they always looked out once again, to bid it good night; and when they were turning round to sleep, they used to say, 'God bless the star!'

But while she was still very young – oh, very, very young! – the sister drooped, and came to be so weak that she could no longer stand in the window at night; and then the child looked sadly out by himself, and when he saw the star, turned round and said to the patient pale face on the bed, 'I see the star!' and then a smile would come upon the face, and a little weak voice used to say, 'God bless my brother and the star!'

And so the time came all too soon when the child looked out alone, and when there was no face on the bed, and when there was a little grave among the graves, not there before; and when the star made long rays down towards him, as he saw it through his tears.

Now, these rays were so bright, and they seemed to make such a shining way from earth to Heaven, that when the child went to his solitary bed, he dreamed about the star; and dreamed that, lying where he was, he saw a train of people taken up that sparkling road by angels. And the star, opening, showed him a great world of light, where many more such angels waited to receive them.

All these angels, who were waiting, turned their beaming

eyes upon the people who were carried up into the star; and some came out from the long rows in which they stood, and fell upon the people's necks, and kissed them tenderly, and went away with them down avenues of light, and were so happy in their company, that lying in his bed he wept for joy.

But, there were many angels who did not go with them, and among them one he knew. The patient face that once had lain upon the bed was glorified and radiant, but his heart found out his sister among all the host.

His sister's angel lingered near the entrance of the star, and said to the leader among those who had brought the people thither, 'Is my brother come?'

And he said, 'No.'

She was turning hopefully away, when the child stretched out his arms and cried, 'Oh, sister, I am here! Take me!' and then she turned her beaming eyes upon him, and it was night; and the star was shining into the room, making long rays down towards him as he saw it through his tears.

From that hour forth, the child looked out upon the star as on the home he was to go to, when his time should come; and he thought that he did not belong to the earth alone, but to the star too, because of his sister's angel gone before.

There was a baby born to be a brother to the child; and while he was so little that he never yet had spoken a word, he stretched his tiny form out on his bed, and died.

Again the child dreamed of the opened star, and of the company of angels, and the train of people, and the rows of angels with their beaming eyes all turned upon those people's faces.

Said his sister's angel to the leader, 'Is my brother come?'

And he said, 'Not that one, but another.'

As the child beheld his brother's angel in her arms, he cried, 'Oh, sister, I am here! Take me!' And she turned and smiled upon him, and the star was shining.

He grew to be a young man, and was busy at his books when an old servant came to him and said, 'Thy mother is no more. I bring her blessing on her darling son!'

Again at night he saw the star, and all that former company. Said his sister's angel to the leader, 'Is my brother come?'

And he said, 'Thy mother!'

A mighty cry of joy went forth through all the star, because the mother was reunited to her two children. And he stretched out his arms and cried, 'Oh, mother, sister, and brother, I am here! Take me!' And they answered him, 'Not yet,' and the star was shining.

He grew to be a man, whose hair was turning grey, and he was sitting in his chair by the fireside, heavy with grief, and with his face bedewed with tears, when the star opened once again.

Said his sister's angel to the leader, 'Is my brother come?'

And he said, 'Nay, but his maiden daughter.'

And the man who had been the child saw his daughter, newly lost to him, a celestial creature among those three, and he said, 'My daughter's head is on my sister's bosom, and her arm is round my mother's neck, and at her feet there is the baby of old time, and I can bear the parting from her, God be praised!'

And the star was shining.

Thus the child came to be an old man, and his once smooth face was wrinkled, and his steps were slow and feeble, and his back was bent. And one night as he lay upon his bed, his children standing round, he cried, as he had cried so long ago, 'I see the star!'

They whispered to one another, 'He is dying.'

And he said, 'I am. My age is falling from me like a garment, and I move towards the star as a child. And oh, my Father, now I thank thee that it has so often opened to receive those dear ones who await me!'

And the star was shining; and it shines upon his grave.

CHRISTMAS GHOSTS

I like to come home at Christmas. We all do, or we all *should*. We ought to come home for a holiday – the longer the better – from the great boarding school where we are for ever working at our arithmetical slates, to take and give a rest.

We travel home across a winter prospect; by low-lying mist grounds, through fens and fogs, up long hills, winding dark as caverns between thick plantations, almost shutting out the sparkling stars; so, out on broad heights, until we stop at last, with sudden silence, at an avenue. The gate bell has a deep, half-awful sound in the frosty air; the gate swings open on its hinges; and, as we drive up to a great house, the glancing lights grow larger in the windows, and the opposing rows of trees seem to fall solemnly back on either side, to give us place. At intervals, all day, a frightened hare has shot across this whitened turf; or the distant clatter of a herd of deer trampling the hard frost has, for the minute, crushed the silence too. Their watchful eyes beneath the fern may be shining now, if we could see them, like the icy dewdrops on the leaves; but they are still, and all is still. And so, the lights growing larger, and the trees falling back before us, and closing up again behind us, as if to forbid retreat, we come to the house.

There is probably a smell of roasted chestnuts and other good comfortable things all the time, for we are telling Winter Stories – Ghost Stories, or more shame for us – round the Christmas fire; and we have never stirred, except to draw a little nearer to it. But, no matter for that. We come to the house, and it is an old house, full of great chimneys where wood is burnt on ancient dogs upon the hearth, and grim portraits (some of them with grim legends, too) lower distrustfully from the oaken panels of the walls. We are a middle-aged nobleman, and we make a generous supper with our host and hostess and their guests – it being Christmastime, and the old house full of company – and then we go to bed. Our room is a very old room. It is hung with tapestry. We don't like the portrait of a cavalier in green, over the fireplace. There are great black beams in the ceiling, and there is a great black bedstead, supported at the foot by two great black figures, who seem to have come off a couple of tombs in the old baronial church in the park, for our particular accommodation. But, we are not a superstitious nobleman, and we don't mind. Well! we dismiss our servant, lock the door, and sit before the fire in our dressing-gown, musing about a great many things. At length we go to bed. Well! we can't sleep. We toss and tumble, and can't sleep. The embers on the hearth burn fitfully, and make the room look ghostly. We can't help peeping out, over the counterpane, at the two black figures and the cavalier – that wicked-looking cavalier in green. In the flickering light they seem to advance and retire: which, though we are not by any means a superstitious nobleman, is not agreeable. Well! we get nervous – more and more nervous. We say, 'This is very foolish, but we can't stand this; we'll pretend to be ill, and knock up somebody.' Well! we are just going to do it, when the locked door opens, and there comes in a young woman, deadly pale, and with long fair hair, who glides to the fire, and sits down in the chair we have left there, wringing her hands. Then, we notice that her clothes are wet. Our tongue cleaves to the roof of our mouth, and we can't speak; but, we observe her accurately. Her clothes are wet; her long hair is dabbled with moist mud; she is dressed in the fashion of two hundred years ago; and she has at her girdle a bunch of rusty keys. Well! there she sits, and we can't even faint, we are in such a state about it. Presently she gets up, and tries all the locks in the room with the rusty keys, which won't fit one of them; then, she fixes her eyes on the portrait of the cavalier in green, and says, in a low, terrible voice, 'The stags know it!' After that, she wrings her hands again, passes the bedside, and goes out at the door. We hurry on our dressing-gown, seize our pistols (we always travel with pistols), and are following, when we find the door locked. We turn the key, look out into the dark gallery; no one there. We wander away, and try to find our servant. Can't be done. We pace the gallery till daybreak; then return to our deserted room, fall asleep, and are awakened by our servant (nothing ever haunts *him*) and the shining sun. Well! we make a wretched breakfast, and all the company say we look queer. After breakfast, we go over the house with our host, and then we take him to the portrait of the cavalier in green, and then it all comes out. He was false to a young housekeeper once attached to that family, and famous for her beauty, who drowned herself in a pond, and whose body was discovered, after a long time, because the stags refused to drink the water. Since which, it has been whispered that she traverses the house at midnight (but goes especially to that room, where the cavalier in green was wont to sleep), trying the old locks with the rusty keys. Well! we tell our host of what we have seen, and a shade comes over his features, and he begs it may be hushed up; and so it is. But, it's all true; and we said so, before we died (we are dead now), to many responsible people.

There is no end to the old houses, with resounding galleries, and dismal state bedchambers, and haunted wings shut up for many years, through which we may ramble, with an agreeable creeping up our back, and encounter any number of ghosts, but (it is worthy of remark perhaps) reducible to a very few general types and classes; for, ghosts have little originality, and 'walk' in a beaten track. Thus, it comes to pass that a certain room in a certain old hall, where a certain bad lord, baronet, knight, or gentleman shot himself, has certain planks in the floor from which the blood *will not* be taken out. You may scrape and scrape, as the present owner has done, or plane and plane, as his father did, or scrub and scrub, as his grandfather did, or burn and burn with strong acids, as his great-grandfather did, but there the blood will still be – no redder and no paler – no more and no less – always just the same. Thus, in such another house there is a haunted door that never will keep open; or another door that never will keep shut; or a haunted sound of a spinning-wheel, or a hammer, or a footstep, or a cry, or a sigh, or a horse's tramp, or the rattling of a chain. Or else there is a turret clock, which, at the midnight hour, strikes thirteen when the head of the family is going to die; or a shadowy, immovable black carriage which at such a time is always seen by somebody, waiting near the great gates in the stable-yard. Or thus, it came to pass how Lady Mary went to pay a visit at a large wild house in the Scottish Highlands, and, being fatigued with her long journey, retired to bed early, and innocently said, next morning, at the breakfast-table, 'How odd to have so late a party last night in this remote place, and not to tell me of it before I went to bed!' Then, every one asked Lady Mary what she meant. Then, Lady Mary, replied, 'Why, all night long, the carriages were driving round and round the terrace, underneath my window!' Then, the owner of the house turned pale, and so did his Lady, and Charles Macdoodle of Macdoodle signed to Lady Mary to say no more, and everyone was silent. After breakfast, Charles Macdoodle told Lady Mary that it was a tradition in the family that those rumbling carriages on the terrace betokened death. And so it proved, for, two months afterwards, the Lady of the mansion died. And Lady Mary, who was a Maid of Honour at Court, often told this story to the old Queen Charlotte; by this token, that the old King always said, 'Eh, eh? What, what? Ghosts, ghosts? No such thing, no such thing!' And never left off saying so until he went to bed.

Or, a friend of somebody's, whom most of us know, when he was a young man at college, had a particular friend, with whom he made the compact that, if it were possible for the Spirit to return to this earth after its separation from the body, he of the twain who first died should reappear to the other. In course of time this compact was forgotten by our friend; the two young men having progressed in life, and taken diverging paths that were wide asunder. But one night, many years afterwards, our friend being in the North of England, and staying for the night in an inn on the Yorkshire Moors, happened to look out of bed; and there, in the moonlight, leaning on a bureau near the window, steadfastly regarding him, saw his old college friend! The appearance being solemnly addressed, replied, in a kind of whisper, but very audibly, 'Do not come near me. I am dead. I am here to redeem my promise. I come from another world, but may not disclose its secrets!' Then, the whole form becoming paler, melted, as it were, into the moonlight, and faded away.

Or, there was the daughter of the first occupier of the picturesque Elizabethan house, so famous in our neighbourhood. You have heard about her? No! Why, *she* went out one summer evening at twilight, when she was a beautiful girl, just seventeen years of age, to gather flowers in the garden; and presently came running, terrified, into the hall to her father, saying, 'Oh, dear father, I have met myself!' He took her in his arms, and told her it was fancy, but she said, 'Oh no! I met myself in the broad walk, and I was pale and gathering withered flowers, and I turned my head, and held them up!' And, that night, she died; and a picture of her story was begun, though never finished, and they say it is somewhere in the house to this day, with its face to the wall.

Or, the uncle of my brother's wife was riding home on horseback, one mellow evening at sunset, when, in a green lane close to his own house, he saw a man standing before him, in the very centre of the narrow way. 'Why does that man in the cloak stand there?' he thought. 'Does he want me to ride over him?' But the figure never moved. He felt a strange sensation at seeing it so still, but slackened his trot and rode forward. When he was so close to it as almost to touch it with his stirrup, his horse shied, and the figure glided up the bank in a curious, unearthly manner – backward, and without seeming to use its feet – and was gone. The uncle of my brother's wife exclaiming, 'Good Heaven! It's my cousin Harry, from Bombay!' put spurs to his horse, which was suddenly in a profuse sweat, and wondering at such strange behaviour, dashed round to the front of his house. There, he saw the same figure, just passing in at the long French window of the drawing-room opening on the ground. He threw his bridle to a servant, and hastened in after it. His sister was sitting there alone.

'Alice, where's my cousin Harry?'

'Your cousin Harry, John?'

'Yes. From Bombay. I met him in the lane just now, and saw him enter here this instant.'

Not a creature had been seen by any one; and in that hour and minute, as it afterwards appeared, this cousin died in India.

Or, it was a certain sensible old maiden lady, who died at ninety-nine, and retained her faculties to the last, who really did see the Orphan Boy; a story which has often been incorrectly told, but of which the real truth is this – because it is, in fact, a story belonging to our family – and she was a connection of our family. When she was about forty years of age, and still an uncommonly fine woman (her lover died young, which was the reason why she never married, though she had many offers), she went to stay at a place in Kent, which her brother, an Indian merchant, had newly bought.

There was a story that this place had once been held in trust by the guardian of a young boy; who was himself the next heir, and who killed the young boy by harsh and cruel treatment. She knew nothing of that. It has been said that there was a cage in her bedroom, in which the guardian used to put the boy. There was no such thing. There was only a closet. She went to bed, made no alarm whatever in the night, and in the morning said composedly to her maid, when she came in, 'Who is the pretty forlorn-looking child who has been peeping out of that closet all night?' The maid replied by giving a loud scream, and instantly decamping. She was surprised; but, she was a woman of remarkable strength of mind, and she dressed herself and went downstairs, and closeted herself with her brother. 'Now, Walter,' she said, 'I have been disturbed all night by a pretty, forlorn-looking boy, who has been constantly peeping out of that closet in my room, which I can't open. This is some trick.'

I am afraid not, Charlotte,' said he, 'for it is the legend of the house. It is the Orphan Boy. What did he do?'

'He opened the door softly,' said she, 'and peeped out. Sometimes, he came a step or two into the room. Then, I called to him, to encourage him, and he shrunk, and shuddered, and crept in again, and shut the door.'

The closet has no communication, Charlotte,' said her brother, 'with any other part of the house, and it's nailed up.'

This was undeniably true, and it took two carpenters a whole forenoon to get it open for examination. Then, she was satisfied that she had seen the Orphan Boy. But the wild and terrible part of the story is, that he was also seen by three of her brother's sons in succession, who all died young. On the occasion of each child being taken ill, he came home in a heat, twelve hours before, and said, Oh, mamma, he had been playing under a particular oak-tree, in a certain meadow, with a strange boy – a pretty, forlorn-looking boy, who was very timid, and made signs! From fatal experience, the parents came to know that this was the Orphan Boy, and that the course of that child whom he chose for his little playmate was surely run.

TO BE READ AT DUSK

One, two, three, four, five. There were five of them.

Five couriers, sitting on a bench outside the convent on the summit of the Great St Bernard in Switzerland, looking at the remote heights, stained by the setting sun, as if a mighty quantity of red wine had been broached upon the mountain top, and had not yet had time to sink into the snow.

This is not my simile. It was made for the occasion by the stoutest courier, who was a German. None of the others took any more notice of it than they took of me, sitting on another bench on the other side of the convent door, smoking my cigar, like them, and – also like them – looking at the reddened snow, and at the lonely shed hard by, where the bodies of belated travellers, dug out of it, slowly wither away, knowing no corruption in that cold region.

The wine upon the mountain top soaked in as we looked; the mountain became white; the sky, a very dark blue; the wind rose; and the air turned piercing cold. The five couriers buttoned their rough coats. There being no safer man to imitate in all such proceedings than a courier, I buttoned mine.

The mountain in the sunset had stopped the five couriers in a conversation. It is a sublime sight, likely to stop conversation. The mountain being now out of the sunset, they resumed.

Not that I had heard any part of their previous discourse; for indeed, I had not then broken away from the American gentleman, in the travellers' parlour of the convent, who, sitting with his face to the fire, had undertaken to realise to me the whole progress of events which had led to the accumulation by the Honourable Ananias Dodger of one of the largest acquisitions of dollars ever made in our country.

'My God!' said the Swiss courier, speaking in French, which I do not hold (as some authors appear to do) to be such an all-sufficient excuse for a naughty word, that I have only to write it in that language to make it innocent; 'if you talk of ghosts——'

'But I *don't* talk of ghosts,' said the German.

'Of what then?' asked the Swiss.

'If I knew of what then,' said the German, 'I should probably know a great deal more.'

It was a good answer, I thought, and it made me curious. So, I moved my position to that corner of my bench which was nearest to them, and leaning my back against the convent wall, heard perfectly, without appearing to attend.

'Thunder and lightning!' said the German, warming, 'when a certain man is coming to see you, unexpectedly; and, without his own knowledge, sends some invisible messenger, to put the idea of him into your head all day, what do you call that? When you walk along a crowded street – at

Frankfurt, Milan, London, Paris – and think that a passing stranger is like your friend Heinrich, and then that another passing stranger is like your friend Heinrich, and so begin to have a strange foreknowledge that presently you'll meet your friend Heinrich – which you do, though you believed him at Trieste – what do you call *that*?'

'It's not uncommon, either,' murmured the Swiss and the other three.

'Uncommon!' said the German. 'It's as common as cherries in the Black Forest. It's as common as maccaroni at Naples. And Naples reminds me! When the old Marchesa Senzanima shrieks at a card-party on the Chiaja – as I heard and saw her, for it happened in a Bavarian family of mine, and I was overlooking the service that evening – I say, when the old Marchesa starts up at the card-table, white through her rouge, and cries, "My sister in Spain is dead! I felt her cold touch on my back!" – and when that sister *is* dead at the moment – what do you call that?'

'Or when the blood of San Gennaro liquefies at the request of the clergy – as all the world knows that it does regularly once a-year, in my native city,' said the Neapolitan courier after a pause, with a comical look, 'what do you call that?'

'*That*!' cried the German. 'Well, I think I know a name for that.'

'Miracle?' said the Neapolitan, with the same sly face.

The German merely smoked and laughed; and they all smoked and laughed.

'Bah!' said the German, presently. 'I speak of things that really do happen. When I want to see the conjurer, I pay to see a professed one, and have my money's worth. Very strange things do happen without ghosts. Ghosts! Giovanni Baptista, tell your story of the English bride. There's no ghost in that, but something full as strange. Will any man tell me what?'

As there was a silence among them, I glanced around. He whom I took to be Baptista was lighting a fresh cigar. He presently went on to speak. He was a Genoese, as I judged.

'The story of the English bride?' said he. 'Basta! one ought not to call so slight a thing a story. Well, it's all one. But it's true. Observe me well, gentlemen, it's true. That which glitters is not always gold; but what I am going to tell, is true.'

He repeated this more than once.

Ten years ago, I took my credentials to an English gentleman at Long's Hotel, in Bond Street, London, who was about to travel – it might be for one year, it might be for two. He approved of them; likewise of me. He was pleased to make inquiry. The testimony that he received was favourable. He engaged me by the six months, and my entertainment was generous.

He was young, handsome, very happy. He was enamoured of a fair young English lady, with a sufficient fortune, and they were going to be married. It was the wedding-trip, in short, that we were going to take. For three months' rest in the hot weather (it was early summer then) he had hired an old place on the Riviera, at an easy distance from my city, Genoa, on the road to Nice. Did I know that place? Yes; I told him I knew it well. It was an old palace with great gardens. It was a little bare, and it was a little dark and gloomy, being close surrounded by trees; but it was spacious, ancient, grand, and on the seashore. He said it had been so described to him exactly, and he was well pleased that I knew it. For its being a little bare of furniture, all such places were. For its being a little gloomy, he had hired it principally for the gardens, and he and my mistress would pass the summer weather in their shade.

'So all goes well, Baptista?' said he.

'Indubitably, signore; very well.'

We had a travelling chariot for our journey, newly built for us, and in all respects complete. All we had was complete; we wanted for nothing. The marriage took place. They were happy. *I* was happy, seeing all so bright, being so well situated, going to my own city, teaching my language in the rumble to the maid, la bella Carolina, whose heart was gay with laughter: who was young and rosy.

The time flew. But I observed – listen to this, I pray! (and here the courier dropped his voice) – I observed my mistress sometimes brooding in a manner very strange; in a frightened manner; in an unhappy manner; with a cloudy, uncertain alarm upon her. I think that I began to notice this when I was walking up hills by the carriage side, and master had gone on in front. At any rate, I remember that it impressed itself upon my mind one evening in the South of France, when she called to me to call master back; and when he came back, and walked for a long way, talking encouragingly and affectionately to her, with his hand upon the open window, and hers in it. Now and then, he laughed in a merry way, as if he were bantering her out of something. By-and-by, she laughed, and then all went well again.

It was curious. I asked la bella Carolina, the pretty little one, Was mistress unwell? – No. Out of spirits? – No. Fearful of bad roads, or brigands? – No. And what made it more mysterious was, the pretty little one would not look at me in giving answer, but *would* look at the view.

But, one day she told me the secret.

'If you must know,' said Carolina, 'I find, from what I have overheard, that mistress is haunted.'

'How haunted?'

'By a dream.'

'What dream?'

'By a dream of a face. For three nights before her marriage, she saw a face in a dream – always the same face, and only one.'

'A terrible face?'

'No. The face of a dark, remarkable-looking man, in black, with black hair and a grey moustache – a handsome man except for a reserved and secret air. Not a face she ever saw, or at all like a face she ever saw. Doing nothing in the dream but looking at her fixedly, out of darkness.'

'Does the dream come back?'

'Never. The recollection of it is all her trouble.'

'And why does it trouble her?'

Carolina shook her head.

'That's master's question,' said la bella. 'She don't know. She wonders why, herself. But I heard her tell him, only last night, that if she was to find a picture of that face in our Italian house (which she is afraid she will) she did not know how she could ever bear it.'

Upon my word I was fearful after this (said the Genoese courier) of our coming to the old palazzo, lest some such ill-starred picture should happen to be there. I knew there were many there; and, as we got nearer and nearer to the place, I wished the whole gallery in the crater of Vesuvius. To mend the matter, it was a stormy dismal evening when we, at last, approached that part of the Riviera. It thundered;

and the thunder of my city and its environs, rolling among the high hills, is very loud. The lizards ran in and out of the chinks in the broken stone wall of the garden, as if they were frightened; the frogs bubbled and croaked their loudest; the sea-wind moaned, and the wet trees dripped; and the lightning – body of San Lorenzo, how it lightened!

We all know what an old palace in or near Genoa is – how time and the sea air have blotted it – how the drapery painted on the outer walls has peeled off in great flakes of plaster – how the lower windows are darkened with rusty bars of iron – how the court-yard is overgrown with grass – how the outer buildings are dilapidated – how the whole pile seems devoted to ruin. Our palazzo was one of the true kind. It had been shut up close for months. Months? Years! – it had an earthy smell, like a tomb. The scent of the orange trees on the broad back terrace, and of the lemons ripening on the wall, and of some shrubs that grew around a broken fountain, had got into the house somehow, and had never been able to get out again. There was, in every room, an aged smell, grown faint with confinement. It pined in all the cupboards and drawers. In the little rooms of communication between great rooms, it was stifling. If you turned a picture – to come back to the pictures – there it still was, clinging to the wall behind the frame, like a sort of bat.

The lattice-blinds were close shut, all over the house.

There were two ugly grey old women in the house, to take care of it; one them with a spindle, who stood winding and mumbling in the doorway, and who would as soon have let in the devil as the air. Master, mistress, la bella Carolina, and I, went all through the palazzo. I went first, though I have named myself last, opening the windows and the lattice-blinds, and shaking down on myself splashes of rain, and scraps of mortar, and now and then a dozing mosquito, or a monstrous, fat, blotchy, Genoese spider.

When I had let the evening light into a room, master, mistress, and la bella Carolina, entered. Then, we looked round at all the pictures, and I went forward again into another room. Mistress secretly had great fear of meeting with the likeness of that face – we all had; but there was no such thing. The Madonna and Bambino, San Francisco, San Sebastiano, Venus, Santa Caterina, Angels, Brigands, Frairs, Temples at Sunset, Battles, White Horses, Forests, Apostles, Doges, all my old acquaintances many times repeated? – yes. Dark handsome man in black, reserved and secret, with black hair and grey moustache, looking fixedly at mistress out of darkness? – no.

At last we got through all the rooms and all the pictures, and came out into the gardens. They were pretty well kept, being rented by a gardener, and were large and shady. In one place there was a rustic theatre, open to the sky; the stage a green slope; the coulisses, three entrances upon a side, sweet-smelling, leafy screens. Mistress moved her bright eyes, even there, as if she looked to see the face come – in upon the scene; but all was well.

'Now, Clara,' master said, in a low voice, 'you see that it is nothing? You are happy.'

Mistress was much encouraged. She soon accustomed herself to that grim palazzo, and would sing, and play the harp, and copy the old pictures, and stroll with master under the green trees and vines all day. She was beautiful. He was happy. He would laugh and say to me, mounting his horse for his morning ride before the heat, 'All goes well, Baptista!'

'Yes, signore, thank God, very well.'

We kept no company. I took la bella to the Duomo and Annunciata, to the Café, to the Opera, to the village Festa, to the Public Garden, to the Day Theatre, to the Marionetti. The pretty little one was charmed with all she saw. She learnt Italian – heavens! miraculously! Was mistress quite forgetful of that dream? I asked Carolina sometimes. Nearly, said la bella – almost. It was wearing out.

One day master received a letter, and called me.

'Baptista!'

'Signore!'

'A gentleman who is presented to me will dine here today. He is called the Signor Dellombra. Let me dine like a prince.'

It was an odd name. I did not know that name. But, there had been many noblemen and gentlemen pursued by Austria on political suspicions, lately, and some names had changed. Perhaps this was one. Altro! Dellombra was as good a name to me as another.

When the Signor Dellombra came to dinner (said the Genoese courier in the low voice, into which he had subsided once before), I showed him into the reception-room, the great sala of the old palazzo. Master received him with cordiality, and presented him to mistress. As she rose, her faced changed, she gave a cry, and fell upon the marble floor.

Then, I turned my head to the Signor Dellombra, and saw that he was dressed in black, and had a reserved and secret air, and was a dark remarkable-looking man, with black hair and a grey moustache.

Master raised mistress in his arms, and carried her to her own room, where I sent la bella Carolina straight. La bella told me afterwards that mistress was nearly terrified to death, and that she wandered in her mind about her dream all night.

Master was vexed and anxious – almost angry, and yet full of solicitude. The Signor Dellombra was a courtly gentleman, and spoke with great respect and sympathy of mistress's being so ill. The African wind had been blowing for some days (they had told him at his hotel of the Maltese Cross), and he knew that it was often hurtful. He hoped the beautiful lady would recover soon. He begged permission to retire, and to renew his visit when he should have the happiness of hearing that she was better. Master would not allow of this, and they dined alone.

He withdrew early. Next day he called at the gate, on horseback, to inquire for mistress. He did so two or three times in that week.

What I observed myself, and what la bella Carolina told me, united to explain to me that master had now set his mind on curing mistress of her fanciful terror. He was all kindness, but he was sensible and firm. He reasoned with her, that to encourage such fancies was to invite melancholy, if not madness. That it rested with herself to be herself. That if she once resisted her strange weakness, so successfully as to receive the Signor Dellombra as an English lady would receive any other guest, it was for ever conquered. To make an end, the signore came again, and mistress received him without marked distress (though with constraint and apprehension still), and the evening passed serenely. Master was so delighted with this change, and so anxious to confirm it, that the Signor Dellombra became a constant guest. He was accomplished in pictures, books, and music; and his society, in any grim palazzo, would have been welcome.

I used to notice, many times, that mistress was not quite recovered. She would cast down her eyes and droop her head, before the Signor Dellombra, or would look at him with a terrified and fascinated glance, as if his presence had some evil influence or power upon her. Turning from her to him, I used to see him in the shaded gardens, or the large half-lighted sala, looking, as I might say, 'fixedly upon her out of darkness.' But, truly, I had not forgotten la bella Carolina's words describing the face in the dream.

After his second visit I heard master say, 'Now, see, my dear Clara, it's over! Dellombra has come and gone, and your apprehension is broken like glass.'

'Will he – will he ever come again?' asked mistress.

'Again? Why, surely, over and over again! Are you cold?' (She shivered.)

'No, dear – but – he terrifies me: are you sure that he need come again?'

'The surer for the question, Clara!' replied master, cheerfully.

But, he was very hopeful of her complete recovery now, and grew more and more so every day. She was beautiful. He was happy.

'All goes well, Baptista?' he would say to me again.

'Yes, signore, thank God; very well.'

We were all (said the Genoese courier, constraining himself to speak a little louder), we were all at Rome for the carnival. I had been out, all day, with a Sicilian, a friend of mine, and a courier, who was there with an English family. As I returned at night to our hotel, I met the little Carolina, who never stirred from home alone, running distractedly along the Corso.

'Carolina! What's the matter?'

'O Baptista! O, for the Lord's sake! where is my mistress?'

'Mistress, Carolina?'

'Gone since morning – told me, when master went out on his day's journey, not to call her, for she was tired with not resting in the night (having been in pain) and would lie in bed until the evening; then get up refreshed. She is gone! – she is gone! Master has come back, broken down the door, and she is gone! My beautiful, my good, my innocent mistress!'

The pretty little one so cried, and raved, and tore herself that I could not have held her, but for her swooning on my arm as if she had been shot. Master came up – in manner, face, or voice, no more the master that I knew, than I was he. He took me (I laid the little one upon her bed in the hotel, and left her with the chamber-women), in a carriage, furiously through the darkness, across the desolate campagna. When it was day, and we stopped at a miserable post-house, all the horses had been hired twelve hours ago, and sent away in different directions. Mark me! by the Signor Dellombra, who had passed there in a carriage, with a frightened English lady crouching in one corner.

I never heard (said the Genoese courier, drawing a long breath) that she was ever traced beyond that spot. All I know is, that she vanished into infamous oblivion, with the dreaded face beside her that she had seen in her dream.

'What do you call *that*?' said the German courier, triumphantly. 'Ghosts! There are no ghosts *there*! What do you call this, that I am going to tell you? Ghosts! There are no ghosts *here*!

I took an engagement once (pursued the German courier) with an English gentleman, elderly and a bachelor, to travel through my country, my Fatherland. He was a merchant who traded with my country and knew the language, but who had never been there since he was a boy – as I judge, some sixty years before.

His name was James, and he had a twin-brother John, also a bachelor. Between these brothers there was a great affection. They were in business together, at Goodman's Fields, but they did not live together. Mr James dwelt in Poland Street, turning out of Oxford Street, London; Mr John resided by Epping Forest.

Mr James and I were to start for Germany in about a

week. The exact day depended on business. Mr John came to Poland Street (where I was staying in the house), to pass that week with Mr James. But, he said to his brother on the second day, 'I don't feel very well, James. There's not much the matter with me; but I think I am a little gouty. I'll go home and put myself under the care of my old housekeeper, who understands my ways. If I get quite better, I'll come back and see you before you go. If I don't feel well enough to resume my visit where I leave it off, why *you* will come and see *me* before you go.' Mr James, of course, said he would, and they shook hands – both hands, as they always did – and Mr John ordered out his old-fashioned chariot and rumbled home.

It was on the second night after that – that is to say, the fourth in the week – when I was awoke out of my sound sleep by Mr James coming into my bedroom in his flannel-gown, with a lighted candle. He sat upon the side of my bed, and looking at me, said, 'Wilhelm, I have reason to think I have got some strange illness upon me.'

I then perceived that there was a very unusual expression in his face.

'Wilhelm,' said he, 'I am not afraid or ashamed to tell you what I might be afraid or ashamed to tell another man. You come from a sensible country, where mysterious things are inquired into and are not settled to have been weighed and measured – or to have been unweighable and unmeasurable – or in either case to have been completely disposed of, for all time – ever so many years ago. I have just now seen the phantom of my brother.'

I confess (said the German courier) that it gave me a little tingling of the blood to hear it.

'I have just now seen,' Mr James repeated, looking full at me, that I might see how collected he was, 'the phantom of my brother John. I was sitting up in bed, unable to sleep, when it came into my room, in a white dress, and regarding me earnestly, passed up to the end of the room, glanced at some papers on my writing-desk, turned, and, still looking earnestly at me as it passed the bed, went out at the door. Now, I am not in the least mad, and am not in the least disposed to invest that phantom with any external existence out of myself. I think it is a warning to me that I am ill; and I think I had better be bled.'

I got out of bed directly (said the German courier) and began to get on my clothes, begging him not to be alarmed, and telling him that I would go myself to the doctor. I was just ready, when we heard a loud knocking and ringing at the street door. My room being an attic at the back, and Mr James's being the second-floor room in the front, we went down to his room, and put up the window, to see what was the matter.

'Is that Mr James?' said a man below, falling back to the opposite side of the way to look up.

'It is,' said Mr James, 'and you are my brother's man, Robert.'

'Yes, Sir. I am sorry to say, Sir, that Mr John is ill. He is very bad, Sir. It is even feared that he may be lying at the point of death. He wants to see you, Sir. I have a chaise here. Pray come to him. Pray lose no time.'

Mr James and I looked at one another. 'Wilhelm,' said he, 'this is strange. I wish you to come with me!' I helped him to dress, partly there and partly in the chaise; and no grass grew under the horses' iron shoes between Poland Street and the Forest.

Now, mind! (said the German courier) I went with Mr James into his brother's room, and I saw and heard myself what follows.

His brother lay upon his bed, at the upper end of a long bedchamber. His old housekeeper was there, and others were there: I think three others were there, if not four, and they had been with him since early in the afternoon. He was in white, like the figure – necessarily so, because he had his night-dress on. He looked like the figure – necessarily so, because he looked earnestly at his brother when he saw him come into the room.

But, when his brother reached the bedside, he slowly

raised himself in bed, and looking full upon him, said these words:

'*James, you have seen me before, tonight – and you know it!*'

And so died!

I waited, when the German courier ceased, to hear something said of this strange story. The silence was unbroken. I looked round, and the five couriers were gone: so noiselessly that the ghostly mountain might have absorbed them into its eternal snows. By this time, I was by no means in a mood to sit alone in that awful scene, with the chill air coming solemnly upon me – or, if I may tell the truth, to sit alone anywhere. So I went back into the convent parlour, and, finding the American gentleman still disposed to relate the biography of the Honourable Ananias Dodger, heard it all out.

THE GHOST CHAMBER

The house was a genuine old house of a very quaint description, teeming with old carvings, and beams, and panels, and having an excellent old staircase, with a gallery or upper staircase, cut off from it by a curious fence-work of old oak, or of the old Honduras Mahogany wood. It was, and is, and will be, for many a long year to come, a remarkably picturesque house; and a certain grave mystery lurking in the depth of the old mahogany panels, as if they were so many deep pools of dark water – such, indeed, as they had been much among when they were trees – gave it a very mysterious character after nightfall.

When Mr Goodchild and Mr Idle had first alighted at the door, and stepped into the sombre handsome old hall, they had been received by half-a-dozen noiseless old men in black, all dressed exactly alike, who glided up the stairs with the obliging landlord and waiter – but without appearing to get into their way, or to mind whether they did or no – and who had filed off to the right and left on the old staircase, as the guests entered their sitting-room. It was then broad, bright day. But, Mr Goodchild had said, when their door was shut, 'Who on earth are those old men?' And afterwards, both on going out and coming in, he had noticed that there were no old men to be seen.

Neither, had the old men, or any one of the old men, reappeared since. The two friends had passed a night in the house, but had seen nothing more of the old men. Mr Goodchild, in rambling about it, had looked along passages, and glanced in at doorways, but had encountered no old men; neither did it appear that any old men were, by any member of the establishment, missed or expected.

Another odd circumstance impressed itself on their attention. It was, that the door of their sitting-room was never left untouched for a quarter of an hour. It was opened with hesitation, opened with confidence, opened a little way, opened a good way, always clapped-to again without a word of explanation. They were reading, they were writing, they were eating, they were drinking, they were talking, they were dozing; the door was always opened at an unexpected moment, and they looked towards it, and it was clapped-to again, and nobody was to be seen. When this had happened fifty times or so, Mr Goodchild had said to his companion, jestingly: 'I begin to think, Tom, there was something wrong with those six old men.'

Night had come again, and they had been writing for two or three hours: writing, in short, a portion of the lazy notes from which these lazy sheets are taken. They had left off writing, and glasses were on the table between them. The house was closed and quiet. Around the head of Thomas

Idle, as he lay upon his sofa, hovered light wreaths of fragrant smoke. The temples of Francis Goodchild, as he leaned back in his chair, with his two hands clasped behind his head, and his legs crossed, were similarly decorated.

They had been discussing several idle subjects of speculation, not omitting the strange old men, and were still so occupied, when Mr Goodchild abruptly changed his attitude to wind up his watch. They were just becoming drowsy enough to be stopped in their talk by any such slight check. Thomas Idle, who was speaking at the moment, paused and said, 'How goes it?'

'One,' said Goodchild.

As if he had ordered one old man, and the order were promptly executed (truly, all orders were so, in that excellent hotel), the door opened, and one old man stood there.

He did not come in, but stood with the door in his hand.

'One of the six, Tom, at last!' said Mr Goodchild, in a surprised whisper. 'Sir, your pleasure?'

'Sir, *your* pleasure?' said the one old man.

'I didn't ring.'

'The bell did,' said the one old man.

He said *bell*, in a deep strong way, that would have expressed the church bell.

'I had the pleasure, I believe, of seeing you, yesterday?'

said Goodchild.

'I cannot undertake to say for certain,' was the grim reply of the one old man.

'I think you saw me. Did you not?'

'Saw *you*?' said the old man. 'O yes, I saw *you*. But, I see many who never see me.'

A chilled, slow, earthy, fixed old man. A cadaverous old man of measured speech. An old man who seemed as unable to wink, as if his eyelids had been nailed to his forehead. An old man whose eyes – two spots of fire – had no more motion than if they had been connected with the back of his skull by screws driven through it, and riveted and bolted outside, among his grey hair.

The night had turned so cold, to Mr Goodchild's sensations, that he shivered. He remarked lightly, and half apologetically, 'I think somebody is walking over my grave.'

'No,' said the weird old man, 'there is no one there.'

Mr Goodchild looked at Idle, but Idle lay with his head enwreathed in smoke.

'No one there?' said Goodchild.

'There is no one at your grave, I assure you,' said the old man.

He had come in and shut the door, and he now sat down. He did not bend himself to sit, as other people do, but seemed to sink bolt upright, as if in water, until the chair stopped him.

'My friend, Mr Idle,' said Goodchild, extremely anxious to introduce a third person into the conversation.

'I am,' said the old man, without looking at him, 'at Mr Idle's service.'

'If you are an old inhabitant of this place,' Francis Goodchild resumed:

'Yes.'

'Perhaps you can decide a point my friend and I were in doubt upon, this morning. They hang condemned criminals at the castle, I believe?'

'*I* believe so,' said the old man.

'Are their faces turned towards that noble prospect?'

'Your face is turned,' replied the old man, 'to the castle wall. When you are tied up, you see its stones expanding and contracting violently, and a similar expansion and contraction seem to take place in your own head and breast. Then, there is a rush of fire and an earthquake, and the castle springs into the air, and you tumble down a precipice.'

His cravat appeared to trouble him. He put his hand to his throat, and moved his neck from side to side. He was an old man of a swollen character of face, and his nose was immovably hitched up on one side, as if by a little hook inserted in that nostril. Mr Goodchild felt exceedingly uncomfortable, and began to think the night was hot, and not cold.

'A strong description, sir,' he observed.

'A strong sensation,' the old man rejoined.

Again, Mr Goodchild looked to Mr Thomas Idle; but Thomas lay on his back with his face attentively turned towards the one old man, and made no sign. At this time Mr Goodchild believed that he saw threads of fire stretch from the old man's eyes to his own, and there attach themselves. (Mr Goodchild writes the present account of his experience, and, with the utmost solemnity, protests that he had the strongest sensation upon him of being forced to look at the old man along those two fiery films, from that moment.)

'I must tell it to you,' said the old man, with a ghastly and a stony stare.

'What?' asked Francis Goodchild.

'You know where it took place. Yonder!'

Whether he pointed to the room above, or to the room below, or to any room in that old house, or to a room in some other old house in that old town, Mr Goodchild was not, nor is, nor ever can be, sure. He was confused by the circumstance that the right forefinger of the one old man seemed to dip itself in one of the threads of fire, light itself, and make a fiery start in the air, as it pointed somewhere. Having pointed somewhere, it went out.

'You know she was a bride,' said the old man.

'I know they still send up bride-cake,' Mr Goodchild faltered. This is a very oppressive air.'

She was a bride, said the old man. She was a fair, flaxen-haired, large-eyed girl, who had no character, no purpose. A weak, credulous, incapable, helpless nothing. Not like her mother. No, no. It was her father whose character she reflected.

Her mother had taken care to secure everything to herself, for her own life, when the father of this girl (a child at that time) died – of sheer helplessness; no other disorder – and then he renewed the acquaintance that had once subsisted between the mother and him. He had been put aside for the flaxen-haired, large-eyed man (or nonentity) with money. He could overlook that for money. He wanted compensation in money.

So, he returned to the side of that woman the mother, made love to her again, danced attendance on her, and submitted himself to her whims. She wreaked upon him every whim she had, or could invent. He bore it. And the more he bore, the more he wanted compensation in money, and the more he was resolved to have it.

But, lo! Before he got it, she cheated him. In one of her imperious states, she froze, and never thawed again. She put her hands to her head one night, uttered a cry, stiffened, lay in that attitude certain hours, and died. And he had got no compensation from her in money, yet. Blight and Murrain on her! Not a penny.

He had hated her throughout that second pursuit, and had longed for retaliation on her. He now counterfeited her signature to an instrument, leaving all she had to leave, to her daughter – ten years old then – to whom the property passed absolutely, and appointing himself the daughter's Guardian. When he slid it under the pillow of the bed on which she lay, he bent down in the deaf ear of Death, and whispered: 'Mistress Pride, I have determined a long time that, dead or alive, you must make me compensation in money.'

So, now there were only two left. Which two were, he, and the fair flaxen-haired, large-eyed foolish daughter, who afterwards became the bride.

He put her to school. In a secret, dark, oppressive, ancient house, he put her to school with a watchful and unscrupulous woman. 'My worthy lady,' he said, 'here is a mind to be formed; will you help me to form it?' She accepted the trust. For which she, too, wanted compensation in money, and had it.

The girl was formed in the fear of him, and in the conviction, that there was no escape from him. She was taught, from the first, to regard him as her future husband- the man who must marry her – the destiny that overshadowed her – the appointed certainty that could never be evaded. The poor fool was soft white wax in their hands, and took the impression that they put upon her. It hardened with time. It became a part of herself. Inseparable from herself, and only to be torn away from her, by tearing life away from her.

Eleven years she had lived in the dark house and its gloomy garden. He was jealous of the very light and air getting to her, and they kept her close. He stopped the wide chimneys, shaded the little windows, left the strong- stemmed ivy to wander where it would over the house- front, the moss to accumulate on the untrimmed fruit-trees in the red-walled garden, the weeds to over-run its green and yellow walks. He surrounded her with images of sorrow and desolation. He caused her to be filled with fears of the place and of the stories that were told of it, and then on pretext of correcting them, to be left in it in solitude, or made to shrink about it in the dark. When her mind was most depressed and fullest of terrors, then, he would come out of one of the hiding-places from which he overlooked her, and present himself as her sole resource.

Thus, by being from her childhood the one embodiment her life presented to her of power to coerce and power to relieve, power to bind and power to loose, the ascendency over her weakness was secured. She was twenty-one years and twenty-one days old, when he brought her home to the gloomy house, his half-witted, frightened, and submissive bride of three weeks.

He had dismissed the governess by that time – what he had left to do, he could best do alone – and they came back, upon a rainy night, to the scene of her long preparation. She turned to him upon the threshold, as the rain was dripping from the porch, and said, 'Oh sir, it is the Death-watch ticking for me!'

'Well!' he answered. 'And if it were?'

'O sir!' she returned to him, 'look kindly on me, and be merciful to me! I beg your pardon. 'I will do anything you wish, if you will only forgive me!'

That had become the poor fool's constant song: 'I beg your pardon,' and 'Forgive me!'

She was not worth hating; he felt nothing but contempt for her. But, she had long been in the way, and he had long been weary, and the work was near its end, and had to be worked out.

'You fool,' he said. 'Go up the stairs!'

She obeyed very quickly, murmuring, 'I will do anything you wish!' When he came into the bride's chamber, having been a little retarded by the heavy fastenings of the great door (for they were alone in the house, and he had arranged that the people who attended on them should come and go in the day), he found her withdrawn to the furthest corner, and there standing pressed against the panelling as if she would have shrunk through it: her flaxen hair all wild about her face, and her large eyes staring at him in vague terror.

'What are you afraid of? Come and sit down by me.'

I will do anything you wish. I beg your pardon, sir. Forgive me!' Her monotonous tune as usual.

'Ellen, here is a writing that you must write out tomorrow, in your own hand. You may as well be seen by others, busily engaged upon it. When you have written it all fairly, and corrected all mistakes, call in any two people there may be about the house, and sign your name to it before them. Then, put it in your bosom to keep it safe, and when I sit here again tomorrow night, give it to me.'

'I will do it all, with the greatest care. I will do anything you wish.'

'Don't shake and tremble, then.'

'I will try my utmost not to do it – if you will only forgive me!'

Next day, she sat down at her desk, and did as she had been told. He often passed in and out of the room, to observe her, and always saw her slowly and laboriously writing: repeating to herself the words she copied, in appearance quite mechanically, and without caring or endeavouring to comprehend them, so that she did her task. He saw her follow the directions she had received, in all particulars; and at night, when they were alone again in the same bride's chamber, and he drew his chair to the hearth, she timidly approached him from her distant seat, took the paper from her bosom, and gave it into his hand.

It secured all her possessions to him, in the event of her death. He put her before him, face to face, that he might look at her steadily; and he asked her, in so many plain words, neither fewer nor more, did she know that?

There were spots of ink upon the bosom of her white dress, and they made her face look whiter and her eyes look larger as she nodded her head. There were spots of ink upon the hand with which she stood before him, nervously plaiting and folding her white skirts.

He took her by the arm, and looked her, yet more closely and steadily, in the face. 'Now, die! I have done with you.'

She shrunk, and uttered a low, suppressed cry.

'I am not going to kill you. I will not endanger my life for yours. Die!'

He sat before her in the gloomy bride's chamber, day after day, night after night, looking the word at her when he did not utter it. As often as her large unmeaning eyes were raised from the hands in which she rocked her head, to the stern figure, sitting with crossed arms and knitted forehead, in the chair, they read in it, 'Die!' When she dropped asleep in exhaustion, she was called back to shuddering consciousness, by the whisper, 'Die!' When she fell upon her old entreaty to be pardoned, she was answered, 'Die!' When she had out-watched and out-suffered the long night, and the rising sun flamed into the sombre room, she heard it hailed with, 'Another day and not dead? Die!'

Shut up in the deserted mansion, aloof from all mankind, and engaged alone in such a struggle without any respite, it came to this – that either he must die, or she. He knew it very well, and concentrated his strength against her feebleness. Hours upon hours he held her by the arm when her arm was black where he held it, and bade her Die!

It was done, upon a windy morning, before sunrise. He computed the time to be half-past four; but, his forgotten watch had run down, and he could not be sure. She had broken away from him in the night, with loud and sudden cries – the first of that kind to which she had given vent – and he had had to put his hands over her mouth. Since then, she had been quiet in the corner of the panelling where she had sunk down; and he had left her, and had gone back with his folded arms and his knitted forehead to his chair.

Paler in the pale light, more colourless than ever in the leaden dawn, he saw her coming, trailing herself along the floor towards him – a white wreck of hair, and dress, and wild eyes, pushing itself on by an irresolute and bending hand.

'O, forgive me! I will do anything. O, sir, pray tell me I

may live!'

'Die!'

'Are you so resolved? Is there no hope for me?'

'Die!'

Her large eyes strained themselves with wonder and fear; wonder and fear changed to reproach; reproach to blank nothing. It was done. He was not at first so sure it was done, but that the morning sun was hanging jewels in her hair – he saw the diamond, emerald, and ruby, glittering among it in little points, as he stood looking down at her – when he lifted her and laid her on her bed.

She was soon laid in the ground. And now they were all gone, and he had compensated himself well.

He had a mind to travel. Not that he meant to waste his money, for he was a pinching man and liked his money dearly (like nothing else, indeed), but, that he had grown tired of the desolate house and wished to turn his back upon it and have done with it. But, the house was worth money, and money must not be thrown away. He determined to sell it before he went. That it might look the less wretched and bring a better price, he hired some labourers to work in the overgrown garden; to cut out the dead wood, trim the ivy that drooped in heavy masses over the windows and gables, and clear the walks in which the weeds were growing mid-leg high.

He worked, himself, along with them. He worked later than they did, and, one evening at dusk, was left working alone, with his bill-hook in his hand. One autumn evening, when the bride was five weeks dead.

'It grows too dark to work longer,' he said to himself, 'I must give over for the night.'

He detested the house, and was loath to enter it. He looked at the dark porch waiting for him like a tomb, and felt that it was an accursed house. Near to the porch, and near to where he stood, was a tree whose branches waved before the old bay-window of the bride's chamber, where it had been done. The tree swung suddenly, and made him start. It swung again, although the night was still. Looking up into it, he saw a figure among the branches.

It was the figure of a young man. The face looked down, as his looked up; the branches cracked and swayed; the figure rapidly descended, and slid upon its feet before him. A slender youth of about her age, with long light brown hair.

'What thief are you?' he said, seizing the youth by the collar.

The young man, in shaking himself free, swung him a blow with his arm across the face and throat. They closed, but the young man got from him and stepped back, crying, with great eagerness and horror, 'Don't touch me! I would as lieve be touched by the Devil!'

He stood still, with his bill-hook in his hand, looking at the young man. For, the young man's look was the counterpart of her last look, and he had not expected ever to see that again.

'I am no thief. Even if I were, I would not have a coin of your wealth, if it would buy me the Indies. You murderer!'

'What!'

'I climbed it,' said the young man, pointing up into the tree, 'for the first time, nigh four years ago. I climbed it, to look at her. I saw her. I spoke to her. I have climbed it, many a time, to watch and listen for her. I was a boy, hidden among its leaves, when from that bay-window she gave me this!'

He showed a tress of flaxen hair, tied with a mourning ribbon.

'Her life,' said the young man, 'was a life of mourning. She gave me this, as a token of it, and a sign that she was dead to every one but you. If I had been older, if I had seen her sooner, I might have saved her from you. But, she was fast in the web when I first climbed the tree, and what could I do then to break it!'

In saying these words, he burst into a fit of sobbing and crying: weakly at first, then passionately, 'Murderer! I climbed the tree on the night when you brought her back. I heard her, from the tree, speak of the Death-watch at the door. I was three times in the tree while you were shut up with her, slowly killing her. I saw her, from the tree, lie dead upon her bed. I have watched you, from the tree, for proofs and traces of your guilt. The manner of it, is a mystery to me yet, but I will pursue you until you have rendered up your life to the hangman. You shall never, until then, be rid of me. I loved her! I can know no relenting towards you. Murderer, I loved her!'

The youth was bare-headed, his hat having fluttered away in his descent from the tree. He moved towards the gate. He had to pass – him – to get to it. There was breadth for two old-fashioned carriages abreast; and the youth's abhorrence, openly expressed in every feature of his face and limb of his body, and very hard to bear, had verge enough to keep itself at a distance in. He (by which I mean the other) had not stirred hand or foot, since he had stood still to look at the boy. He faced round, now, to follow him with his eyes. As the back of the bare light brown head was turned to him, he saw a red curve stretch from his hand to it. He knew, before he threw the bill-hook, where it had alighted – I say, had alighted, and not would alight; for, to his clear perception the thing was done before he did it. It cleft the head, and it remained there, and the boy lay on his face.

He buried the body in the night, at the foot of the tree. As soon as it was light in the morning, he worked at turning up all the ground near the tree, and hacking and hewing at the neighbouring bushes and undergrowth. When the labourers came, there was nothing suspicious, and nothing suspected.

But, he had, in a moment, defeated all his precautions, and destroyed the triumph of the scheme he had so long concerted, and so successfully worked out. He had got rid of the bride, and had acquired her fortune without endangering his life; but now, for a death by which he had gained nothing, he had evermore to live with a rope around his neck.

Beyond this, he was chained to the house of gloom and horror, which he could not endure. Being afraid to sell it or to quit it, lest discovery should be made, he was forced to live in it. He hired two old people, man and wife, for his servants; and dwelt in it, and dreaded it. His great difficulty, for a long time, was the garden. Whether he should keep it trim, whether he should suffer it to fall into its former state of neglect, what would be the least likely way of attracting attention to it?

He took the middle course of gardening, himself, in his evening leisure, and of then calling the old serving-man to help him; but, of never letting him work there alone. And he made himself an arbour over against the tree, where he could sit and see that it was safe.

As the seasons changed, and the tree changed, his mind perceived dangers that were always changing. In the leafy time, perceived that the upper boughs were growing into the form of the young man – that they made the shape of him exactly, sitting in a forked branch swinging in the wind. In the time of the falling leaves, he perceived that they came down from the tree, forming tell-tale letters on the path, or that they had a tendency to heap themselves into a churchyard-mound above the grave. In the winter, when the trees were bare, he perceived that the boughs swung at him the ghost of the blow the young man had given, and that they threatened him openly. In the spring, when the sap was mounting in the trunk, he asked himself, were the dried-up particles of blood mounting with it: to make out more obviously this year than last, the leaf-screened figure of the young man, swinging in the wind?

However, he turned his money over and over, and still over. He was in the dark trade, and gold-dust trade, and most secret trades that yielded great returns. In ten years, he had turned his money over, so many times, that the traders and shippers who had dealings with him, absolutely did not lie – for once – when they declared that he had increased his fortune, twelve hundred per cent.

He possessed his riches one hundred years ago, when people could be lost easily. He had heard who the youth was, from hearing of the search that was made after him; but, it died away, and the youth was forgotten.

The annual round of changes in the tree had been repeated ten times since the night of the burial at its foot, when there was a great thunder-storm over this place. It broke at midnight, and raged until morning. The first intelligence he heard from his old serving-man that morning, was, that the tree had been struck by lightning.

It had been driven down the stem, in a very surprising manner, and the stem lay in two blighted shafts: one resting against the house, and one against a portion of the old red garden-wall in which its fall had made a gap. The fissure went down the tree to a little above the earth, and there stopped. There was great curiosity to see the tree, and, with most of his former fears revived, he sat in his arbour – grown quite an old man – watching the people who came to see it.

They quickly began to come, in such dangerous numbers, that he closed his garden-gate and refused to admit any more. But, there were certain men of science who travelled from a distance to examine the tree, and, in an evil hour, he let them in – Blight and Murrain on them, let them in!

They wanted to dig up the ruin by the roots, and closely examine it, and the earth about it. Never, while he lived! They offered money for it. They! Men of science, whom he could have bought by the gross, with a scratch of his pen! He showed them the garden-gate again, and locked and barred it.

But they were bent on doing what they wanted to do, and they bribed the old serving-man – a thankless wretch who regularly complained when he received his wages, of being underpaid – and they stole into the garden by night with their lanterns, picks, and shovels, and fell to at the tree. He was lying in a turret-room on the other side of the house (the bride's chamber had been unoccupied ever since), but he soon dreamed of picks and shovels, and got up.

He came to an upper window on that side, whence he could see their lanterns, and them, and the loose earth in a heap which he had himself disturbed and put back, when it was last turned to the air. It was found! They had that minute lighted on it. They were all bending over it. One of them said, 'The skull is fractured;' and another, 'See here the bones;' and another, 'See here the clothes;' and then the first struck in again, and said, 'A rusty bill-hook!'

He became sensible, next day, that he was already put under a strict watch, and that he could go nowhere without being followed. Before a week was out, he was taken and laid in hold. The circumstances were gradually pieced together against him, with a desperate malignity, and an appalling ingenuity. But, see the justice of men, and how it was extended to him! He was further accused of having poisoned that girl in the bride's chamber. He, who had carefully and expressly avoided imperilling a hair of his head for her, and who had seen her die of her own incapacity!

There was doubt for which of the two murders he should be first tried; but, the real one was chosen, and he was found guilty, and cast for death. Bloodthirsty wretches! They would have made him guilty of anything, so set they were upon having his life.

His money could do nothing to save him, and he was hanged. *I* am he, and I was hanged at Lancaster Castle with my face to the wall, a hundred years ago!

At this terrific announcement, Mr Goodchild tried to rise and cry out. But, the two fiery lines extending from the old man's eyes to his own, kept him down, and he could not utter a sound. His sense of hearing, however, was acute, and he could hear the clock strike two. No sooner had he heard the clock strike Two, than he saw before him two old men!

Two.

The eyes of each, connected with his eyes by two films of fire: each, exactly like the other: each, addressing him at precisely one and the same instant: each, gnashing the same teeth in the same head, with the same twitched nostril above them, and the same suffused expression around it. Two old men. Differing in nothing, equally distinct to the sight, the copy no fainter than the original, the second as real as the first.

'At what time,' said the two old men, 'did you arrive at the door below?'

'At six.'

'And there were six old men upon the stairs!'

Mr Goodchild having wiped the perspiration from his brow, or tried to do it, the two old men proceeded in one voice, and in the singular number:

I had been anatomised, but had not yet had my skeleton put together and rehung on an iron hook, when it began to be whispered that the bride's chamber was haunted. It *was* haunted, and I was there.

We were there. She and I were there. I, in the chair upon the hearth; she, a white wreck again, trailing itself towards me on the floor. But, I was the speaker no more, and the one word that she said to me from midnight until dawn was, 'Live!'

The youth was there, likewise. In the tree outside the window. Coming and going in the moonlight, as the tree bent and gave. He has, ever since, been there, peeping in at me in my torment; revealing to me by snatches, in the pale lights and slaty shadows where he comes and goes, bareheaded – a bill-hook, standing edgewise in his hair.

In the bride's chamber, every night from midnight until dawn – one month in the year excepted, as I am going to tell you – he hides in the tree, and she comes towards me on the floor; always approaching; never coming nearer; always visible as if by moonlight, whether the moon shines or no; always saying, from midnight until dawn, her one word, 'Live!'

But, in the month wherein I was forced out of this life – this present month of thirty days – the bride's chamber is empty and quiet. Not so my old dungeon. Not so the rooms where I was restless and afraid, ten years. Both are fitfully haunted then. At one in the morning, I am what you saw me when the clock struck that hour – one old man. At two in the morning, I am two old men. At three, I am three. By twelve at noon, I am twelve old men, one for every hundred per cent of old gain. Every one of the twelve, with twelve times my old power of suffering and agony. From that hour until twelve at night, I, twelve old men in anguish and fearful foreboding, wait for the coming of the executioner. At twelve at night, I, twelve old men turned off, swing invisible outside Lancaster Castle, with twelve faces to the wall!

When the bride's chamber was first haunted, it was known to me that this punishment would never cease, until I could make its nature, and my story, known to two living men together. I waited for the coming of two living men together into the bride's chamber, years upon years. It was infused into my knowledge (of the means I am ignorant) that if two living men, with their eyes open, could be in the bride's chamber at one in the morning, they would see me sitting in my chair.

At length, the whispers that the room was spiritually troubled, brought two men to try the adventure. I was scarcely struck upon the hearth at midnight (I came there as if the lightning blasted me into being), when I heard them ascending the stairs. Next, I saw them enter. One of them was a bold, gay, active man, in the prime of life, some five and forty years of age; the other, a dozen years younger. They brought provisions with them in a basket, and bottles. A young woman accompanied them, with wood and coals for the lighting of the fire. When she had lighted it, the bold, gay, active man accompanied her along the gallery outside the room, to see her safely down the staircase, and came back laughing.

He locked the door, examined the chamber, put out the contents of the basket on the table before the fire – little recking of me, in my appointed station on the hearth, close to him – and filled the glasses, and ate and drank. His companion did the same, and was as cheerful and confident as he: though he was the leader. When they had supped, they laid pistols on the table, turned to the fire, and began to smoke their pipes of foreign make.

They had travelled together, and had been much together, and had an abundance of subjects in common. In the midst of their talking and laughing, the younger man made a reference to the leader's being always ready for any adventure; that one, or any other. He replied in these words: 'Not quite so, Dick; if I am afraid of nothing else, I am afraid of myself.'

His companion seeming to grow a little dull, asked him, in what sense? How?

'Why, thus,' he returned. 'Here is a Ghost to be disproved. Well! I cannot answer for what my fancy might do if I were alone here, or what tricks my senses might play with me if they had me to themselves. But, in company with another man, and especially with you, Dick, I would consent to outface all the ghosts that were ever told of in the universe.'

'I had not the vanity to suppose that I was of so much importance tonight,' said the other.

'Of so much,' rejoined the leader, more seriously than he had spoken yet, 'that I would, for the reason I have given, on no account have undertaken to pass the night here alone.'

It was within a few minutes of one. The head of the younger man had drooped when he made his last remark, and it drooped lower now.

'Keep awake, Dick!' said the leader, gaily. 'The small hours are the worst.'

He tried, but his head drooped again.

'Dick!' urged the leader. 'Keep awake!'

'I can't,' he indistinctly muttered. 'I don't know what strange influence is stealing over me. I can't.'

His companion looked at him with a sudden horror, and I, in my different way, felt a new horror also; for, it was on the stroke of one, and I felt that the second watcher was yielding to me, and that the curse was upon me that I must send him to sleep.

'Get up and walk, Dick,' cried the leader. 'Try!'

It was in vain to go behind the slumberer's chair and shake him. One o'clock sounded, and I was present to the elder man, and he stood transfixed before me.

To him alone, I was obliged to relate my story, without hope of benefit. To him alone, I was an awful phantom making a quite useless confession. I foresee it will ever be the same. The two living men together will never come to release me. When I appear, the senses of one of the two will be locked in sleep; he will neither see nor hear me; my communication will ever be made to a solitary listener, and will ever be unserviceable. Woe! Woe! Woe!

As the two old men, with these words, wrung their hands, it shot into Mr Goodchild's mind that he was in the terrible situation of being virtually alone with the spectre, and that Mr Idle's immovability was explained by his having been charmed asleep at one o'clock. In the terror of this sudden discovery which produced an indescribable dread, he struggled so hard to get free from the four fiery threads, that he snapped them, after he had pulled them out to a great width. Being then out of bonds, he caught up Mr Idle from the soafa and rushed downstairs with him.

'What are you about, Francis?' demanded Mr Idle. 'My bedroom is not down here. What the deuce are you carrying me at all for? I can walk with a stick now. I don't want to be carried. Put me down.'

Mr Goodchild put him down in the old hall, and looked about him wildly.

'What are you doing? Idiotically plunging at your own sex, and rescuing them or perishing in the attempt?' asked Mr Idle, in a highly petulant state.

'The one old man!' cried Mr Goodchild, distractedly, 'and the two old men!'

Mr Idle deigned no other reply than, 'The one old woman, I think you mean,' as he began hobbling his way back up the staircase, with the assistance of its broad balustrade.

'I assure you, Tom,' began Mr Goodchild, attending at his side, 'that since you fell asleep——'

'Come, I like that!' said Thomas Idle, 'I haven't closed an eye!'

With the peculiar sensitiveness on the subject of the disgraceful action of going to sleep out of bed, which is the lot of all mankind, Mr Idle persisted in this declaration. The same peculiar sensitiveness impelled Mr Goodchild, on being taxed with the same crime, to repudiate it with honourable resentment. The settlement of the question of the one old man and the two old men was thus presently complicated, and soon made quite impracticable. Mr Idle said it was all bride-cake, and fragments, newly arranged, of things seen and thought about in the day. Mr Goodchild said how could that be, when he hadn't been asleep, and what right could Mr Idle have to say so, who had been asleep? Mr Idle said he had never been asleep, and never did go to sleep, and that Mr Goodchild, as a general rule, was always asleep. They consequently parted for the rest of the night, at their bedroom doors, a little ruffled. Mr Goodchild's last words were, that he had had, in that real and tangible old sitting-room of that real and tangible old Inn (he supposed Mr Idle denied its existence?), every sensation and experience, the present record of which is now within a line or two of completion; and that he would write it out and print it every word. Mr Idle returned that he might if he liked – and he did like, and has now done it.

MR TESTATOR'S VISITATION

Mr Testator took a set of chambers in Lyons Inn when he had but very scanty furniture for his bedroom, and none for his sitting-room. He had lived some wintry months in this condition, and had found it very bare and cold. One night, past midnight, when he sat writing, and still had writing to do that must be done before he went to bed, he found himself out of coals. He had coals downstairs, but had never been to his cellar; however, the cellar key was on his mantel-shelf, and, if he went down and opened the cellar it fitted, he might fairly assume the coals in that cellar to be his. As to his laundress, she lived among the coal-waggons and Thames watermen – for there were Thames watermen at that time – in some unknown rat-hole by the river, down lanes and alleys on the other side of the Strand. As to any other person to meet him or obstruct him, Lyons Inn was dreaming, drunk, maudlin, moody, betting, brooding over bill discounting or renewing – asleep or awake, minding its own affairs. Mr Testator took his coal-scuttle in one hand, his candle and key in the other, and descended to the dismallest underground dens of Lyons Inn, where the late vehicles in the streets became thunderous, and all the water-pipes in the neighbourhood seemed to have Macbeth's Amen sticking in their throats, and to be trying to get it out. After groping here and there among low doors to no purpose, Mr Testator at length came to a door with a rusty padlock which his key fitted. Getting the door open with much trouble, and looking in, he found, no coals, but a confused pile of furniture. Alarmed by this intrusion on another man's property, he locked the door again, found his own cellar, filled his scuttle, and returned upstairs.

But the furniture he had seen ran on casters across and across Mr Testator's mind incessantly, when, in the chill hour of five in the morning, he got to bed. He particularly wanted a table to write at, and a table expressly made to be written at had been the piece of furniture in the foreground of the heap. When his laundress emerged from her burrow in the morning to make his kettle boil he artfully led up to the subject of cellars and furniture; but the two ideas had evidently no connection in her mind. When she left him, and he sat at his breakfast, thinking about the furniture, he recalled the rusty state of the padlock, and inferred that the furniture must have been stored in the cellars for a long time – was perhaps forgotten – owner dead, perhaps? After thinking it over a few days, in the course of which he could pump nothing out of Lyons Inn about the furniture, he became desperate, and resolved to borrow that table. He did so that night. He had not had the table long, when he determined to borrow an easy-chair; he had not had that long, when he made up his mind to borrow a book-case; then, a couch; then, a carpet and rug. By that time, he felt he was 'in furniture stepped in so far,' as that it could be no worse to borrow it all. Consequently, he borrowed it all, and locked up the cellar for good. He had always locked it after every visit. He had carried up every separate article in the dead of the night, and, at the best, had felt as wicked as a resurrection man. Every article was blue and furry when brought into his rooms, and he had had, in a murderous and guilty sort of way, to polish it up while London slept.

Mr Testator lived in his furnished chambers two or three years, or more, and gradually lulled himself into the opinion that the furniture was his own. This was his convenient state of mind when, late one night, a step came up the stairs, and a hand passed over his door, feeling for his knocker, and then one deep and solemn rap was rapped, that might have been a spring in Mr Testator's easy-chair to shoot him out of it; so promptly was it attended with that effect.

With a candle in his hand, Mr Testator went to the door, and found there a very pale and very tall man; a man who stooped; a man with very high shoulders, a very narrow chest, and a very red nose; a shabby-genteel man. He was wrapped in a long threadbare black coat, fastened up the front with more pins than buttons, and under his arm he squeezed an umbrella without a handle, as if he were playing bagpipes. He said, 'I ask your pardon, but can you tell me——' and stopped; his eyes resting on some object within the chambers.

'Can I tell you what?' asked Mr Testator, noting his stoppage with quick alarm.

'I ask your pardon,' said the stranger, 'but – this is not the inquiry I was going to make – *do* I see in there any small article of property belonging to *me*?'

Mr Testator was beginning to stammer that he was not aware – when the visitor slipped past him into the chambers. There, in a goblin way which froze Mr Testator to the marrow, he examined, first, the writing-table, and said, 'Mine', then, the easy-chair, and said 'Mine', then, the book-case, and said, 'Mine'; then, turned up a corner of the carpet, and said, 'Mine!' In a word, inspected every item of furniture from the cellar in succession, and said, 'Mine!' Towards the end of this investigation, Mr Testator perceived that he was sodden with liquor, and that the liquor was gin. He was not unsteady with gin, either in his speech or carriage; but he was stiff with gin in both particulars.

Mr Testator was in a dreadful state, for (according to his making out of the story) the possible consequences of what he had done in recklessness and hardihood flashed upon him in their fulness for the first time. When they had stood gazing at one another for a little while, he tremulously began, 'Sir,

I am conscious that the fullest explanation, compensation, and restitution are your due. They shall be yours. Allow me to entreat that, without temper, without even natural irritation on your part, we may have a little——'

'Drop of something to drink,' interposed the stranger. 'I am agreeable.'

Mr Testator had intended to say, 'a little quiet conversation,' but with great relief of mind adopted the amendment. He produced a decanter of gin, and was bustling about for hot water and sugar, when he found that his visitor had already drunk half the decanter's contents. With hot water and sugar the visitor drank the remainder before he had been an hour in the chambers by the chimes of the church of St Mary in the Strand; and during the process he frequently whispered to himself, 'Mine!'

The gin gone, and Mr Testator wondering what was to follow it, the visitor rose and said, with increased stiffness, 'At what hour of the morning, sir, will it be convenient?'

Mr Testator hazarded, 'At ten?'

'Sir,' said the visitor, 'at ten, to the moment, I shall be here.' He then contemplated Mr Testator somewhat at leisure, and said, 'God bless you! How is your wife?'

Mr Testator (who never had a wife) replied, with much feeling, 'Deeply anxious, poor soul, but otherwise well.'

The visitor thereupon turned and went away, and fell

twice in going downstairs. From that hour he was never heard of. Whether he was a ghost, or a spectral illusion of conscience, or a drunken man who had no business there, or the drunken rightful owner of the furniture, with a transitory gleam of memory; whether he got safe home, or had no home to get to; whether he died of liquor on the way, or lived in liquor ever afterwards; he never was heard of more. This was the story, received with the furniture, and held to be as substantial, by its second possessor in an upper set of chambers in grim Lyons Inn.

THE TRIAL FOR MURDER

I have always noticed a prevalent want of courage, even among persons of superior intelligence and culture, as to imparting their own psychological experiences when those have been of a strange sort. Almost all men are afraid that what they could relate in such wise would find no parallel or response in a listener's internal life, and might be suspected or laughed at. A truthful traveller, who should have seen some extraordinary creature in the likeness of a sea-serpent, would have no fear of mentioning it; but the same traveller, having had some singular presentiment, impulse, vagary of thought, vision (so-called), dream, or other remarkable mental impression, would hesitate considerably before he would own to it. To this reticence I attribute much of the obscurity in which such subjects are involved. We do not habitually communicate our experiences of these subjective things as we do our experiences of objective creation. The consequence is, that the general stock of experience in this regard appears exceptional, and really is so, in respect of being miserably imperfect.

In what I am going to relate, I have no intention of setting up, opposing, or supporting, any theory whatever. I know the history of the bookseller in Berlin. I have studied the case of the wife of a late Astronomer Royal as related by Sir

David Brewster, and I have followed the minutest details of a much more remarkable case of spectral illusion occurring within my private circle of friends. It may be necessary to state as to this last, that the sufferer (a lady) was in no degree, however distant, related to me. A mistaken assumption on that head might suggest an explanation of a part of my own case – but only a part – which would be wholly without foundation. It cannot be referred to my inheritance of any developed peculiarity, nor had I ever before any at all similar experience, nor have I ever had any at all similar experience since.

It does not signify how many years ago, or how few, a certain murder was committed in England, which attracted great attention. We hear more than enough of murderers as they rise in succession to their atrocious eminence, and I would bury the memory of this particular brute, if I could, as his body was buried, in Newgate Jail. I purposely abstain from giving any direct clue to the criminal's individuality.

When the murder was first discovered, no suspicion fell – or I ought rather to say, for I cannot be too precise in my facts, it was nowhere publicly hinted that any suspicion fell – on the man who was afterwards brought to trial. As no reference was at that time made to him in the newspapers, it is obviously impossible that any description of him can at that time have been given in the newspapers. It is essential that this fact be remembered.

Unfolding at breakfast my morning paper, containing the account of that first discovery, I found it to be deeply interesting, and I read it with close attention. I read it twice, if not three times. The discovery had been made in a bedroom, and, when I laid down the paper, I was aware of a flash – rush, flow – I do not know what to call it, no word I can find is satisfactorily descriptive, in which I seemed to see that bedroom passing through my room, like a picture impossibly painted on a running river. Though almost instantaneous in its passing, it was perfectly clear; so clear that I distinctly, and with a sense of relief, observed the absence of the dead body from the bed.

It was in no romantic place that I had this curious sensation, but in chambers in Piccadilly, very near to the corner of St James's Street. It was entirely new to me. I was in my easy-chair at the moment, and the sensation was accompanied with a peculiar shiver which started the chair from its position. (But it is to be noted that the chair ran easily on castors.) I went to one of the windows (there are two in the room, and the room is on the second floor) to refresh my eyes with the moving objects down in Piccadilly. It was a bright autumn morning, and the street was sparkling and cheerful. The wind was high. As I looked out; it brought down from the park a quantity of fallen leaves, which a gust took, and whirled into a spiral pillar. As the pillar fell and the leaves dispersed, I saw two men on the opposite side of the way, going from west to east. They were one behind the other. The foremost man often looked back over his shoulder. The second man followed him, at a distance of some thirty paces, with his right hand menacingly raised. First, the singularity and steadiness of this threatening gesture in so public a thoroughfare attracted my attention; and next, the more remarkable circumstance that nobody heeded it. Both men threaded their way among the other passengers with a smoothness hardly consistent even with the action of walking on a pavement; and no single creature, that I could see, gave them place, touched them, or looked after them. In passing before my windows, they both stared up at me. I saw their two faces very distinctly, and I knew that I could recognise them anywhere. Not that I had consciously noticed anything very remarkable in either face, except that the man who went first had an unusually lowering appearance, and that the face of the man who followed him was of the colour of impure wax.

I am a bachelor, and my valet and his wife constitute my whole establishment. My occupation is in a certain branch bank, and I wish that my duties as head of a department were as light as they are popularly supposed to be. They kept me in town that autumn, when I stood in need of change. I was not ill, but I was not well. My reader is to make the most that can be reasonably made of my feeling jaded, having a depressing sense upon me of a monotonous life, and being 'slightly dyspeptic.' I am assured by my renowned doctor that my real state of health at that time justifies no stronger description, and I quote his own from his written answer to my request for it.

As the circumstances of the murder, gradually unravelling, took stronger and stronger possession of the public mind, I kept them away from mine by knowing as little about them as was possible in the midst of the universal excitement. But I knew that a verdict of wilful murder had been found against the suspected murderer, and that he had been committed to Newgate for trial. I also knew that his trial had been postponed over one Sessions of the Central Criminal Court, on the ground of general prejudice and want of time for the preparation of the defence. I may further have known, but I believe I did not, when, or about when, the Sessions to which his trial stood postponed would come on.

My sitting-room, bedroom, and dressing-room, are all on one floor. With the last there is no communication but through the bedroom. True, there is a door in it, once communicating with the staircase; but a part of the fitting of my bath has been – and had then been for some years – fixed across it. At the same period, and as a part of the same arrangement, the door had been nailed up and canvased over.

I was standing in my bedroom late one night, giving some directions to my servant before he went to bed. My face was towards the only available door of communication with the dressing-room, and it was closed. My servant's back was towards that door. While I was speaking to him, I saw it open, and a man look in, who very earnestly and mysteriously beckoned to me. That man was the man who had gone second of the two along Piccadilly, and whose face was of the colour of impure wax.

The figure, having beckoned, drew back, and closed the door. With no longer pause than was made by my crossing the bedroom, I opened the dressing-room door, and looked in. I had a lighted candle already in my hand. I felt no inward expectation of seeing the figure in the dressing-room, and I did not see it there.

Conscious that my servant stood amazed, I turned round to him, and said, 'Derrick, could you believe that in my cool senses I fancied I saw a—

As I there laid my hand upon his breast, with a sudden start he trembled violently, and said, 'O Lord, yes, sir! A dead man beckoning!'

Now I do not believe that this John Derrick, my trusty and attached servant for more than twenty years, had any impression whatever of having seen any such figure, until I touched him. The change in him was so startling, when I touched him, that I fully believe he derived his impression in some occult manner from me at that instant.

I bade John Derrick bring some brandy, and I gave him a dram, and was glad to take one myself. Of what had preceded that night's phenomenon, I told him not a single word. Reflecting on it, I was absolutely certain that I had never seen that face before, except on the one occasion in Piccadilly. Comparing its expression when beckoning at the door with its expression when it had stared up at me as I stood at my window, I came to the conclusion that on the first occasion it had sought to fasten itself upon my memory, and that on the second occasion it had made sure of being immediately remembered.

I was not very comfortable that night, though I felt a certainty difficult to explain, that the figure would not return. At daylight I fell into a heavy sleep, from which I was awakened by John Derrick's coming to my bedside with a paper in his hand.

This paper, it appeared, had been the subject of an altercation at the door between its bearer and my servant. It was a summons to me to serve upon a jury at the forthcoming Sessions at the Central Criminal Court at the Old Bailey. I had never before been summoned on such a jury, as John

Derrick well knew. He believed – I am not certain at this hour whether with reason or otherwise – that that class of jurors were customarily chosen on a lower qualification than mine, and he had at first refused to accept the summons. The man who served it had taken the matter very coolly. He had said that my attendance or non-attendance was nothing to him; there the summons was; and I should deal with it at my own peril, and not at his.

For a day or two I was undecided whether to respond to this call, or take no notice of it. I was not conscious of the slighest mysterious bias, influence, or attraction, one way or other. Of that I am as strictly sure as of every other statement that I make here. Ultimately I decided, as a break in the monotony of my life, that I would go.

The appointed morning was a raw morning in the month of November. There was a dense brown fog in Piccadilly, and it became positively black and in the last degree oppressive east of Temple Bar. I found the passages and staircases of the court-house flaringly lighted with gas, and the court itself similarly illuminated. I *think* that, until I was conducted by officers into the old court and saw its crowded state, I did not know that the murderer was to be tried that day. I *think* that, until I was so helped into the old court with considerable difficulty, I did not know into which of the two courts sitting my summons would take me. But this must not be received as a positive assertion, for I am not completely satisfied in my mind on either point.

I took my seat in the place appropriated to jurors in waiting, and I looked about the court as well as I could through the cloud of fog and breath that was heavy in it. I noticed the black vapour hanging like a murky curtain outside the great windows, and I noticed the stifled sound of wheels on the straw or tan that was littered in the street; also, the hum of the people gathered there, which a shrill whistle, or a louder song or hail than the rest, occasionally pierced. Soon afterwards the judges, two in number, entered, and took their seats. The buzz in the court was awfully hushed. The direction was given to put the murderer to the bar. He appeared there. And in that same instant I recognised in him the first of the two men who had gone down Piccadilly.

If my name had been called then, I doubt if I could have answered it audibly. But it was called about sixth or eighth in the panel, and I was by that time able to say, 'Here!' Now, observe. As I stepped into the box, the prisoner, who had been looking on attentively, but with no sign of concern, became violently agitated, and beckoned to his attorney. The prisoner's wish to challenge me was so manifest, that it occasioned a pause, during which the attorney, with his hand upon the dock, whispered with his client, and shook his head. I afterwards had it from that gentleman, that the prisoner's first affrighted words to him were, 'At all hazards, challenge that man!' But that, as he would give no reason for it, and admitted that he had not even known my name until he heard it called and I appeared, it was not done.

Both on the ground already explained, that I wish to avoid reviving the unwholesome memory of that murderer, and also because a detailed account of his long trial is by no means indispensable to my narrative, I shall confine myself closely to such incidents in the ten days and nights during which we, the jury, were kept together, as directly bear on my own curious personal experience. It is in that, and not in the murderer, that I seek to interest my reader. It is to that, and not to a page of the Newgate Calendar, that I beg attention.

I was chosen foreman of the jury. On the second morning of the trial, after evidence had been taken for two hours (I heard the church clocks strike), happening to cast my eyes over my brother jurymen, I found an inexplicable difficulty in counting them. I counted them several times, yet always with the same difficulty. In short, I made them one too many.

I touched the brother juryman whose place was next me, and I whispered to him, 'Oblige me by counting us.'

He looked surprised by the request, but turned his head and counted. 'Why,' says he, suddenly, 'we are Thirt——;

but no, it's not possible. No. We are twelve.'

According to my counting that day, we were always right in detail, but in the gross we were always one too many. There was no appearance – no figure – to account for it; but I had now an inward foreshadowing of the figure that was surely coming.

The jury were housed at the London Tavern. We all slept in one large room on separate tables, and we were constantly in the charge and under the eye of the officer sworn to hold us in safe-keeping. I see no reason for suppressing the real name of that officer. He was intelligent, highly polite, and obliging, and (I was glad to hear) much respected in the City. He had an agreeable presence, good eyes, enviable black whiskers, and a fine sonorous voice. His name was Mr Harker.

When we turned into our twelve beds at night, Mr Harker's bed was drawn across the door. On the night of the second day, not being disposed to lie down, and seeing Mr Harker sitting on his bed, I went and sat beside him, and offered him a pinch of snuff. As Mr Harker's hand touched mine in taking it from my box, a peculiar shiver crossed him, and he said, 'Who is this?'

Following Mr Harker's eyes, and looking along the room, I saw again the figure I expected – the second of the two men who had gone down Piccadilly. I rose, and advanced a few steps; then stopped, and looked round at Mr Harker. He was quite unconcerned, laughed, and said in a pleasant way, 'I thought for a moment we had a thirteenth juryman, without a bed. But I see it is the moonlight.'

Making no revelation to Mr Harker, but inviting him to take a walk with me to the end of the room, I watched what the figure did. It stood for a few moments by the bedside of each of my eleven brother jurymen, close to the pillow. It always went to the right-hand side of the bed, and always passed out crossing the foot of the next bed. It seemed, from the action of the head, merely to look down pensively at each recumbent figure. It took no notice of me, or of my bed, which was that nearest to Mr Harker's. It seemed to go out where the moonlight came in, through a high window, as by an aerial flight of stairs.

Next morning at breakfast, it appeared that everybody present had dreamed of the murdered man last night, except myself and Mr Harker.

I now felt as convinced that the second man who had gone down Piccadilly was the murdered man (so to speak), as if it had been borne into my comprehension by his immediate testimony. But even this took place, and in a manner for which I was not at all prepared.

On the fifth day of the trial, when the case for the prosecution was drawing to a close, a miniature of the murdered man, missing from his bedroom upon the discovery of the deed, and afterwards found in a hiding-place where the murderer had been seen digging, was put in evidence. Having been identified by the witness under examination, it was handed up to the bench, and thence handed down to be inspected by the jury. As an officer in a black gown was making his way with it across to me, the figure of the second man who had gone down Piccadilly impetuously started from the crowd, caught the miniature from the officer, and gave it to me with his own hands, at the same time saying, in a low and hollow tone – before I saw the miniature, which was in a locket – 'I was younger then, and my face was not then drained of blood.' It also came between me and the brother juryman to whom I would have given the miniature, and between him and the brother juryman to whom he would have given it, and so passed it on through the whole of our number, and back into my possession. Not one of them, however, detected this.

At table, and generally when we were shut up together in Mr Harker's custody, we had from the first naturally discussed the day's proceedings a good deal. On that fifth day, the case for the prosecution being closed, and we having that side of the question in a completed shape before us, our discussion was more animated and serious. Among our number was a vestryman – the densest idiot I have ever seen at large – who met the plainest evidence with the most preposterous objections, and who was sided with by two flabby parochial parasites; all the three impanelled from a district so delivered over to fever that they ought to have been upon their own trial for five hundred murders. When these mischievous blockheads were at their loudest, which was towards midnight, while some of us were already preparing for bed, I again saw the murdered man. He stood grimly behind them, beckoning to me. On my going towards them, and striking into the conversation, he immediately retired. This was the beginning of a separate series of appearances, confined to that long room in which *we* were confined. Whenever a knot of my brother jurymen laid their heads together, I saw the head of the murdered man among theirs. Whenever their comparison of notes was going against him, he would solemnly and irresistibly beckon to me.

It will be borne in mind that down to the production of the miniature, on the fifth day of the trial, I had never seen the appearance in court. Three changes occurred now that we entered on the case for the defence. Two of them I will mention together, first. The figure was now in court continually, and it never there addressed itself to me, but always to the person who was speaking at the time. For instance: the throat of the murdered man had been cut straight across. In the opening speech for the defence, it was suggested that the deceased might have cut his own throat. At that very moment, the figure, with its throat in the dreadful condition referred to (this it had concealed before), stood at the speaker's elbow, motioning across and across its windpipe, now with the right hand, now with the left, vigorously suggesting to the speaker himself the impossibility of such a wound having been self-inflicted by either hand. For another instance: a witness to character, a woman, deposed to the prisoner's being the most amiable of mankind. The figure in that instant stood on the floor before her, looking her full in the face, and pointing out the prisoner's evil countenance with an extended arm and an outstretched finger.

The third change now to be added impressed me strongly as the most marked and striking of all. I do not theorise upon it; I accurately state it, and there leave it. Although the appearance was not itself perceived by those whom it addressed, its coming close to such persons was invariably attended by some trepidation or disturbance on their part. It seemed to me as if it were prevented, by laws to which I was not amenable, from fully revealing itself to others, and yet as if it could invisibly, dumbly, and darkly overshadow their minds. When the leading counsel for the defence suggested that hypothesis of suicide, and the figure stood at the learned gentleman's elbow, frightfully sawing at its severed throat, it is undeniable that the counsel faltered in his speech, lost for a few seconds the thread of his ingenious discourse, wiped his forehead with his handkerchief, and turned extremely pale. When the witness to character was confronted by the appearance, her eyes most certainly did follow the direction of its pointed finger, and rest in great hesitation and trouble upon the prisoner's face. Two additional illustrations will suffice. On the eighth day of the trial, after the pause which was every day made early in the afternoon for a few minutes' rest and refreshment, I came back into court with the rest of the jury some little time before the return of the judges. Standing up in the box and looking about me, I thought the figure was not there, until, chancing to raise my eyes to the gallery, I saw it bending forward, and leaning over a very decent woman, as if to assure itself whether the judges had resumed their seats or not. Immediately afterwards that woman screamed, fainted, and was carried out. So with the venerable, sagacious, and patient judge who conducted the trial. When the case was over, and he settled himself and his papers to sum up, the murdered man, entering by the judges' door, advanced to his Lordship's desk, and looked eagerly over his shoulder at the pages of his notes which he was turning. A change came over his Lordship's face; his hand stopped; the peculiar shiver, that I knew so well, passed over him; he faltered, 'Excuse me, gentlemen, for a few moments. I am somewhat oppressed by the vitiated air;' and did not recover until he had drunk a glass of water.

Through all the monotony of six of those interminable ten days – the same judges and others on the bench, the same murderer in the dock, the same lawyers at the table, the same tones of question and answer rising to the roof of the court, the same scratching of the judge's pen, the same ushers going in and out, the same lights kindled at the same hour when there had been any natural light of day, the same foggy curtain outside the great windows when it was foggy, the same rain pattering and dripping when it was rainy, the same footmarks and turnkeys and prisoner day after day on the same sawdust, the same keys locking and unlocking the same heavy doors – through all the wearisome montony which made me feel as if I had been foreman of the jury for a vast period of time, and Piccadilly had flourished coevally with Babylon, the murdered man never lost one trace of his distinctness in my eyes, nor was he at any moment less distinct than anybody else. I must not omit, as a matter of fact, that I never once saw the appearance which I call by the name of the murdered man look at the murderer. Again and. again I wondered, 'Why does he not?' But he never did.

Nor did he look at me, after the production of the miniature, until the last closing minutes of the trial arrived. We retired to consider, at seven minutes before ten at night. The idiotic vestryman and his two parochial parasites gave us so much trouble that we twice returned into court to beg to have certain extracts from the judge's notes re-read. Nine of us had not the smallest doubt about those passages, neither, I believe, had any one in the court; the dunder-headed triumvirate, however, having no idea but obstruction, disputed them for that very reason. At length we prevailed, and finally the jury returned into court at ten minutes past twelve.

The murdered man at that time stood directly opposite the jury-box, on the other side of the court. As I took my place, his eyes rested on me with great attention; he seemed satisfied, and slowly shook a great grey veil, which he carried on his arm for the first time, over his head and whole form. As I gave in our verdict, 'Guilty,' the veil collapsed, all was gone, and his place was empty.

The murderer, being asked by the judge, according to usage, whether he had anything to say before sentence of death should be passed upon him, indistinctly muttered something which was described in the leading newspapers of the following day as 'a few rambling, incoherent, and half-audible words, in which he was understood to complain that he had not had a fair trial, because the foreman of the jury was prepossessed against him'. The remarkable declaration that he really made was this: 'My Lord, I knew I was a doomed man, when the foreman of my jury came into the box. My Lord, I knew he would never let me off, because before I was taken, he somehow got to my bedside in the night, woke me, and put a rope round my neck.'

THE SIGNAL-MAN

'Halloa! Below there!'

When he heard a voice thus calling to him, he was standing at the door of his box, with a flag in his hand, furled round its short pole. One would have thought, considering the nature of the ground, that he could not have doubted from what quarter the voice came; but instead of looking up to where I stood on the top of the steep cutting nearly over his head, he turned himself about, and looked down the line. There was something remarkable in his manner of doing so, though I could not have said for my life what. But I know it was remarkable enough to attract my notice, even though his figure was foreshortened and shadowed, down in the deep trench, and mine was high above him, so steeped in the glow of an angry sunset, that I had shaded my eyes with my hand before I saw him at all.

'Halloa! Below!'

From looking down the line, he turned himself about again, and raising his eyes, saw my figure high above him.

'Is there any path by which I can come down and speak to you?'

He looked up at me without replying, and I looked down at him without pressing him too soon with a repetition of my idle question. Just then there came a vague vibration in the earth and air, quickly changing into a violent pulsation, and an oncoming rush that caused me to start back, as though it had force to draw me down. When such vapour as rose to my height from this rapid train had passed me, and was skimming away over the landscape, I looked down again, and saw him refurling the flag he had shown while the train went by.

I repeated my inquiry. After a pause, during which he seemed to regard me with fixed attention, he motioned with his rolled-up flag towards a point on my level, some two or three hundred yards distant. I called down to him, 'All right!' and made for that point. There, by dint of looking closely about me, I found a rough zigzag descending path notched out, which I followed.

The cutting was extremely deep, and unusually precipitate. It was made through a clammy stone, that became oozier and wetter as I went down. For these reasons, I found the way long enough to give me time to recall a singular air of reluctance or compulsion with which he had pointed out the path.

When I came down low enough upon the zigzag descent to see him again, I saw that he was standing between the rails on the way by which the train had lately passed, in an attitude as if he were waiting for me to appear. He had his left hand at his chin, and that left elbow rested on his right hand, crossed over his breast. His attitude was one of such expectation and watchfulness that I stopped a moment, wondering at it.

I resumed my downward way, and stepping out upon the level of the railroad, and drawing nearer to him, saw that he was a dark sallow man, with a dark beard and rather heavy eyebrows. His post was in as solitary and dismal a place as ever I saw. On either side, a dripping-wet wall of jagged stone, excluding all view but a strip of sky; the perspective one way only a crooked prolongation of this great dungeon; the shorter perspective in the other direction terminating in a gloomy red light, and the gloomier entrance to a black tunnel, in whose massive architecture there was a barbarous, depressing, and forbidding air. So little sunlight ever found its way to this spot, that it had an earthy, deadly smell; and so much cold wind rushed through it, that it struck chill to me, as if I had left the natural world.

Before he stirred, I was near enough to him to have touched him. Not even then removing his eyes from mine, he stepped back one step, and lifted his hand.

This was a lonesome post to occupy (I said), and it had riveted my attention when I looked down from up yonder. A visitor was a rarity, I should suppose; not an unwelcome rarity, I hoped? In me, he merely saw a man who had been shut up within narrow limits all his life, and who, being at last set free, had a newly-awakened interest in these great works. To such purpose I spoke to him; but I am far from sure of the terms I used; for, besides that I am not happy in opening any conversation, there was something in the man that daunted me.

He directed a most curious look towards the red light near the tunnel's mouth, and looked all about it, as if something were missing from it, and then looked at me.

That light was part of his charge? Was it not?

He answered in a low voice, 'Don't you know it is?'

The monstrous thought came into my mind, as I perused the fixed eyes and the saturnine face, that this was a spirit, not a man. I have speculated since, whether there may have been infection in his mind.

In my turn, I stepped back. But in making the action, I detected in his eyes some latent fear of me. This put the monstrous thought to flight.

'You look at me,' I said, forcing a smile, 'as if you had a dread of me.'

'I was doubtful,' he returned, 'whether I had seen you before.'

'Where?'

He pointed to the red light he had looked at.

'There?' I said.

Intently watchful of me, he replied (but without

sound), 'Yes.'

'My good fellow, what should I do there? However, be that as it may, I never was there, you may swear.'

'I think I may,' he rejoined. 'Yes; I am sure I may.'

His manner cleared, like my own. He replied to my remarks with readiness, and in well-chosen words. Had he much to do there? Yes; that was to say, he had enough responsibility to bear; but exactness and watchfulness were what was required of him, and of actual work – manual labour – he had next to none. To change that signal, to trim those lights, and to turn this iron handle now and then, was all he had to do under that head. Regarding those many long and lonely hours of which I seemed to make so much, he could only say that the routine of his life had shaped itself into that form, and he had grown used to it. He had taught himself a language down here, if only to know it by sight, and to have formed his own crude ideas of its pronunciation, could be called learning it. He had also worked at fractions and decimals, and tried a little algebra; but he was, and had been as a boy, a poor hand at figures. Was it necessary for him when on duty always to remain in that channel of damp air, and could he never rise into the sunshine between those high stone walls? Why, that depended upon times and circumstances. Under some conditions there would be less upon the line than under others, and the same held good as to certain hours of the day and night. In bright weather, he did choose occasions for getting a little above these lower shadows; but, being at all times liable to be called by his electric bell, and at such times listening for it with redoubled anxiety, the relief was less than I would suppose.

He took me into his box, where there was a fire, a desk for an official book in which he had to make certain entries, a telegraphic instrument with its dial, face, and needles, and the little bell of which he had spoken. On my trusting that he would excuse the remark that he had been well educated, and (I hoped I might say without offence), perhaps educated above that station, he observed that instances of slight incongruity in such wise would rarely be found wanting among large bodies of men; that he had heard it was so in workhouses, in the police force, even in that last desperate resource, the army; and that he knew it was so, more or less, in any great railway staff. He had been, when young (if I could believe it, sitting in that hut – he scarcely could), a student of natural philosphy, and had attended lectures; but he had run wild, misused his opportunities, gone down, and never risen again. He had no complaint to offer about that. He had made his bed, and he lay upon it. It was far too late to make another.

All that I have here condensed he said in a quiet manner, with his grave dark regards divided between me and the fire.

He threw in the word, 'Sir,' from time to time, and especially when he referred to his youth, as though to request me to understand that he claimed to be nothing but what I found him. He was several times interrupted by the little bell, and had to read off messages, and send replies. Once he had to stand without the door, and display a flag as a train passed, and make some verbal communication to the driver. In the discharge of his duties, I observed him to be remarkably exact and vigilant, breaking off his discourse at a syllable, and remaining silent until what he had to do was done.

In a word, I should have set this man down as one of the safest of men to be employed in that capacity, but for the circumstance that while he was speaking to me he twice broke off with a fallen colour, turned his face towards the little bell when it did *not* ring, opened the door of the hut (which was kept shut to exclude the unhealthy damp), and looked out towards the red light near the mouth of the tunnel. On both of those occasions, he came back to the fire with the inexplicable air upon him which I had remarked, without being able to define, when we were so far asunder.

Said I, when I rose to leave him, 'You almost make me think that I have met with a contented man.'

(I am afraid I must acknowledge that I said it to lead him on.)

'I believe I used to be so,' he rejoined, in the low voice

in which he had first spoken; 'but I am troubled, sir, I am troubled.'

He would have recalled the words if he could. He had said them, however, and I took them up quickly.

'With what? What is your trouble?'

'It is very difficult to impart, sir. It is very, very difficult to speak of. If ever you make me another visit, I will try to tell you.'

'But I expressly intend to make you another visit. Say, when shall it be?'

'I go off early in the morning, and I shall be on again at ten tomorrow night, sir.'

'I will come at eleven.'

He thanked me, and went out at the door with me. 'I'll show my white light, sir,' he said, in his peculiar low voice, 'till you have found the way up. When you have found it, don't call out! And when you are at the top, don't call out!'

His manner seemed to make the place strike colder to me, but I said no more than, 'Very well.'

'And when you come down tomorrow night, don't call out! Let me ask you a parting question. What made you cry, "Halloa! Below there!" tonight?'

'Heaven knows,' said I. 'I cried something to that effect——'

'Not to that effect, sir. Those were the very words. I know

them well.'

'Admit those were the very words. I said them, no doubt, because I saw you below.'

'For no other reason?'

'What other reason could I possibly have?'

'You had no feeling that they were conveyed to you in any supernatural way?'

'No.'

He wished me good night, and held up his light. I walked by the side of the down line of rails (with a very disagreeable sensation of a train coming behind me) until I found the path. It was easier to mount than to descend, and I got back to my inn without any adventure.

Punctual to my appointment, I placed my foot on the first notch of the zigzag next night, as the distant clocks were striking eleven. He was waiting for me at the bottom, with his white light on. 'I have not called out,' I said, when we came close together; 'may I speak now?' 'By all means, sir.' 'Good night, then, and here's my hand.' 'Good night, sir, and here's mine.' With that we walked side by side to his box, entered it, closed the door, and sat down by the fire.

'I have made up my mind, sir,' he began, bending forward as soon as we were seated, and speaking in a tone but a little above a whisper, 'that you shall not have to ask me twice what troubles me. I took you for someone else yesterday evening. That troubles me.'

'That mistake?'

'No. That someone else.'

'Who is it?'

'I don't know.'

'Like me?'

'I don't know. I never saw the face. The left arm is across the face, and the right arm is waved – violently waved. This way.'

I followed his action with my eyes, and it was the action of an arm gesticulating, with the utmost passion and vehemence, 'For God's sake, clear the way!'

'One moonlight night,' said the man, 'I was sitting here, when I heard a voice cry, "Halloa! Below there!" I started up, looked from that door, and saw this someone else standing by the red light near the tunnel, waving as I just now showed you. The voice seemed hoarse with shouting, and it cried, "Look out! Look out!" And then again, "Halloa! Below there! Look out!" I caught up my lamp, turned it on red, and ran towards the figure, calling, "What's wrong? What has happened? Where?" It stood just outside the blackness of the tunnel. I advanced so close upon it that I wondered at its keeping the sleeve across its eyes. I ran right up at it, and had my hand stretched out to pull the sleeve away, when it was gone.'

'Into the tunnel?' said I.

'No. I ran on into the tunnel, five hundred yards. I stopped, and held my lamp above my head, and saw the figures of the measured distance, and saw the wet stains stealing down the walls and trickling through the arch. I ran out again faster than I had run in (for I had a mortal abhorrence of the place upon me), and I looked all round the red light with my own red light, and I went up the iron ladder to the gallery atop of it, and I came down again, and ran back here. I telegraphed both ways, "An alarm has been given. Is anything wrong?" The answer came back, both ways, "All well." '

Resisting the slow touch of a frozen finger tracing out my spine, I showed him how that this figure must be a deception of his sense of sight; and how that figures, originating in disease of the delicate nerves that minister to the functions of the eye, were known to have often troubled patients, some of whom had become conscious of the nature of their affliction, and had even proved it by experiments upon themselves. 'As to an imaginary cry,' said I, 'do but listen for a moment to the wind in this unnatural valley while we speak so low, and to the wild harp it makes of the telegraph wires.'

That was all very well, he returned, after we had sat listening for a while, and he ought to know something of the wind and the wires – he who so often passed long winter nights there, alone and watching. But he would beg to remark that he had not finished.

I asked his pardon, and he slowly added these words, touching my arm, 'Within six hours after the appearance, the memorable accident on this line happened, and within ten hours the dead and wounded were brought along through the tunnel over the spot where the figure had stood.'

A disagreeable shudder crept over me, but I did my best against it. It was not to be denied, I rejoined, that this was a remarkable coincidence, calculated deeply to impress his mind. But it was unquestionable that remarkable coincidences did continually occur, and they must be taken into account in dealing with such a subject. Though to be sure I must admit, I added (for I thought I saw that he was going to bring the objection to bear upon me), men of common sense did not allow much for coincidences in making the ordinary calculations of life.

He again begged to remark that he had not finished.

I again begged his pardon for being betrayed into interruptions.

'This,' he said, again laying his hand upon my arm, and glancing over his shoulder with hollow eyes, 'was just a year ago. Six or seven months passed, and I had recovered from the surprise and shock, when one morning, as the day was breaking, I, standing at the door, looked towards the red light, and saw the spectre again.' He stopped, with a fixed look at me.

'Did it cry out?'

'No. It was silent.'

'Did it wave its arm?'

'No. It leaned against the shaft of the light, with both hands before the face. Like this.'

Once more I followed his action with my eyes. It was an action of mourning. I have seen such an attitude in stone figures on tombs.

'Did you go up to it?'

'I came in and sat down, partly to collect my thoughts, partly because it had turned me faint. When I went to the door again, daylight was above, and the ghost was gone.'

'But nothing followed? Nothing came of this?'

He touched me on the arm with his forefinger twice or thrice, giving a ghastly nod each time: 'That very day, as a train came out of the tunnel, I noticed, at a carriage window on my side, what looked like a confusion of hands and heads, and something waved. I saw it just in time to signal the driver, Stop! He shut off, and put his brake on, but the train drifted past here a hundred and fifty yards or more. I ran after it, and, as I went along, heard terrible screams and cries. A beautiful young lady had died instantaneously in one of the compartments, and was brought in here, and laid down on this floor between us.'

Involuntarily I pushed my chair back, as I looked from the boards at which he pointed to himself.

'True, sir, True. Precisely as it happened, so I tell it you.'

I could think of nothing to say, to any purpose, and my mouth was very dry. The wind and the wires took up the story with a long lamenting wail.

He resumed. 'Now, sir, mark this, and judge how my mind is troubled. The spectre came back a week ago. Ever since, it has been there, now and again, by fits and starts.'

'At the light?'

'At the danger-light.'

'What does it seem to do?'

He repeated, if possible with increased passion and vehemence, that former gesticulation of, 'For God's sake, clear the way!'

Then he went on. 'I have no peace or rest for it. It calls to me, for many minutes together, in an agonised manner, "Below there! Look out! Look out!" It stands waving to me. It rings my little bell——'

I caught at that. 'Did it ring your bell yesterday evening when I was here, and you went to the door?'

'Twice.'

'Why, see,' said I, 'how your imagination misleads you. My eyes were on the bell, and my ears were open to the bell, and if I am a living man, it did *not* ring at those times. No, nor at any other time, except when it was rung in the natural course of physical things by the station communicating with you.'

He shook his head. 'I have never made a mistake as to that yet, sir. I have never confused the spectre's ring with the man's. The ghost's ring is a strange vibration in the bell that it derives from nothing else, and I have not asserted that the bell stirs to the eye. I don't wonder that you failed to hear it. But *I* heard it.'

'And did the spectre seem to be there, when you looked out?'

'It *was* there.'

'Both times?'

He repeated firmly, 'Both times.'

'Will you come to the door with me, and look for it now?'

He bit his underlip as though he were somewhat unwilling, but arose. I opened the door, and stood on the step, while he stood in the doorway. There was the danger-light. There was the dismal mouth of the tunnel. There were the high, wet stone walls of the cutting. There were the stars above them.

'Do you see it?' I asked him, taking particular note of his face. His eyes were prominent and strained, but not very much more so, perhaps, than my own had been when I had directed them earnestly towards the same spot.

'No,' he answered, 'it is not there.'

'Agreed,' said I.

We went in again, shut the door, and resumed our seats. I was thinking how best to improve this advantage, if it might be called one, when he took up the conversation in such a matter-of-course way, so assuming that there could be no serious question of fact between us, that I felt myself placed in the weakest positions.

'By this time you will fully understand, sir,' he said, 'that what troubles me so dreadfully is the question, What does the spectre mean?'

I was not sure, I told him, that I did fully understand.

'What is its warning against?' he said, ruminating, with his eyes on the fire, and only by times turning them on me. 'What is the danger? Where is the danger? There is danger overhanging somewhere on the line. Some dreadful calamity will happen. It is not to be doubted this third time, after what has gone before. But surely this is a cruel haunting of *me*. What can *I* do?'

He pulled out his handkerchief, and wiped the drops from his heated forehead.

'If I telegraphed danger on either side of me, or on both, I can give no reason for it,' he went on, wiping the palms of his hands. 'I should get into trouble, and do no good. They would think I was mad. This is the way it would work:

Message – "Danger! Take care!" Answer – "What Danger? Where?" Message – "Don't know. But, for God's sake, take care!" They would displace me. What else could they do?'

His pain of mind was most pitiable to see. It was the mental torture of a conscientious man, oppressed beyond endurance by an unintelligible responsibility involving life.

'When it first stood under the danger-light,' he went on, putting his dark hair back from his head, and drawing his hands outward across and across his temples in an extremity of feverish distress, 'why not tell me where that accident was to happen – if it must happen? Why not tell me how it could be averted – if it could have been averted? When on its second coming it hid its face, why not tell me, instead, "She is going to die. Let them keep her at home"? If it came, on those two occasions, only to show me that its warnings were true, and so to prepare me for the third, why not warn me plainly now? And I, Lord help me! A mere poor signal-man on this solitary station! Why not go to somebody with credit to be believed, and power to act?'

When I saw him in this state, I saw that for the poor man's sake, as well as for the public safety, what I had to do for the time was to compose his mind. Therefore, setting aside all question of reality or unreality between us, I represented to him that whoever thoroughly discharged his duty must do well, and that at least it was his comfort that he understood his duty, though he did not understand these confounding appearances. In this effort I succeeded far better than in the attempt to reason him out of his conviction. He became calm; the occupations incidental to his post as the night advanced began to make larger demands on his attention: and I left him at two in the morning. I had offered to stay through the night, but he would not hear of it.

That I more than once looked back at the red light as I ascended the pathway, that I did not like the red light, and that I should have slept but poorly if my bed had been under it, I see no reason to conceal. Nor did I like the two sequences of the accident and the dead girl. I see no reason to conceal that either.

But what ran most in my thoughts was the consideration how ought I to act, having become the recipient of this disclosure? I had proved the man to be intelligent, vigilant, painstaking, and exact; but how long might he remain so, in his state of mind? Though in a subordinate position, still he held a most important trust, and would I (for instance) like to stake my own life on the chances of his continuing to execute it with precision?

Unable to overcome a feeling that there would be something treacherous in my communicating what he had told me to his superiors in the company, without first being plain with himself and proposing a middle course to him,

I ultimately resolved to offer to accompany him (otherwise keeping his secret for the present) to the wisest medical practitioner we could hear of in those parts, and to take his opinion. A change in his time of duty would come round next night, he had apprised me, and he would be off an hour or two after sunrise, and on again soon after sunset. I had appointed to return accordingly.

Next evening was a lovely evening, and I walked out early to enjoy it. The sun was not yet quite down when I traversed the field path near the top of the deep cutting. I would extend my walk for an hour, I said to myself, half an hour on and half an hour back, and it would then be time to go to my signal-man's box.

Before pursuing my stroll, I stepped to the brink, and mechanically looked down, from the point from which I had first seen him. I cannot describe the thrill that seized upon me, when, close at the mouth of the tunnel, I saw the appearance of a man, with his left sleeve across his eyes, passionately waving his right arm.

The nameless horror that oppressed me passed in a moment, for in a moment I saw that this appearance of a man was a man indeed, and that there was a little group of other men, standing at a short distance, to whom he seemed to be rehearsing the gesture he made. The danger-light was not yet lighted. Against its shaft, a little low hut, entirely new to me, had been made of some wooden supports and tarpaulin. It looked no bigger than a bed.

With an irresistible sense that something was wrong, with a flashing self-reproachful fear that fatal mischief had come of my leaving the man there, and causing no one to be sent to overlook or correct what he did, I descended the notched path with all the speed I could make.

'What is the matter?' I asked the men.

'Signal-man killed this morning, sir.'

'Not the man belonging to that box?'

'Yes, sir.'

'Not the man I know?'

'You will recognise him, sir, if you knew him,' said the man who spoke for the others, solemnly uncovering his own head, and raising an end of the tarpaulin, 'for his face is quite composed.'

'O, how did this happen, how did this happen?' I asked, turning from one to another as the hut closed in again.

'He was cut down by an engine, sir. No man in England knew his work better. But somehow he was not clear of the outer rail. It was just at broad day. He had struck the light, and had the lamp in his hand. As the engine came out of the tunnel, his back was towards her, and she cut him down. That man drove her, and was showing how it happened. Show the gentleman, Tom.'

The man, who wore rough dark dress, stepped back to his former place at the mouth of the tunnel.

'Coming round the curve in the tunnel, sir,' he said, 'I saw him at the end, like as if I saw him down a perspective-glass. There was no time to check speed, and I knew him to be very careful. As he didn't seem to take heed of the whistle, I shut it off when we were running down upon him, and called to him as loud as I could call.'

'What did you say?'

'I said, "Below there! Look out! Look out! For God's sake, clear the way!" '

I started.

'Ah! it was a dreadful time, sir. I never left off calling to him. I put this arm before my eyes not to see, and I waved this arm to the last; but it was no use.'

Without prolonging the narrative to dwell on any one of its curious circumstances more than on any other, I may, in closing it, point out the coincidence that the warning of the engine-driver included, not only the words which the unfortunate signal-man had repeated to me as haunting him, but also the words which I myself – not he – had attached, and that only in my own mind, to the gesticulation he had imitated.

FOUR GHOST STORIES

I

Some few years ago a well-known English artist received a commission from Lady F. to paint a portrait of her husband. It was settled that he should execute the commission at F. Hall, in the country, because his engagements were too many to permit his entering upon a fresh work till the London season should be over. As he happened to be on terms of intimate acquaintance with his employers, the arrangement was satisfactory to all concerned, and on the 13th of September he set out in good heart to perform his engagement.

He took the train for the station nearest to F. Hall, and found himself, when first starting, alone in a carriage. His solitude did not, however, continue long. At the first station out of London, a young lady entered the carriage, and took the corner opposite to him. She was very delicate-looking, with a remarkable blending of sweetness and sadness in her countenance, which did not fail to attract the notice of a man of observation and sensibility. For some time neither uttered a syllable. But at length the gentleman made the remarks usual under such circumstances, on the weather and the country, and, the ice being broken, they entered into conversation. They spoke of painting. The artist was much surprised by the intimate knowledge the young lady seemed to have of himself and his doings. He was quite certain that he had never seen her before. His surprise was by no means lessened when she suddenly inquired whether he could make, from recollection, the likeness of a person whom he had seen only once, or at most twice? He was hesitating what to reply, when she added, 'Do you think, for example, that you could paint me from recollection?'

He replied that he was not quite sure, but that perhaps he could.

'Well,' she said, 'look at me again. You may have to take a likeness of me.'

He complied with this odd request, and she asked, rather eagerly, 'Now, do you think you could?'

'I think so,' he replied; 'but I cannot say for certain.'

At this moment the train stopped. The young lady rose from her seat, smiled in a friendly manner on the painter, and bade him goodbye; adding, as she quitted the carriage, 'We shall meet again soon.' The train rattled off, and Mr H. (the artist) was left to his own reflections.

The station was reached in due time, and Lady F.'s carriage was there, to meet the expected guest. It carried him to the place of his destination, one of 'the stately homes of England', after a pleasant drive, and deposited him at the hall door, where his host and hostess were standing to receive him. A kind greeting passed, and he was shown to his room: for the dinner-hour was close at hand.

Having completed his toilet, and descended to the drawing-room, Mr H. was much surprised, and much pleased, to see, seated on one of the ottomans, his young companion of the railway carriage. She greeted him with a smile and a bow of recognition. She sat by his side at dinner, spoke to him two or three times, mixed in the general conversation, and seemed perfectly at home. Mr H. had no doubt of her being an intimate friend of his hostess. The evening passed away pleasantly. The conversation turned a good deal upon the fine arts in general, and on painting in particular, and Mr H. was entreated to show some of the sketches he had brought down with him from London. He readily produced them, and the young lady was much interested in them.

At a late hour the party broke up, and retired to their several apartments.

Next morning, early, Mr H. was tempted by the bright sunshine to leave his room, and stroll out into the park. The drawing-room opened into the garden; passing through it, he inquired of a servant who was busy arranging the furniture, whether the young lady had come down yet?

'What young lady, sir?' asked the man, with an appearance of surprise.

'The young lady who dined here last night.'

'No young lady dined here last night, sir,' replied the man, looking fixedly at him.

The painter said no more: thinking within himself that the servant was either very stupid or had a very bad memory. So, leaving the room, he sauntered out into the park.

He was returning to the house, when his host met him, and the usual morning salutations passed between them.

'Your fair young friend has left you?' observed the artist.

'What young friend?' inquired the lord of the manor.

'The young lady who dined here last night,' returned Mr H.

'I cannot imagine to whom you refer,' replied the gentleman, very greatly surprised.

'Did not a young lady dine and spend the evening here yesterday?' persisted Mr H., who in his turn was beginning to wonder.

'No,' replied his host; 'most certainly not. There was no one at table but yourself, my lady, and I.'

The subject was never reverted to after this occasion, yet our artist could not bring himself to believe that he was labouring under a delusion. If the whole were a dream, it was a dream in two parts. As surely as the young lady had been his companion in the railway carriage, so surely she had sat beside him at the dinner-table. Yet she did not come again; and everybody in the house, except himself, appeared to be ignorant of her existence.

He finished the portrait on which he was engaged, and returned to London.

For two whole years he followed up his profession: growing in reputation, and working hard. Yet he never all the while forgot a single lineament in the fair young face of his fellow-traveller. He had no clue by which to discover where she had come from, or who she was. He often thought of her, but spoke to no one about her. There was a mystery about the matter which imposed silence on him. It was wild, strange, utterly unaccountable.

Mr H. was called by business to Canterbury. An old friend of his – whom I will call Mr Wylde – resided there. Mr H., being anxious to see him, and having only a few hours at his disposal, wrote as soon as he reached the hotel, begging Mr Wylde to call upon him there. At the time appointed the door of his room opened, and Mr Wylde was announced. He was a complete stranger to the artist; and the meeting between the two was a little awkward. It appeared, on explanation, that Mr H.'s friend had left Canterbury some time; that the gentleman now face to face with the artist was another Mr Wylde; that the note intended for the absentee had been given to him; and that he had obeyed the summons, supposing some business matter to be the cause of it.

The first coldness and surprise dispelled, the two gentlemen entered into a more friendly conversation; for Mr

H. had mentioned his name, and it was not a strange one to his visitor. When they had conversed a little while, Mr Wylde asked Mr H. whether he had ever painted, or could undertake to paint, a portrait from mere description? Mr H. replied, never.

'I ask you this strange question,' said Mr Wylde, 'because, about two years ago, I lost a dear daughter. She was my only child, and I loved her dearly. Her loss was a heavy affliction to me, and my regrets are the deeper that I have no likeness of her. You are a man of unusual genius. If you could paint me a portrait of my child, I should be very grateful.'

Mr Wylde then described the features and appearance of his daughter, and the colour of her eyes and hair, and tried to give an idea of the expression of her face. Mr H. listened attentively, and, feeling great sympathy with his grief, made a sketch. He had no thought of its being like, but hoped the bereaved father might possibly think it so. But the father shook his head on seeing the sketch, and said, 'No, it was not at all like.' Again the artist tried, and again he failed. The features were pretty well, but the expression was not hers; and the father turned away from it, thanking Mr H. for his kind endeavours, but quite hopeless of any successful result. Suddenly a thought struck the painter; he took another sheet of paper, made a rapid and vigorous sketch, and handed it to his companion. Instantly, a bright look of recognition and pleasure lighted up the father's face, and he exclaimed, 'That is she! Surely you must have seen my child, or you never could have made so perfect a likeness!'

'When did your daughter die?' inquired the painter, with agitation.

'Two years ago; on the 13th of September. She died in the afternoon, after a few days' illness.'

Mr H. pondered, but said nothing. The image of that fair young face was engraven on his memory as with a diamond's point, and her strangely prophetic words were now fulfilled.

A few weeks after, having completed a beautiful full-length portrait of the young lady, he sent it to her father, and the likeness was declared, by all who had ever seen her, to be perfect.

II

Among the friends of my family was a young Swiss lady, who, with an only brother, had been left an orphan in her childhood. She was brought up, as well as her brother, by an aunt; and the children, thus thrown very much upon each other, became very strongly attached. At the age of twenty-two the youth got some appointment in India, and the terrible day drew near when they must part. I need not describe the agony of persons so circumstanced. But the mode in which these two sought to mitigate the anguish of separation was singular. They agreed that if either should die before the young man's return, the dead should appear to the living.

The youth departed. The young lady by-and-by married a Scotch gentleman, and quitted her home, to be the light and ornament of his. She was a devoted wife, but she never forgot her brother. She corresponded with him regularly, and her brightest days in all the year were those which brought letters from India.

One cold winter's day, two or three years after her marriage, she was seated at work near a large bright fire, in her own bedroom upstairs. It was about midday, and the room was full of light. She was very busy, when some strange impulse caused her to raise her head and look round. The door was slightly open, and, near the large antique bed, stood a figure, which she, at a glance, recognised as that of her brother. With a cry of delight she started up, and ran forward to meet him, exclaiming, 'Oh, Henry! How could you surprise me so! You never told me you were coming!' But he waved his hand sadly, in a way that forbade approach, and she remained rooted to the spot. He advanced a step towards her, and said, in a low soft voice, 'Do you remember our agreement? I have come to fulfil it;' and approaching nearer he laid his hand on her wrist. It was icy cold, and the touch made her shiver. Her brother smiled, a faint sad smile, and, again waving his hand, turned and left the room.

When the lady recovered from a long swoon there was a mark on her wrist, which never left it to her dying day. The next mail from India brought a letter, informing her that her brother had died on the very day, and at the very hour, when he presented himself to her in her room.[*]

III

Overhanging the waters of the Firth of Forth there lived, a good many years ago, a family of old standing in the kingdom of Fife: frank, hospitable, and hereditary Jacobites. It consisted of the squire, or laird – a man well advanced in years – his wife, three sons, and four daughters. The sons were sent out into the world, but not into the service of the reigning family. The daughters were all young and unmarried, and the eldest and the youngest were much attached to each other. They slept in the same room, shared the same bed, and had no secrets one from the other. It chanced that among the visitors to the old house there came a young naval officer, whose gun-brig often put in to the neighbouring harbours. He was well received, and between him and the elder of the two sisters a tender attachment sprang up.

But the prospect of such an alliance did not quite please the lady's mother, and, without being absolutely told that it should never take place, the lovers were advised to separate. The plea urged, was, that they could not then afford to marry, and that they must wait for better times. Those were times when parental authority – at all events in Scotland – was like the decree of fate, and the lady felt that she had nothing left to do, but to say farewell to her lover. Not so he. He was a fine gallant fellow, and, taking the old lady at her word, her determined to do his utmost to push his worldly fortunes.

There was war at that time with some northern power – I think with Prussia – and the lover, who had interest at the Admiralty, applied to be sent to the Baltic. He obtained his wish. Nobody interfered to prevent the young people from taking a tender farewell of each other, and, he full of hope, and she desponding, they parted. It was settled that he should write by every opportunity; and twice a week – on the post days at the neighbouring village – the younger sister would mount her pony and ride in for letters. There was much hidden joy over every letter that arrived. And often and often the sisters would sit at the window a whole winter's night listening to the roar of the sea among the rocks, and hoping and praying that each light, as it shone far away, might be the signal-lamp hung at the mast-head to apprise them that the gun-brig was coming. So weeks stole on in hope deferred, and there came a lull in the correspondence. Post-day after post-day brought no letters from the Baltic, and the agony of the sisters, especially of the betrothed, became almost unbearable.

They slept, as I have said, in the same room, and their window looked down well-nigh into the waters of the Firth. One night, the younger sister was awakened by the heavy moanings of the elder. They had taken to burning a candle in their room, and placing it in the window: thinking, poor girls, that it would serve as a beacon to the brig. She saw by its light that her sister was tossing about, and was greatly disturbed in her sleep. After some hesitation she determined to awaken the sleeper, who sprang up with a wild cry, and, pushing back her long hair with her hands, exclaimed, 'What have you done, what have you done!' Her sister tried to soothe her, and asked tenderly if anything had alarmed her. 'Alarmed!' she answered, still very wildly, 'no! But I saw him! He entered at that door, and came near the foot of the bed. He looked very pale, and his hair was wet. He was just going to speak to me, when you drove him away. O what have you done, what have you done!'

I do not believe that her lover's ghost really appeared, but the fact is certain that the next mail from the Baltic brought intelligence that the gun-brig had gone down in a gale of wind, with all on board.

IV

When my mother was a girl about eight or nine years old, and living in Switzerland, the Count R. of Holstein, coming to Switzerland for his health, took a house at Vevay, with the intention of remaining there for two or three years. He soon became acquainted with my mother's parents, and between him and them acquaintance ripened into friendship. They met constantly, and liked each other more and more. Knowing the count's intentions respecting his stay in Switzerland, my grandmother was much surprised by receiving from him one morning a short hurried note, informing her that urgent and unexpected business obliged him to return that very day to Germany. He added, that he was very sorry to go, but that he must go; and he ended by bidding her farewell, and hoping they might meet again some day. He quitted Vevay that evening, and nothing more was heard of him or his mysterious business.

A few years after this departure, my grandmother and one of her sons went to spend some time at Hamburg. Count R., hearing that they were there, went to see them, and brought them to his castle at Breitenburg, where they were to stay a few days. It was a wild but beautiful district, and the castle, a huge pile, was a relic of the feudal times, which, like most old places of the sort, was said to be haunted. Never having heard the story upon which this belief was founded, my grandmother entreated the count to tell it. After some little hesitation and demur, he consented:

'There is a room in this house,' he began, 'in which no one is able to sleep. Noises are heard in it continually, which have never been accounted for, and which sound like the ceaseless turning over and upsetting of furniture. I have had the room emptied, I have had the old floor taken up and a new one laid down, but nothing would stop the noises. At last, in despair, I had it walled up. The story attached to the room is this.'

Some hundreds of years ago, there lived in this castle a countess, whose charity to the poor and kindness to all people were unbounded. She was known far and wide as 'the good Countess R.' and everybody loved her. The room in question was her room. One night, she was awakened from her sleep by a voice near her; and looking out of bed, she saw, by the faint light of her lamp, a little tiny man, about a foot in height, standing near her bedside. She was greatly surprised, but he spoke, and said, 'Good Countess of R., I have come to ask you to be godmother to my child. Will you consent?' She said she would, and he told her that he would come and fetch her in a few days, to attend the christening; with those words he vanished out of the room.

Next morning, recollecting the incidents of the night, the countess came to the conclusion that she had had an odd dream, and thought no more of the matter. But, about a fortnight afterwards, when she had well-nigh forgotten the dream, she was again roused at the same hour and by the same small individual, who said he had come to claim the fulfilment of her promise. She rose, dressed herself, and followed her tiny guide down the stairs of the castle. In the centre of the courtyard there was, and still is, a large square well, very deep, and stretching underneath the building nobody knew how far. Having reached the side of this well, the little man blindfolded the countess, and bidding her not fear, but follow him, descended some unknown stairs. This was for the countess a strange and novel position, and she felt uncomfortable; but she determined at all hazards to see the adventure to the end, and descended bravely. They reached the bottom, and when her guide removed the bandage from her eyes, she found herself in a room full of small people like himself. The christening was performed, the countess stood godmother, and at the conclusion of the ceremony, as the lady was about to say goodbye, the mother of the baby took a handful of wood shavings which lay in a corner, and put them into her visitor's apron.

'You have been very kind, good Countess of R.,' she said, 'in coming to be godmother to my child, and your kindness shall not go unrewarded. When you rise tomorrow, these shavings will have turned into metal, and out of them you must immediately get made, two fishes and thirty silberlingen (a German coin). When you get them back, take great care of them, for so long as they all remain in your family everything will prosper with you; but, if one of them ever gets lost, then you will have troubles without end.' The countess thanked her, and bade them all farewell. Having again covered her eyes, the little man led her out of the well, and landed her safe in her own courtyard, where he removed the bandage, and she never saw him more.

Next morning the countess awoke with a confused notion of some extraordinary dream. While at her toilet, she recollected all the incidents quite plainly, and racked her brain for some cause which might account for it. She was so employed when, stretching out her hand for her apron, she was astounded to find it tied up, and, within the folds, a number of metal shavings. How came they there? Was it a reality? Had she not dreamed of the little man and the christening? She told the story to the members of her family at breakfast, who all agreed that whatever the token might mean, it should not be disregarded. It was therefore settled that the fishes and the silberlingen should be made, and carefully kept among the archives of the family. Time passed; everything prospered with the house of R. The King of Denmark loaded them with honours and benefits, and gave the count high office in his household. For many years all went well with them.

Suddenly, to the consternation of the family, one of the fishes disappeared, and, though strenuous efforts were made to discover what had become of it, they all failed. From this time everything went wrong. The count then living, had two sons; while out hunting together, one killed the other; whether accidentally or not, is uncertain, but, as the youths were known to be perpetually disagreeing, the case seemed doubtful. This was the beginning of sorrows. The king, hearing what had occurred, thought it necessary to deprive the count of the office he held. Other misfortunes followed. The family fell into discredit. Their lands were sold, or forfeited to the crown; till little was left but the old castle of Breitenburg and the narrow domain which surrounded it. This deteriorating process went on through two or three generations, and, to add to all other misfortunes, there was always in the family one mad member.

'And now,' continued the count, 'comes the strange part of the mystery. I had never placed much faith in these mysterious little relics, and I regarded the story in connexion with them as a fable. I should have continued in this belief, but for a very extraordinary circumstance. You remember my sojourn in Switzerland a few years ago, and how abruptly it terminated? Well. Just before leaving Holstein, I had received a curious wild letter from some knight in Norway, saying that he was very ill, but that he could not die without first seeing arid conversing with me. I thought the man mad, because I had never heard of him before, and he could have no possible business to transact with me. So, throwing the letter aside, I did not give it another thought.

'My correspondent, however, was not satisfied. He wrote again. My agent, who in my absence opened and answered my letters, told him that I was in Switzerland for my health, and that, if he had anything to say, he had better say it in writing, as I could not possibly travel so far as Norway.

'This, however, did not satisfy the knight. He wrote a third time, beseeching me to come to him, and declaring that what he had to tell me was of the utmost importance to us both. My agent was so struck by the earnest tone of the letter, that he forwarded it to me: at the same time advising me not to refuse the entreaty. This was the cause of my sudden departure from Vevay, and I shall never cease to rejoice that I did not persist in my refusal.

'I had a long and weary journey, and once or twice I felt sorely tempted to stop short, but some strange impulse kept me going. I had to traverse well-nigh the whole of Norway; often for days on horseback, riding over wild moorland, heathery bogs, mountains and crags and lonely places, and ever at my left the rocky coast, lashed and torn by the surging waters.

'At last, after some fatigue and hardship, I reached the village named in the letter, on the northern coast of Norway. The knight's castle – a large round tower – was built on a small island off the coast, and communicated with the land by a drawbridge. I arrived there, late at night, and must admit that I felt misgivings when I crossed the bridge by the lurid glare of torchlight, and heard the dark waters surging under me. The gate was opened by a man, who, as soon as I entered, closed it behind me. My horse was taken from me, and I was led up to the knight's room. It was a small circular apartment, nearly at the top of the tower, and scantily furnished. There, on a bed, lay the old knight, evidently at the point of death. He tried to rise as I entered, and gave me such a look of gratitude and relief that it repaid me for my pains.

' "I cannot thank you sufficiently, Count of R.," said he, "for granting my request. Had I been in a state to travel I should have gone to you; but that was impossible, and I could not die without first seeing you. My business is short, though important. Do you know this?" And he drew from under his pillow, my long-lost fish. Of course I knew it; and he went on. "How long it has been in this house, I do not know, nor by what means it came here, nor, till quite lately, was I at all aware to whom it rightfully belonged. It did not come here in my time, nor in my father's time, and who brought it is a mystery. When I fell ill, and my recovery was pronounced to be impossible, I heard one night, a voice telling me that I should not die till I had restored the fish to the Count R. of Breitenburg. I did not know you; I had never heard of you; and at first I took no heed of the voice. But it came again, every night, until at length in despair I wrote to you. Then the voice stopped. Your answer came, and again I heard the warning, that I must not die till you arrived. At last I heard that you were coming, and I have no language in which to thank you for your kindness. I feel sure I could not have died without seeing you."

'That night the old man died. I waited to bury him, and then returned home, bringing my recovered treasure with me. It was carefully restored to its place. That same year, my eldest brother, whom you know to have been the inmate of a lunatic asylum for years, died, and I became the owner of this place. Last year, to my great surprise, I received a kind letter from the King of Denmark, restoring to me the office which my fathers once held. This year, I have been named governor to his eldest son, and the king has returned a great part of the confiscated property; so that the sun of prosperity seems to shine once more upon the house of Breitenburg. Not long ago, I sent one of the silberlingen to Paris, and another to Vienna, in order that they might be analysed, and the metal of which they are composed made known to me;

but no one is able to decide that point.'

Thus ended the Count of R.'s story, after which he led his eager listener to the place where these precious articles were kept, and showed them to her.

* In the Beresford story, a similar ineffaceable marl is said to have been made by an apparition on a lady's wrist. It may be worth consideration whether, under very exceptional and rare conditions, there is thus developed in women and erratic manifestation of the power a mother sometimes has, of marking the body of her unborn child.

THE PORTRAIT-PAINTER'S STORY

There was lately published in these pages a paper entitled 'Four Ghost Stories'. The first of those stories related the strange experience of 'a well-known English artist, Mr H.'. On the publication of that account, Mr H. himself addressed the Editor of this journal – to his great surprise – and forwarded to him his own narrative of the occurrences in question. As Mr H. wrote, without any concealment, in his own name in full, and from his own studio in London, and as there was no possible doubt of his being a real existing person and a responsible gentleman, it became a duty to read his communication attentively. And great injustice having been unconsciously done to it, in the version published as the first of the 'Four Ghost Stories', it follows here exactly as received. It is, of course, published with the sanction and authority of Mr H., and Mr H. has himself corrected the proofs. Entering on no theory of our own towards the explanation of any part of this remarkable narrative, we have prevailed on Mr H. to present it without any introductory remarks whatever. It only remains to add, that no one has for a moment stood between us and Mr H. in this matter. The whole communication is at first hand. On seeing the article, 'Four Ghost Stories', Mr H. frankly and good humouredly wrote, 'I am the Mr H., the living man, of whom mention is made; how my story has been picked up, I do not know, but it is correctly

277

told. I have it by me, written by myself, and here it is.'

I am a painter. One morning in May, 1858, I was seated in my studio at my usual occupation. At an earlier hour than that at which visits are usually made, I received one from a friend whose acquaintance I had made some year or two previously in Richmond Barracks, Dublin. My acquaintance was a captain in the 3rd West York Militia, and from the hospitable manner in which I had been received while a guest with that regiment, as well as from the intimacy that existed between us personally, it was incumbent on me to offer my visitor suitable refreshments; consequently, two o'clock found us well occupied in conversation, cigars, and a decanter of sherry. About that hour a ring at the bell reminded me of an engagement I had made with a model, or a young person who, having a pretty face and neck, earned a livelihood by sitting for artists. Not being in the humour for work, I arranged with her to come on the following day, promising, of course, to remunerate her for her loss of time, and she went away. In about five minutes she returned, and, speaking to me privately, stated that she had looked forward to the money for the day's sitting, and would be inconvenienced by the want of it; would I let her have a part? There being no difficulty on this point, she again went. Close to the street in which I live there is another of a very similar name, and persons who are not familiar with my address often go to it by mistake. The model's way lay directly through it, and, on arriving there, she was accosted by a lady and gentleman, who asked if she could inform them where I lived? They had forgotten my right address, and were endeavouring to find me by inquiring of persons whom they met; in a few more minutes they were shown into my room.

My new visitors were strangers to me. They had seen a portrait I had painted, and wished for likenesses of themselves and their children. The price I named did not deter them, and they asked to look round the studio to select the style and size they should prefer. My friend of the 3rd West York, with infinite address and humour, took upon himself the office of showman, dilating on the merits of the respective works in a manner that the diffidence that is expected in a professional man when speaking of his own productions would not have allowed me to adopt. The inspection proving satisfactory, they asked whether I could paint the pictures at their house in the country, and there being no difficulty on this point, an engagement was made for the following autumn, subject to my writing to fix the time when I might be able to leave town for the purpose. This being adjusted, the gentleman gave me his card, and they left. Shortly afterwards my friend went also, and on looking for the first time at the card left by the strangers, I was somewhat disappointed to find that though it contained the name of Mr and Mrs Kirkbeck, there was no address. I tried to find it by looking at the Court Guide, but it contained no such name, so I put the card in my writing-desk, and forgot for a time the entire transaction.

Autumn came, and with it a series of engagements I had made in the north of England. Towards the end of September, 1858, I was one of a dinner-party at a country-house on the confines of Yorkshire and Lincolnshire. Being a stranger to the family, it was by a mere accident that I was at the house at all. I had arranged to pass a day and a night with a friend in the neighbourhood who was intimate at the house, and had received an invitation, and the dinner occurring on the evening in question, I had been asked to accompany him. The party was a numerous one, and as the meal approached its termination, and was about to subside into the dessert, the conversation became general. I should here mention that my hearing is defective; at some times more so than at others, and on this particular evening I was extra deaf – so much so, that the conversation only reached me in the form of a continued din. At one instant, however, I heard a word distinctly pronounced, though it was uttered by a person at a considerable distance from me, and that word was Kirkbeck. In the business of the London season I had forgotten all about the visitors of the spring, who had left their card without the address. The word reaching me under such circumstances, arrested my attention, and immediately recalled the transaction to my remembrance. On the first opportunity that offered, I asked a person whom I was conversing with if a family of the name in question was resident in the neighbourhood. I was told in reply, that a Mr Kirkbeck lived at A——, at the farther end of the county. The next morning I wrote to this person, saying that I believed he called at my studio in the spring, and had made an arrangement with me, which I was prevented fulfilling by there being no address on his card; furthermore, that I should shortly be in his neighbourhood on my return from the north, but should I be mistaken in addressing him, I begged he would not trouble himself to reply to my note. I gave as my address, The Post Office, York. On applying there three days afterwards, I received a note from Mr Kirkbeck, stating that he was very glad he had heard from me, and that if I would call on my return, he would arrange about the pictures; he also told me to write a day before I proposed coming, that he might not otherwise engage himself. It was ultimately arranged that I should go to his house the succeeding Saturday, stay till Monday morning, transact afterwards what matters I had to attend to in London, and return in a fortnight to execute the commissions.

The day having arrived for my visit, directly after breakfast I took my place in the morning train from York to London.

The train would stop at Doncaster, and after that at Retford junction, where I should have to get out in order to take the line through Lincoln to A——. The day was cold, wet, foggy, and in every way as disagreeable as I have ever known a day to be in an English October. The carriage in which I was seated had no other occupant than myself, but at Doncaster a lady got in. My place was back to the engine and next to the door. As that is considered the ladies' seat, I offered it to her; she, however, very graciously declined it, and took the corner opposite, saying, in a very agreeable voice, that she liked to feel the breeze on her cheek. The next few minutes were occupied in locating herself. There was the cloak to be spread under her, the skirts of the dress to be arranged, the gloves to be tightened, and such other trifling arrangements of plumage as ladies are wont to make before settling themselves comfortably at church or elsewhere, the last and most important being the placing back over her hat the veil that concealed her features. I could then see that the lady was young, certainly not more than two- or three-and-twenty; but being moderately tall, rather robust in make, and decided in expression, she might have been two or three years younger. I suppose that her complexion would be termed a medium one; her hair being of a bright brown, or auburn, while her eyes and rather decidedly marked eyebrows were nearly black. The colour of her cheek was of that pale transparent hue that sets off to such advantage large expressive eyes, and an equable firm expression of mouth. On the whole, the ensemble was rather handsome than beautiful, her expression having that agreeable depth and harmony about it that rendered her face and features, though not strictly regular, infinitely more attractive than if they had been modelled upon the strictest rules of symmetry.

It is no small advantage on a wet day and a dull long journey to have an agreeable companion, one who can converse, and whose conversation has sufficient substance in it to make one forget the length and the dreariness of the journey. In this respect I had no deficiency to complain of, the lady being decidedly and agreeably conversational. When she had settled herself to her satisfaction, she asked to be allowed to look at my Bradshaw, and not being a proficient in that difficult work, she requested my aid in ascertaining at what time the train passed through Retford again on its way back from London to York. The conversation turned afterwards on general topics, and, somewhat to my surprise, she led it into such particular subjects as I might be supposed to be more especially familiar with; indeed, I could not avoid remarking that her entire manner, while it was anything but forward, was that of one who had either known me personally or by report. There was in her manner a kind of confidential reliance when she listened to me that is not usually accorded to a stranger, and sometimes she actually seemed to refer to different circumstances with which I had been connected in times past. After about three-quarters of an hour's conversation the train arrived at Retford, where I was to change carriages. On my alighting and wishing her good morning, she made a slight movement of the hand as if she meant me to shake it, and on my doing so she said, by way of adieu, 'I dare say we shall meet again;' to which I replied, 'I hope that we shall all meet again,' and so parted, she going on the line towards London, and I through Lincolnshire to A——. The remainder of the journey was cold, wet, and dreary. I missed the agreeable conversation, and tried to supply its place with a book I had brought with me from York, and the *Times* newspaper, which I had procured at Retford. But the most disagreeable journey comes to an end at last, and half-past five in the evening found me at the termination of mine. A carriage was waiting for me at the station, where Mr Kirkbeck was also expected by the same train, but as he did not appear it was concluded he would come by the next – half an hour later; accordingly, the carriage drove away with myself only.

The family being from home at the moment, and the dinner hour being seven, I went at once to my room to unpack and to dress; having completed these operations, I descended to the drawing-room. It probably wanted some time to the dinner hour, as the lamps were not lighted, but in their place a large blazing fire threw a flood of light into every corner of the room, and more especially over a lady who, dressed in deep black, was standing by the chimney-piece warming a very handsome foot on the edge of the fender. Her face being turned away from the door by which I had entered, I did not at first see her features; on my advancing into the middle of the room, however, the foot was immediately withdrawn, and she turned round to accost me, when, to my profound astonishment, I perceived that it was none other than my companion in the railway carriage. She betrayed no surprise at seeing me; on the contrary, with one of those agreeable joyous expressions that make the plainest woman appear beautiful, she accosted me with, 'I said we should meet again.'

My bewilderment at the moment almost deprived me of utterance. I knew of no railway or other means by which she could have come. I had certainly left her in a London train, and had seen it start, and the only conceivable way in which she could have come was by going on to Peterborough and then returning by a branch to A——, a circuit of about ninety miles. As soon as my surprise enabled me to speak, I said that I wished I had come by the same conveyance as herself.

'That would have been rather difficult,' she rejoined.

At this moment the servant came with the lamps, and informed me that his master had just arrived and would be down in a few minutes.

The lady took up a book containing some engravings, and having singled one out (a portrait of Lady——), asked me to look at it well and tell her whether I thought it like her.

I was engaged trying to get up an opinion, when Mr and Mrs Kirkbeck entered, and shaking me heartily by the hand, apologised for not being at home to receive me; the gentleman ending by requesting me to take Mrs Kirkbeck in to dinner.

The lady of the house having taken my arm, we marched on. I certainly hesitated a moment to allow Mr Kirkbeck to pass on first with the mysterious lady in black, but Mrs Kirkbeck not seeming to understand it, we passed on at once. The dinner-party consisting of us four only, we fell into our respective places at the table without difficulty, the mistress and master of the house at the top and bottom, the lady in black and myself on each side. The dinner passed much as is usual on such occasions. I, having to play the guest, directed my conversation principally, if not exclusively, to my host and hostess, and I cannot call to mind that I or any one else once addressed the lady opposite. Seeing this, and remembering something that looked light a slight want of attention to her on coming into the dining-room, I at once concluded that she was the governess. I observed, however, that she made an excellent dinner; she seemed to appreciate both the beef and the tart as well as a glass of claret afterwards; probably she had had no luncheon, or the journey had given her an appetite.

The dinner ended, the ladies retired, and after the usual port, Mr Kirkbeck and I joined them in the drawing-room. By this time, however, a much larger party had assembled. Brothers and sisters-in-laws had come in from their residences in the neighbourhood, and several children, with Miss Hardwick, their governess, were also introduced to me. I saw at once that my supposition as to the lady in black being the governess was incorrect. After passing the time necessarily occupied in complimenting the children, and saying something to the different persons to whom I was introduced, I found myself again engaged in conversation with the lady of the railway carriage, and as the topic of the evening had referred principally to portrait-painting, she continued the subject.

'Do you think you could paint my portrait?' the lady inquired.

'Yes, I think I could, if I had the opportunity.'

Now, look at my face well; do you think you should recollect my features?'

'Yes, I am sure I should never forget your features.'

'Of course I might have expected you to say that; but do you think you could do me from recollection?'

'Well, if it be necessary, I will try; but can't you give me any sittings?'

'No, quite impossible; it could not be. It is said that the print I showed to you before dinner is like me; do you think so?'

'Not much,' I replied; 'it has not your expression. If you can give me only one sitting, it would be better than none.'

'No; I don't see how it could be.'

The evening being by this time rather far advanced, and the chamber candles being brought in, on the plea of being rather tired, she shook me heartily by the hand, and wished me good night. My mysterious acquaintance caused me no small pondering during the night. I had never been introduced to her, I had not seen her speak to any one during the entire evening, not even to wish them good night – how she got across the country was an inexplicable mystery. Then, why did she wish me to paint her from memory, and why could she not give me even one sitting? Finding the difficulties of a solution to these questions rather increase upon me, I made up my mind to defer further consideration of them till breakfast-time, when I supposed the matter would receive some elucidation.

The breakfast now came, but with it no lady in black. The

breakfast over, we went to church, came home to luncheon, and so on through the day, but still no lady, neither any reference to her. I then concluded that she must be some relative, who had gone away early in the morning to visit another member of the family living close by. I was much puzzled, however, by no reference whatever being made to her, and finding no opportunity of leading any part of my conversation with the family towards the subject, I went to bed the second night more puzzled than ever. On the servant coming in in the morning, I ventured to ask him the name of the lady who dined at the table on the Saturday evening, to which he answered:

'A lady, sir? No lady, only Mrs Kirkbeck, sir.'

'Yes, the lady that sat opposite me dressed in black?'

'Perhaps, Miss Hardwick, the governess, sir?'

'No, not Miss Hardwick; she came down afterwards.'

'No lady as I see, sir.'

'Oh dear me, yes, the lady dressed in black that was in the drawing-room when I arrived, before Mr Kirkbeck came home?'

The man looked at me with surprise as if he doubted my sanity, and only answered, 'I never see any lady, sir,' and then left.

The mystery now appeared more impenetrable than ever – I thought it over in every possible aspect, but could come to no conclusion upon it. Breakfast was early that morning, in order to allow of my catching the morning train to London. The same cause also slightly hurried us, and allowed no time for conversation beyond that having direct reference to the business that brought me there; so, after arranging to return to paint the portraits on that day three weeks, I made my adieus, and took my departure for town.

It is only necessary for me to refer to my second visit to that house, in order to state that I was assured most positively, both by Mr and Mrs Kirkbeck, that no fourth person dined at the table on the Saturday evening in question. Their recollection was clear on the subject, as they had debated whether they should ask Miss Hardwick, the governess, to take the vacant seat, but had decided not to do so; neither could they recall to mind any such person as I described in the whole circle of their acquaintance.

Some weeks passed. It was close upon Christmas. The light of a short winter day was drawing to a close, and I was seated at my table, writing letters for the evening post. My back was towards the folding-doors leading into the room in which my visitors usually waited. I had been engaged some minutes in writing, when, without hearing or seeing anything, I became aware that a person had come through the folding-doors, and was then standing beside me. I turned, and beheld the lady of the railway carriage. I suppose that my manner indicated that I was somewhat startled, as the lady, after the usual salutation, said, 'Pardon me for disturbing you. You did not hear me come in.' Her manner, though it was more quiet and subdued than I had known it before, was hardly to be termed grave, still less sorrowful. There was a change, but it was that kind of change only which may often be observed from the frank impulsiveness of an intelligent young lady, to the composure of self-possession of that same young lady when she is either betrothed or has recently become a matron. She asked me whether I had made any attempt at a likeness of her. I was obliged to confess that I had not. She regretted it much, as she wished one for her father. She had brought an engraving (a portrait of Lady M. A.) with her that she thought would assist me. It was like the one she had asked my opinion upon at the house in Lincolnshire. It had always been considered very like her, and she would leave it with me. Then (putting her hand impressively on my arm) she added, 'She really would be most thankful and grateful to me if I would do it' (and, if I recollect rightly, she added), '*as much depended on it.*'

Seeing she was so much in earnest, I took up my sketchbook, and by the dim light that was still remaining began to make a rapid pencil sketch of her. On observing my doing so, however, instead of giving me what assistance she was able, she turned away under pretence of looking at the pictures around the room, occasionally passing from one to another so as to enable me to catch a momentary glimpse of her features. In this manner I made two hurried but rather expressive sketches of her, which being all that the declining light would allow me to do, I shut my book, and she prepared to leave. This time, instead of the usual 'Good morning,' she wished me an impressively pronounced 'Goodbye,' firmly holding rather than shaking my hand while she said it. I accompanied her to the door, outside of which she seemed rather to fade into the darkness than to pass through it. But I refer this impression to my own fancy.

I immediately inquired of the servant why she had not announced the visitor to me. She stated that she was not aware there had been one, and that any one who had entered must have done so when she had left the street door open about half an hour previously, while she went across the road for a moment.

Soon after this occurred I had to fulfil an engagement at a house near Bosworth Field, in Leicestershire. I left town on a Friday, having sent some pictures, that were too large to take with me, by the luggage train a week previously, in order that they might be at the house on my arrival, and occasion me no loss of time in waiting for them. On getting to the house, however, I found that they had not been heard of, and on inquiring at the station, it was stated that a case similar to the one I described had passed through and gone on to Leicester, where it probably still was. It being Friday, and past the hour for the post, there was no possibility of getting a letter to Leicester before Monday morning, as the luggage office would be closed there on the Sunday; consequently, I could in no case expect the arrival of the pictures before the succeeding Tuesday or Wednesday. The loss of three days would be a serious one; therefore, to avoid it, I suggested to my host that I should leave immediately to transact some business in South Staffordshire, as I should be obliged to attend to it before my return to town, and if I could see about it in the vacant interval thus thrown upon my hands, it would be saving me the same amount of time after my visit to his house was concluded. This arrangement meeting with his ready assent, I hastened to the Atherstone station on the Trent Valley Railway. By reference to Bradshaw, I found that my route lay through L——, where I was to change carriages, to S——, in Staffordshire. I was just in time for the train that would put me down at L——at eight in the evening, and a train was announced to start from L——for S——at ten minutes after eight, answering, as I concluded, to the train in which I was about to travel. I therefore saw no reason to doubt but that I should get to my journey's end the same night; but on my arriving at L——I found my plans entirely frustrated. The train arrived punctually, and I got out intending to wait on the platform for the arrival of the carriages for the other line. I found, however, that though the two lines crossed at L——, they did not communicate with each other, the L——station on the Trent Valley line being on one side of the town, and the L——station on the South Staffordshire line on the other. I also found that there was not time to get to the other station so as to catch the train the same evening; indeed, the train had just that moment passed on a lower level beneath my feet, and to get to the other side of the town, where it would stop for two minutes only, was out of the question. There was, therefore, nothing for it but to put up at the Swan Hotel for the night. I have an especial dislike to passing an evening at an hotel in a country town. Dinner at such places I never take, as I had rather go without than have such as I am likely to get. Books are never to be had, the country newspapers do not interest me. *The Times* I have spelt through on my journey. The society I am likely to meet have few ideas in common with myself. Under such circumstances, I usually resort to a meat tea to while away the time, and when that is over, occupy myself in writing letters.

This was the first time I had been in L——, and while waiting for the tea, it occurred to me how, on two occasions within the past six months, I had been on the point of coming to that very place, at one time to execute a small commission for an old acquaintance, resident there, and another, to get the materials for a picture I proposed painting of an incident in the early life of Dr Johnson. I should have come on each of these occasions had not other arrangements diverted my purpose and caused me to postpone the journey indefinitely. The thought, however, would occur to me, 'How strange! Here I am at L——, by no intention of my own, though I have twice tried to get here and been balked.' When I had done tea, I thought I might as well write to an acquaintance I had known some years previously, and who lived in the cathedral close, asking him to come and pass an hour or two with me. Accordingly, I rang for the waitress and asked, 'Does Mr Lute live in Lichfield?'

'Yes, sir.'

'Cathedral close?'

'Yes, sir.'

'Can I send a note to him?'

'Yes, sir.'

I wrote the note, saying where I was, and asking if he would come for an hour or two and talk over old matters. The note was taken; in about twenty minutes a person of gentlemanly appearance, and what might be termed the advanced middle age, entered the room with my note in his hand, saying that I had sent him a letter, he presumed, by mistake, as he did not know my name. Seeing instantly that he was not the person I intended to write to, I apologised, and asked whether there was not another Mr Lute living in L——?

'No, there was none other.'

'Certainly,' I rejoined, 'my friend must have given me his right address, for I had written to him on other occasions here. He was a fair young man, he succeeded to an estate in consequence of his uncle having been killed while hunting with the Quorn hounds, and he married about two years since a lady of the name of Fairbairn.'

The stranger very composedly replied, 'You are speaking of Mr Clyne; he did live in the cathedral close, but he has now gone away.'

The stranger was right, and in my surprise I exclaimed, 'Oh dear, to be sure, that is the name; what could have made me address you instead? I really beg your pardon; my writing to you, and unconsciously guessing your name, is one of the most extraordinary and unaccountable things I ever did. Pray pardon me.'

He continued very quietly, 'There is no need of apology; it happens that you are the very person I most wished to see. You are a painter, and I want you to paint a portrait of my daughter; can you come to my house immediately for the purpose?'

I was rather surprised at finding myself known by him,

and the turn matters had taken being so entirely unexpected, I did not at the moment feel inclined to undertake the business; I therefore explained how I was situate, stating that I had only the next day and Monday at my disposal. He, however, pressed me so earnestly, that I arranged to do what I could for him in those two days, and having put up my baggage, and arranged other matters, I accompanied him to his house. During the walk home he scarcely spoke a word, but his taciturnity seemed only a continuance of his quiet composure at the inn. On our arrival he introduced me to his daughter Maria, and then left the room. Maria Lute was a fair and a decidedly handsome girl of about fifteen; her manner was, however, in advance of her years, and evinced that self-possession, and, in the favourable sense of the term, that womanliness, that is only seen at such an early age in girls that have been left motherless, or from other causes thrown much on their own resources.

She had evidently not been informed of the purpose of my coming, and only knew that I was to stay there for the night; she therefore excused herself for a few moments, that she might give the requisite directions to the servants as to preparing my room. When she returned, she told me that I should not see her father again that evening, the state of his health having obliged him to retire for the night; but she hoped I should be able to see him some time on the morrow. In the meantime, she hoped I would make myself quite at home, and call for anything I wanted. She, herself, was sitting in the drawing-room, but perhaps I should like to smoke and take something; if so, there was a fire in the housekeeper's room, and she would come and sit with me, as she expected the medical attendant every minute, and he would probably stay to smoke, and take something. As the little lady seemed to recommend this course, I readily complied. I did not smoke, or take anything, but sat down by the fire, when she immediately joined me. She conversed well and readily, and with a command of language singular in a person so young. Without being disagreeably inquisitive, or putting any question to me, she seemed desirous of learning the business that had brought me to the house. I told her that her father wished me to paint either her portrait or that of a sister of hers, if she had one.

She remained silent and thoughtful for a moment, and then seemed to comprehend it at once. She told me that a sister of hers, an only one, to whom her father was devotedly attached, died near four months previously; that her father had never yet recovered from the shock of her death. He had often expressed the most earnest wish for a portrait of her; indeed, it was his one thought, and she hoped, if something of the kind could be done, it would improve his health. Here she hesitated, stammered, and burst into tears.

After a while she continued, 'It is no use hiding from you what you must very soon be aware of. Papa is insane – he has been so ever since dear Caroline was buried. He says he is always seeing dear Caroline, and he is subject to fearful delusions. The doctor says he cannot tell how much worse he may be, and that everything dangerous, like knives or razors, are to be kept out of his reach. It was necessary you should not see him again this evening, as he was unable to converse properly, and I fear the same may be the case tomorrow; but perhaps you can stay over Sunday, and I may be able to assist you in doing what he wishes.' I asked whether they had any materials for making a likeness – a photograph, a sketch, or anything else for me to go from. No, they had nothing. 'Could she describe her clearly?' She thought she could; and there was a print that was very much like her, but she had mislaid it. I mentioned that with such disadvantages, and in such an absence of materials, I did not anticipate a satisfactory result. I had painted portraits under such circumstances, but their success much depended upon the powers of description of the persons who were to assist me by their recollection; in some instances I had attained a certain amount of success, but in most the result was quite a failure. The medical attendant came, but I did not see him. I learnt, however, that he ordered a strict watch to be kept on his patient till he came again the next morning. Seeing the

299

state of things, and how much the little lady had to attend to, I retired early to bed. The next morning I heard that her father was decidedly better; he had inquired earnestly on waking whether I was really in the house, and at breakfast-time he sent down to say that he hoped nothing would prevent my making an attempt at the portrait immediately, and he expected to be able to see me in the course of the day.

Directly after breakfast I set to work, aided by such description as the sister could give me. I tried again and again, but without success, or, indeed, the least prospect of it. The features, I was told, were separately like, but the expression was not. I toiled on the greater part of the day with no better result. The different studies I made were taken up to the invalid, but the same answer was always returned – no resemblance. I had exerted myself to the utmost, and, in fact, was not a little fatigued by so doing – a circumstance that the little lady evidently noticed, as she expressed herself most grateful for the interest she could see I took in the matter, and referred the unsuccessful result entirely to her want of powers of description. She also said it was so provoking. She had a print – a portrait of a lady – that was so like, but it had gone – she had missed it from her book for three weeks past. It was the more disappointing, as she was sure it would have been of such great assistance. I asked if she could tell me who the print was of, as if I knew, I could easily procure one in London. She answered, Lady M. A. Immediately the name was uttered the whole scene of the lady of the railway carriage presented itself to me. I had my sketch-book in my port-manteau upstairs, and, by a fortunate chance, fixed in it was the print in question, with the two pencil sketches. I instantly brought them down, and showed them to Maria Lute. She looked at them for a moment, turned her eyes full upon me, and said slowly, and with something like fear in her manner, 'Where did you get these?' Then quicker, and without waiting for my answer, 'Let me take them instantly to papa.' She was away ten minutes, or more; when she returned, her father came with her. He did not wait for salutations, but said, in a tone and manner I had not observed in him before, 'I was right all the time; it was you that I saw with her, and these sketches are from her, and from no one else. I value them more than all my possessions, except this dear child.' The daughter also assured me that the print I had brought to the house must be the one taken from the book about three weeks before, in proof of which she pointed out to me the gum marks at the back, which exactly corresponded with those left on the blank leaf. From the moment the father saw these sketches his mental health returned.

I was not allowed to touch either of the pencil drawings

in the sketch-book, as it was feared I might injure them; but an oil picture from them was commenced immediately, the father sitting by me hour after hour, directing my touches, conversing rationally, and indeed cheerfully, while he did so. He avoided direct reference to his delusions, but from time to time led the conversation to the manner in which I had originally obtained the sketches. The doctor came in the evening, and, after extolling the particular treatment he had adopted, pronounced his patient decidedly, and he believed permanently, improved.

The next day being Sunday, we all went to church. The father, for the first time since his bereavement. During a walk which he took with me after luncheon, he again approached the subject of the sketches, and after some seeming hesitation as to whether he should confide in me or not, said, 'Your writing to me by name, from the inn at L——, was one of those inexplicable circumstances that I suppose it is impossible to clear up. I knew you, however, directly I saw you; when those about me considered that my intellect was disordered, and that I spoke incoherently, it was only because I saw things that they did not. Since her death, I know, with a certainty that nothing will ever disturb, that at different times I have been in the actual and visible presence of my dear daughter that is gone – oftener, indeed, just after her death than latterly. Of the many times that this has occurred, I distinctly remember once seeing her in a railway carriage, speaking to a person seated opposite; who that person was I could not ascertain, as my position seemed to be immediately behind him. I next saw her at a dinner-table, with others, and amongst those others unquestionably I saw yourself. I afterwards learnt that at that time I was considered to be in one of my longest and most violent paroxysms, as I continued to see her speaking to you, in the midst of a large assembly, for some hours. Again I saw her, standing by your side, while you were engaged in either writing or drawing. I saw her once again afterwards, but the next time I saw yourself was in the inn parlour.'

The picture was proceeded with the next day, and on the day after the face was completed, and I afterwards brought it with me to London to finish.

I have often seen Mr L. since that period; his health is perfectly re-established, and his manner and conversation are as cheerful as can be expected within a few years of so great a bereavement.

The portrait now hangs in his bedroom, with the print and the two sketches by the side, and written beneath is: 'C. L., 13th September, 1858, aged 22.'

WELL-AUTHENTICATED RAPPINGS

The writer, who is about to record three spiritual experiences of his own in the present truthful article, deems it essential to state that, down to the time of his being favoured therewith, he had not been a believer in rappings, or tippings. His vulgar notions of the spiritual world, represented its inhabitants as probably advanced, even beyond the intellectual supremacy of Peckham or New York; and it seemed to him, considering the large amount of ignorance, presumption, and folly with which this earth is blessed, so very unnecessary to call in immaterial Beings to gratify mankind with bad spelling and worse nonsense, that the presumption was strongly against those respected films taking the trouble to come here, for no better purpose than to make supererogatory idiots of themselves.

This was the writer's gross and fleshy state of mind at so late a period as the twenty-sixth of December last. On that memorable morning, at about two hours after daylight – that is to say, at twenty minutes before ten by the writer's watch, which stood on a table at his bedside, and which can be seen at the publishing-office, and identified as a demi-chronometer made by Bautte of Geneva, and numbered 67,709 – on that memorable morning, at about two hours after daylight, the writer, starting up in bed with his hand to his forehead, distinctly felt seventeen heavy throbs or beats in that region. They were accompanied by a feeling of pain in the locality, and by a general sensation not unlike that which is usually attendant on biliousness. Yielding to a sudden impulse, the writer asked, 'What is this?'

The answer immediately returned (in throbs or beats upon the forehead) was, 'Yesterday.'

The writer then demanded, being as yet but imperfectly awake, 'What was yesterday?'

Answer: 'Christmas Day.'

The writer, being now quite come to himself, inquired, 'Who is the Medium in this case?'

Answer: 'Clarkins.'

Question: 'Mrs Clarkins, or Mr Clarkins?'

Answer: 'Both.'

Question: 'By Mr, do you mean Old Clarkins, or Young Clarkins?'

Answer: 'Both.'

Now, the writer had dined with his friend Clarkins (who can be appealed to, at the State Paper Office) on the previous day, and spirits had actually been discussed at that dinner, under various aspects. It was in the writer's remembrance, also, that both Clarkins Senior and Clarkins Junior had been very active in such discussion, and had rather pressed it on the company. Mrs Clarkins too had joined in it with animation, and had observed, in a joyous if not an exuberant tone, that it was 'only once a year'.

Convinced by these tokens that the rapping was of spiritual origin, the writer proceeded as follows, 'Who are you?'

The rapping on the forehead was resumed, but in a most incoherent manner. It was for some time impossible to make sense of it. After a pause, the writer (holding his head) repeated the inquiry in a solemn voice, accompanied with a groan, 'Who *are* you?'

Incoherent rappings were still the response.

The writer then asked, solemnly as before, and with another groan, 'What is your name?'

The reply was conveyed in a sound exactly resembling a loud hiccough. It afterwards appeared that this spiritual voice was distinctly heard by Alexander Pumpion, the writer's footboy (seventh son of Widow Pumpion, mangler), in an adjoining chamber.

Question: 'Your name cannot be Hiccough? Hiccough is not a proper name.'

No answer being returned, the writer said, 'I solemnly charge you, by our joint knowledge of Clarkins the Medium – of Clarkins Senior, Clarkins Junior, and Clarkins Mrs – to reveal your name!'

The reply rapped out with extreme unwillingness, was 'Sloe-Juice, Logwood, Blackberry.'

This appeared to the writer sufficiently like a parody on Cobweb, Moth, and Mustard-seed, in the *Midsummer Night's Dream*, to justify the retort, '*That* is not your name?'

The rapping spirit admitted, 'No.'

'Then what do they generally call you?'

A Pause.

'I ask you, what do they generally call you?'

The spirit, evidently under coercion, responded, in a most solemn manner, 'Port!'

This awful communication caused the writer to lie prostrate, on the verge of insensibility, for a quarter of an hour: during which the rappings were continued with violence, and a host of spiritual appearances passed before his eyes, of a black hue, and greatly resembling tadpoles endowed with the power of occasionally spinning themselves out into musical notes as they swam down into space. After contemplating a vast legion of these appearances, the writer demanded of the rapping spirit, 'How am I to present you to myself? What, upon the whole, is most like you?'

The terrific reply was, 'Blacking.'

As soon as the writer could command his emotion, which was now very great, he inquired, 'Had I better take something?'

Answer: 'Yes.'

Question: 'Can I write something?'

Answer: 'Yes.'

A pencil and a slip of paper which were on the table at the bedside immediately bounded into the writer's hand, and he found himself forced to write (in a curiously unsteady character and all downhill, whereas his own writing is remarkably plain and straight), the following spiritual note.

'Mr C.D.S. Pooney presents his compliments to Messrs Bell and Company, Pharmaceutical Chemists, Oxford Street, opposite to Portland Street, and begs them to have the goodness to send him by bearer a five-grain genuine blue pill and a genuine black draught of corresponding power.'

But, before entrusting this document to Alexander Pumpion (who unfortunately lost it on his return, if he did not even lay himself open to the suspicion of having wilfully inserted it into one of the holes of a perambulating chestnut-roaster, to see how it would flare), the writer resolved to test the rapping spirit with one conclusive question. He therefore asked, in a slow and impressive voice, 'Will these remedies make my stomach ache?'

It is impossible to describe the prophetic confidence of the reply. '*Yes.*' The assurance was fully borne out by the result, as the writer will long remember; and after this experience it were needless to observe that he could no longer doubt.

The next communication of a deeply interesting character with which the writer was favoured, occurred on one of the leading lines of railway. The circumstances under which the revelation was made to him – on the second day of January in the present year – were these: He had recovered from the effects of the previously remarkable visitation, and had again been partaking of the compliments of the season. The preceding day had been passed in hilarity. He was on his way to a celebrated town, a well-known commercial emporium where he had business to transact, and had lunched in a somewhat greater hurry than is usual on railways, in consequence of the train being behind time. His lunch had been very reluctantly administered to him by a young lady behind a counter. She had been much occupied at the time with the arrangement of her hair and dress, and her expressive countenance had denoted disdain. It will be seen that this young lady proved to be a powerful medium.

The writer had returned to the first-class carriage in which he chanced to be travelling alone, the train had resumed its motion, he had fallen into a doze, and the unimpeachable watch already mentioned recorded forty-five minutes to have elapsed since his interview with the medium, when he was aroused by a very singular musical instrument. This instrument, he found to his admiration not unmixed with alarm, was performing in his inside. Its tones were of a low and rippling character, difficult to describe; but, if such a comparison may be admitted, resembling a melodious heartburn. Be this as it may, they suggested that humble sensation to the writer.

Concurrently with his becoming aware of the phenomenon in question, the writer perceived that his attention was being solicited by a hurried succession of angry raps in the stomach, and a pressure on the chest. A sceptic no more, he immediately communed with the spirit. The dialogue was as follows:

Question: 'Do I know your name?'

Answer: '*I* should think so!'

Question: 'Does it begin with a P?'

Answer (second time): '*I* should think so!'

Question: 'Have you two names, and does each begin with a P?'

Answer (third time): '*I* should think so!'

Question: 'I charge you to lay aside this levity, and inform me what you are called.'

The spirit, after reflecting for a few seconds, spelt out P.O.R.K. The musical instrument then performed a short and fragmentary strain. The spirit then recommenced, and spelt out the word 'P.I.E.'

Now, this precise article of pastry, this particular viand or comestible, actually had formed – let the scoffer know – the staple of the writer's lunch, and actually had been handed to him by the young lady whom he now knew to be a powerful medium! Highly gratified by the conviction thus forced upon his mind that the knowledge with which he conversed was not of this world, the writer pursued the dialogue.

Question: 'They call you pork pie?'

Answer: 'Yes.'

Question (which the writer timidly put, after struggling with some natural reluctance): 'Are you in fact, Pork Pie?'

Answer: 'Yes.'

It was vain to attempt a description of the mental comfort and relief which the writer derived from this important answer. He proceeded:

Question: 'Let us understand each other. A part of you is pork, and a part of you is pie?'

Answer: 'Exactly so.'

Question: 'What is your pie-part made of?'

Answer: 'Lard.' Then came a sorrowful strain from the musical instrument. Then the word, 'Dripping.'

Question: 'How am I to present you to my mind? What are you most like?'

Answer (very quickly): 'Lead.'

A sense of despondency overcame the writer at this point. When he had in some measure conquered it, he resumed:

Question: 'Your other nature is a porky nature. What has that nature been chiefly sustained upon?'

Answer (in a sprightly manner): 'Pork, to be sure!'

Question: 'Not so. Pork is not fed upon pork?'

Answer: 'Isn't it, though!'

A strange internal feeling, resembling a flight of pigeons, seized upon the writer. He then became illuminated in a surprising manner, and said, 'Do I understand you to hint that the human race, incautiously attacking the indigestible fortresses called by your name, and not having time to storm them, owing to the great solidity of their almost impregnable walls, are in the habit of leaving much of their contents in the hands of the mediums, who with such pig nourish the pigs of the future pies?'

Answer: 'That's it!'

Question: 'Then to paraphrase the words of our immortal bard——'

Answer (interrupting): '*The same pork in its time, makes many pies,*

It's least being seven pasties.'

The writer's emotion was profound. But, again desirous still further to try the spirit, and to ascertain whether, in the poetic phraseology of the advanced seers of the United States, it hailed from one of the inner and more elevated circles, he tested its knowledge with the following:

Question: 'In the wild harmony of the musical instrument within me, of which I am again conscious, what other substances are there airs of, besides those you have mentioned?'

Answer: 'Cape, Gamboge. Camomile. Treacle. Spirits of wine. Distilled potatoes.'

Question: 'Nothing else?'

Answer: 'Nothing worth mentioning.'

Let the scorner tremble and do homage; let the feeble sceptic blush! The writer at his lunch had demanded of the powerful medium, a glass of sherry, and likewise a small glass of brandy. Who can doubt that the articles of commerce indicated by the spirit were supplied to him from that source under those two names?

One other instance may suffice to prove that experiences of the foregoing nature are no longer to be questioned, and that it ought to be made capital to attempt to explain them away. It is an exquisite case of tipping.

The writer's destiny had appointed him to entertain a hopeless affection for Miss L. B., of Bungay, in the county of Suffolk. Miss L. B. had not, at the period of the occurrence of the tipping, openly rejected the writer's offer of his hand and heart; but it has since seemed probable that she had been withheld from doing so, by filial fear of her father, Mr. B., who was favourable to the writer's pretensions. Now, mark the tipping. A young man, obnoxious to all well-constituted minds (since married to Miss L. B.), was visiting at the house. Young B. was also home from school.

The writer was present. The family party were assembled about a round table. It was the spiritual time of twilight in the month of July. Objects could not be discerned with any degree of distinctness. Suddenly, Mr. B., whose senses had been lulled to repose, infused terror into all our breasts, by uttering a passionate roar or ejaculation. His words (his education was neglected in his youth) were exactly these: 'Damn, here's somebody a shoving of a letter into my hand, under my own mahogony!'

Consternation seized the assembled group. Mrs B. augmented the prevalent dismay by declaring that somebody had been softly treading on her toes, at intervals, for half an hour. Greater consternation seized the assembled group. Mr B. called for lights. Now, mark the tipping.

Young B. cried (I quote his expressions accurately), 'It's the spirits, father! They've been at it with me this last fortnight.'

Mr B. demanded with irascibility, 'What do you mean, sir? What have they been at?'

Young B. replied, 'Wanting to make a regular Post-Office of me, father. They're always handing impalpable letters to me, father. A letter must have come creeping round to you by mistake. I must be a medium, father. O here's a go!' cried young B. 'If I ain't a jolly medium!'

The boy now became violently convulsed, sputtering

exceedingly, and jerking out his legs and arms in a manner calculated to cause me (and which did cause me) serious inconvenience; for, I was supporting his respected mother within range of his boots, and he conducted himself like a telegraph before the invention of the electric one. All this time Mr B. was looking about under the table for the letter, while the obnoxious young man, since married to Miss L. B., protected that young lady in an obnoxious manner.

'O here's a go!' Young B. continued to cry without intermission, 'If I an't a jolly medium, father! Here's a go! There'll be a tipping presently, father. Look out for the table!'

Now mark the tipping. The table tipped so violently as to strike Mr B. a good half-dozen times on his bald head while he was looking under it; which caused Mr B. to come out with great agility, and rub it with much tenderness (I refer to his head), and to imprecate it with much violence (I refer to the table). I observed that the tipping of the table was uniformly in the direction of the magnetic current; that is to say, from south to north, or from young B. to Mr B. I should have made some further observations on this deeply interesting point, but that the table suddenly revolved, and tipped over on myself, bearing me to the ground with a force increased by the momentum imparted to it by young B., who came over with it in a state of mental exaltation, and could not be displaced for some time. In the interval, I was aware of being crushed by his weight and the table's, and also of his constantly calling out to his sister and the obnoxious young man, that he foresaw there would be another tipping presently.

None such, however, took place. He recovered after taking a short walk with them in the dark, and no worse effects of the very beautiful experience with which we had been favoured, were perceptible in him during the rest of the evening, than a slight tendency to hysterical laughter, and a noticeable attraction (I might almost term it fascination) of his left hand, in the direction of his heart or waistcoat-pocket.

Was this, or was it not a case of tipping? Will the sceptic and the scoffer reply?

www.ingramcontent.com/pod-product-compliance
Lightning Source LLC
Chambersburg PA
CBHW020842020726
47497CB00005B/1221